"I must confess," Allegra whispered as they danced, "You've been on my mind, too. I kept thinking what it would be like to feel you...to hold you close to me."

Kate wanted to speak, to say something more, but there seemed to be no good reason to interrupt the fine and private conversation in which their bodies were now engaged. She sensed Allegra's arousal, growing acutely aware of her own, as the witch pressed her breast, then her stomach into Kate's, her body gyrating almost imperceptibly beneath the slipping and sliding fabric of her black dress. For a moment, the party, the voices, the people ceased to exist; only the music was left, the rhythm of the woman in her arms, and the secret promise of love to come.

Love Spell

Love Spell

Karen Williams

RISING
TIDE
PRESS

5 KIVY STREET, HUNTINGTON STATION, NY 11746

Rising Tide Press
5 Kivy Street
Huntington Station, NY 11746

Printed in the United States

The publishers wish to thank all of the friends who helped to make this book possible: Edna G., Adriane B., Pat G., Harriet E., Beth H., Bobbi B., Marian S., and Evelyn R. We love you.

In Memoriam: Rising Tide Press dedicates this book to the memory of Marie Harrison, a former staff member, who devoted much of her good will, humor, time, and energy to the success of the Press. We will remember her with love.

Publisher's note:
All characters, places and situations in this book are fictitious and any resemblance to persons (living or dead) is purely coincidental.

First printing May, 1993
10 9 8 7 6 5 4 3 2 1

Edited by Alice Frier and Lee Boojamra
Book cover design and illustration by Evelyn Rysdyk
Photo credits for author's portrait: Gloria Marino

Quote by k.d. lang reprinted, by permission, from Larry Managus, manager/ publisher for k.d. lang.

Williams, Karen, 1953 —
          Love Spell/ Karen Williams

          ISBN 0-9628938-2-X

Library of Congress Catalogue Number: 92-062809

DEDICATION

This is for Gloria
For the love, the humor and the dialogue, and for weathering the
hurricane--didn't they name one after you?

And for Dr. Aline Euler

Who over the years, has been my mentor and confidant. Mother
nature couldn't have a better friend, and neither could I.

And for my readers

The fantasy genre is not so far fetched; there is always poetry to be
heard in truths, and truths to be found in fantasy.

ACKNOWLEDGMENTS

Heartfelt thanks go to the following people for their continued support and respective talents: my editors, Alice Frier and Lee Boojamra, who took the risk; Joyce Marino, Ann Scarpa, Rosie Graci, Carol Leudesdorf, Sonny, Kitty, Annette, and Marria.

Love and special thanks to my brother Barry Williams, who so generously gave me a place to write in the country before I could afford one of my own, and for the late-night philosophy, the coffee, and all those woodland adventures. I also wish to extend my love and appreciation to my parents for their acceptance and encouragement and, of course, their creative genes. (They say it's in the blood —along with everything else, like it or not.)

Special thanks also go to Jean Giunta for her friendship and culinary expertise, not to mention the seafood, cappuccino and black truffle cake—you will always be dear to my heart and my palate.

Last but not least, I wish to acknowledge some furry friends: Ashley, a real aristo*cat* if ever I met one, and three fine canines—Alley, Stormy, and "The Gator," who never fail to remind me of one of life's more important lessons: that sometimes its good to shut off the computer and go play in the woods. I love you all.

drink
drink from my spell
quench
love's drying well

— k.d. lang
from *Ingenue*

1

*K*ate opened her front door and drew in a deep breath of crisp air. The pungent smell of damp earth mingled with the scent of falling leaves, clearing her mind of all thoughts save for the splendor rising before her. Where the valley opened up, an autumn sun swelled against the deep blue northern sky. It was that time of day, that time of year, when October's grandeur dapples the countryside with colors of fire; when cumulus clouds, white and fluffy and dream-like, hover just beyond an arm's reach.

Two cats scurried past her from behind, jumping over the dew-covered pumpkins on the porch, then disappeared into the misty field of wild grass. The morning was quiet, its silence interrupted only by the sound of coffee brewing back in the kitchen, and the clacking of the unlatched picket fence every time a gust of warm air blew in, opening then slamming it shut again. Kate zipped her white windbreaker and ran slender fingers through her still damp hair, pushing her short, dark waves to the left, although the breeze insisted on blowing them up and over to the other side. She gave up the fight finally, stuffed her hands in her pockets, and on quiet feet and with a quiet mind, headed for the pond. The cats followed several feet behind.

They never walked alongside Kate like a real companion, a dog, say; no, that would have been an admission of equality, or even worse, dependency. Keeping the distance allowed them to pretend they weren't following her at all, but simply happened to be heading in the same direction. Cats had such control issues. Kate didn't understand it completely, but supposed it had something to do with having the edge, so to speak. And being a vet had led her to hypothesize that losing control and becoming sick was what made cats such miserable patients. It didn't make her love them any less, though. She knew that underneath it all, they really needed to be loved, and that their attitudinal problems stemmed from some deep-rooted fear of ever appearing vulnerable. Maybe they weren't so different from people. The thought made her smile and she glanced back at them inconspicuously, suddenly feeling that *she* had the edge.

Kate continued on her way, ducking branches and taking in the ever-changing beauty of autumn days; the woody aromas, the feel of soil and stones and crispy leaves crinkling beneath her feet. Having lived in the Catskill Mountains only three months, she had vowed never to take its splendor for granted. Every day, before work, Kate traveled the winding dirt path which led past the woods and through the meadow to the pond.

These morning walks were a habit—one of Kate's better habits. The walk down was always inspirational, and the walk back motivated by fresh-brewed coffee and a rationed cigarette. Then, after reading a bit with a second cup, she would set out to tend to her four-legged patients. The days were pretty much routine. But today wasn't just any day.

Along the water's edge, a teasing breeze jostled the wispy branches of willows, and just as Kate strolled past the last of their golden strands and turned to face the water, she found herself in the company of an altogether beautiful witch.

Coming to an abrupt halt, Kate's mouth dropped wide open and she stood staring at the witch in owl-eyed surprise.

The witch seemed to sense, rather than hear Kate's soft approach, and she slowly turned—that black-cloaked figure—not the least bit surprised to find a stranger in her path. It was as if she were waiting there for someone.

Beneath a tall, black hat, raven hair played upon the witch's shoulders, framing flawless, celery green skin, and cat-shaped eyes of an even deeper, forest green. A black cotton dress gathered at the waist with an orange sash, ended just below her knees. And below that, she wore black stockings and pointy, low-cut boots now obscured by remnants of nocturnal fog still lingering, still swirling over the cool morning ground. She couldn't have been more than two inches taller than Kate's five feet four inches, but her black conical hat seemed to exaggerate her height.

The green witch looked down at herself, then smiled shyly and raised her brows in an expression that hinted of both amusement and apology. "Sorry...." she said, "I didn't mean to frighten you."

"No, I—you—I wasn't expecting a—"

"Witch?"

"Yes. I mean, no...." Kate faltered, "I wasn't."

The witch surveyed Kate with one mischievously arched eyebrow. "But today is Halloween...you should be expecting all sorts of things." Her brow dropped and she paused before narrowing her green eyes questioningly. "You're the new vet in town, aren't you? I saw your picture...and your article in last week's paper."

"Oh, my article." Kate said, giving a humble shrug. "Yes, that's me— can't you tell I have a way with words?"

The witch bit her bottom lip, seemingly holding back a smile, but then she laughed, a beautifully infectious laugh, and took a step closer. Kate tilted her head to meet the witch's gaze. "Well, perhaps your cats have your tongue this morning, but your writing was quite fluent. My name is Allegra," she said, extending her hand. "Welcome to the town of Broome."

Realizing she was holding her breath, Kate let out a sigh in good humor and extended her own hand. "Thank you," she managed to say, aware of the warmth of Allegra's skin, the unnerving confidence in her grip. "I'm Kate. Kate Gallagher. But I guess you already know that."

"Unfortunately, it's one of the penalties of country living." She hesitantly released Kate's hand. "If it's anonymity you're looking for, you'd best lose yourself in a crowded city. A vet in a small town can't help but become a public figure, you know."

"So I'm learning."

"And your companions?" Allegra asked, gesturing toward the cats and crouching down to meet them at eye level.

"Merlin's the gray one. The white one is Gandalf."

"Merlin and Gandalf...two very fine wizards, indeed," Allegra addressed them.

Kate watched stupefied as little Merlin walked in a punch-drunk fashion to greet the witch. Gandalf, maintaining his usual reserve, sat still, although he was obviously fascinated by Allegra. And Kate found it awfully strange to hear them both purring so loudly, their droning filling the morning with sounds of feline contentment.

Kate studied Allegra curiously. The vibrant fall landscape and her black costume contrasted sharply with the green pastels of her skin. The makeup itself, so even and natural, lent a botanical liveliness to her finely sculpted features. And now, crouched with the cats, she seemed to take on their feline grace and agility. It was as if Allegra were, all at once, woman, witch, willow, cat; possessing the secret and magic of life itself. This whole business was making Kate self-conscious. She fingered her unruly hair and rubbed her face, thinking that, next to this hauntingly colorful woman, her own fair skin and still-sleepy hazel eyes must look terribly washed out and—

"You're staring at me," Allegra said, without looking up.

Kate's whole body flinched. "Sorry, I...I was just admiring your costume."

"Costume? Now *that's* a bit presumptuous." And then Allegra did look up to find that owl-eyed expression again, and she smirked.

Kate felt the blood rush to her cheeks. "Well...maybe I am. After all, it is a little early for a party. That's why you startled me."

"Oh...so I *did* startle you." Allegra's voice was teasing. She continued to pet the cat.

Kate looked down and gave a good-natured frown. "Only because you were out of context."

"Ah...context!" The witch nodded as if giving serious thought to the word. "It's everything, isn't it?" Then she rose to meet Kate face to face, and their eyes locked.

A warm feeling rushed through Kate's stomach; a powerful rush, yet one leaving her so weak inside it nearly took her breath away. Kate didn't know how to respond. She hated being at a loss for words, and had often wondered why it was that when she didn't care to impress women, she could come across as bright, witty, downright charming. But when it mattered, really mattered, her wit, articulation, motor skills—her whole mind, basically—failed her in a flash.

For the first time, though, it seemed the witch, too, was at a loss for words. Kate shifted her eyes, feeling strangely exposed, and looked instead at Allegra's sensuous throat, as the witch swallowed hard, then turned her back on Kate to face the water. The sky was growing lighter now, the sun full and flaming like the falling leaves, which whispered on the wind as they sailed away from sleepy trees.

"To tell you the truth," Allegra began with regained composure, "I'm off to give a talk on witches and cats in folklore."

"Really? Well, no wonder mine are so impressed." Kate looked down at Merlin, who moved smoothly between them, rubbing up against Kate's legs, then running over to brush against Allegra's. Gandalf feigned indifference, meticulously cleaning his self-important face. But Kate had lived with him long enough to know he was never indifferent; he was an eavesdropper. He shot her one of his pompous little grins and she stuck her tongue out at him. Kate did that a lot. And every time she turned away, was left with the uncanny feeling that Gandalf stuck his tongue right back out at her.

"My relatives are philanthropists of sorts," Allegra went on, "We contribute a great deal to various causes but, personally, I enjoy giving time as well as money when I can. So...today I'm the guest storyteller for a children's Halloween program at the Stepping Stone." The witch folded her arms, glancing back over her shoulder. "Have you heard of it?"

Kate nodded. It was all she could do to maintain her own composure. Of course she had heard of it. Her best friend Gigi, a chef at one of the finer restaurants in the area, had volunteered to cater a benefit at the place not too long ago. The Stepping Stone sponsored women's programs, concerts, and sometimes held events for children of gay and lesbian parents. Kate didn't know what to make of Allegra's connection with the women's community; maybe she was just as she had said, a philanthropist. Suddenly, though, the pressing question for Kate was not whether Allegra was witch, willow, or cat, but whether she was gay, available and, in fact, flirting with Kate.

The witch stared ahead at the pond and the smoky-red outline of distant mountains beyond. "Anyway, the Stepping Stone will supply the pumpkins and cornstalks...."

"And you'll dispel some myths and cast a few spells?"

"If I'm lucky." Allegra directed a playful glance in Kate's direction.

"So you're not going to a party, after all...."

"No, not really. I don't have definite plans for the evening. But we're expecting a full moon, you know. I thought I'd spend some quiet time outdoors." She hesitated for a moment. "How familiar are you with the night woods?"

"Honestly?" Kate made a face. "I'm trying to learn all I can about the woods and native wildlife, but I'm still working on not getting lost during the day."

Allegra smiled. "Well, then...perhaps you'd like to join me." Kate opened her mouth to speak, but when nothing came out the witch spoke again. "The nocturnal world is quite enchanting. So alive with mysteries and wonders that hide from the light of day. It might help you with your work," she encouraged, "and it would be my way of welcoming you to the country."

For the moment Kate couldn't think of anything she wanted more than to be *welcomed* by this wonderful woman, but she was the one with plans for the evening. Gigi was holding a private Halloween party at her restaurant, and Kate had spent a month convincing Gigi to make her famous black ravioli for the occasion. She couldn't not show. Besides, Halloween was a favorite holiday—if you could call it a holiday. On the other hand, she had no intentions of passing up a moonlit walk with a witch. Not this witch.

Kate's mind, or what little use she had of it at the moment, started working overtime. "I—I'd love to, but...do you have a...an agenda?"

Allegra tilted her head and smirked, as if finding Kate's awkwardness terribly appealing. "No...nothing formal, no time schedule. Just a relaxed...*exploration*, if you will."

"What will you be exploring?" Kate inquired innocently.

Allegra lifted her shoulders, then let them drop in a teasingly matter-of-fact way. "Oh, I don't know...possibilities, perhaps."

"Possibilities?"

"Yes." The witch gave a knowing smile. "Would you care to explore some with me?"

Kate lifted her eyes to counter Allegra's gaze, and that warm feeling washed through her stomach again. This time she knew the witch felt it, too; for in those forest green eyes, playful and nonchalant a moment ago, was now something tender and serious and so full of urgency. Kate caught her breath, and in feeling the power of the witch's magic, began wanting her more than she had ever wanted a woman before.

Kate stumbled over her words. "Listen, I uh...I just made a pot of coffee, if you have time for a cup. I'm right up the path in the white house," she said, nervously pointing in every direction except the one from which she had come.

"Oh, I wouldn't want to intrude."

"No!" Kate heard the urgency in her own voice and began again with conscious ease. "No...*really*, I'd be happy to have you—so would the cats."

After a moment they started up the path, commenting on the day, laughing about the animals—making small talk, mostly—then walked the rest of the way in silence. A southwesterly wind moved across the meadow, brushing the tops of sunlit wheat and dry grass and strawflowers, and turning the whole field into a landscape of glittering gold. Then it changed its course and whirled toward them, stirring in its path pieces of leaves and twigs and dust and, it seemed to Kate, bits of enchantment, too.

Kate resisted a compulsive urge to look over at Allegra; to take in, drink in, the beauty of her green profile the way one would a work of art. Better to keep looking ahead, she told herself, than to get caught staring again. Every so often, though, Kate noticed Allegra glancing at *her*, and out of her peripheral vision was almost sure she saw the witch's hands trembling just a bit.

From behind, Gandalf's eyes pierced her, and Kate was suddenly struck with the notion that both the cats and the witch knew something she didn't know. It occurred to Kate that she had lost the edge. How quickly the tables could turn.

$\mathcal{A}$s they reached the top of the path, Kate's white house came into view, and with it the sound of the picket gate. Its rhythmic clacking somehow soothed Kate—a matter of territory is what it was—that primitive, almost animalistic sense of power that comes with being on your own turf.

The cats pushed ahead, eager to be first in line at the front door, then sat by the pumpkins, watching as Kate and the witch trod along the gravel driveway. It was covered—nearly ankle deep—with myriad gold and red and orange leaves. Kate hadn't gotten around to raking yet, and blamed it on the recent rain. On several afternoons she had returned home with vague intentions of doing the job, but with the wet weather and all, was forced to thank the heavens and spend her raking time curled up by the fire with hot cider and a good book. The truth, though, was that Kate rather enjoyed the colorful mess. Why should she worry, anyway, about raking or shoveling or keeping her lawn at its specified suburban height? This wasn't Long Island, after all, it was the Catskill Mountains. To hell with the Joneses— they weren't her neighbors anymore. If Kate found the autumnal ground cover attractive, well then she'd leave all the leaves right where they were until they turned as brown as rotten apples. Then she'd rake up the whole darn mess.

Gandalf, it seemed, wasn't in complete agreement with the new yard maintenance policy. Kate could tell by the way he stopped in the doorway, stretching his hind legs one at a time, then spreading his toes and violently shaking them to rid his dainty feet of the sticky stuff. Kate never did such silly things with her own feet, and maybe that explained the little yellow leaves strewn about the purple living room carpet. As they walked in, Kate bent down, reaching around to collect them, then stood up and shrugged. "Coffee?" she asked.

"Mmm..." Allegra stood with her arms folded, her eyes moving in every direction, taking in the whole room in one prolonged glance. "It's charming," she whispered.

And it was charming, Kate thought; quite cozy, actually, with all its rattan furniture and purple and green pillows and upholstery. One wall was papered in white on green—the teeniest calico print imaginable—and the other walls, including the bookshelves, were stained whitish gray. In the far left corner sat a big potbelly stove, and behind it a bay window overlooking the hills. "Thank you," Kate said, taking her handful of leaves and retreating to the kitchen waste basket.

"Do you mind if I smoke?" Allegra asked from the living room.

"Not at all. Make yourself at home." Kate took two stoneware cups from a hutch which rested against the brick wall, and had started filling them when a strange aroma drifted into the kitchen. A wild, spicy, flowery fragrance, not at all unpleasant, that reminded Kate of the way a blooming meadow smells after a heavy, summer storm. "What is that you're smoking?" she called to the witch.

"Herbal tobacco...lavender, mostly. "

"Lavender?"

"Do you like it?"

"Yes. It's...heady, kind of medicinal. Do you buy it locally?"

Allegra answered in a voice that suggested she wasn't paying full attention to this long distance conversation. "England," she said.

"*You* buy it in England?"

"I travel overseas on occasion. My family is in the import-export business, spices and the like."

Spices and the like. How appropriate, Kate thought. "How do you take your coffee, anyway?"

"Black, please."

"Black like your hat?" Kate mumbled.

"Pardon?"

"Nothing." Kate was, she decided, feeling a bit giddy just then, and didn't *know* if it was a simple case of nerves, or if it had something to do with the smoke Allegra was blowing her way. Now if she could just carry the coffee in without shaking or tripping or spoiling her chances of— what?— she wasn't sure. But if there was a chance of anything, anything at all, she didn't want to chance blowing it.

Kate made it into the living room with surprising grace, and found the hatless witch facing her books; tilting her head as she read various titles. There were hundreds there: medical and zoology books, a multitude of reference material, children's classics, Shakespeare, and a stack of lesbian romances.

Allegra moved over to the sofa and sat beside her witch's hat. "I see you have an interest in women's literature."

Kate nodded, wanting yet not wanting to give herself away, although the books had already done just that.

Allegra looked at her with the hint of a sultry smile. "And an interest in women, too, I presume?"

Kate took a seat in the chair across from Allegra, holding her steaming cup in both hands and staring into it to stall for time. "Would it be a problem if I said yes?"

"Absolutely not," the witch answered softly, her glimmering green eyes dancing all over Kate's face.

"Well...then, yes, I do." She cleared her throat and hesitated. "And you...?"

Allegra slowly puffed on her herbal cigarette, her eyes never leaving Kate's. And as she exhaled, lavender smoke rose and twisted and curled up in front of her face so that, for a moment, she appeared ethereal. "Yes. Quite interested, as a matter of fact."

Well, there. It was done. Out in the open. Now maybe Kate could continue this psychological hide and seek feeling a bit more grounded. But her heart was still pounding; pounding so hard that somewhere between her breast and shirt pocket she could feel the tickle of its vibrations. Her heart no longer felt like it belonged to her; and maybe it didn't. Maybe she had just given it away without knowing it.

Just about then, the cats strolled into the room. Kate prayed one of them would jump on her lap, break the tension, give her something to do with her hands. Instead, Gandalf hopped in the bay window and Merlin jumped right into Allegra's arms. She began petting, stroking him, as if showing Kate how wonderfully sensual her touch could be. Kate half-closed her eyes for a moment, and under lowered lids, shifted her gaze to the witch-black stockings that hugged Allegra's slender legs. Then she looked up again with her lips slightly parted. "You blend in with this room so well...with the colors, I mean."

Allegra cocked her head. "Are you telling me that if I stayed too long I'd risk becoming part of the furniture?"

"Not a chance." Kate smiled, shaking her head coyly.

Allegra lifted Merlin from her lap and sat him beside her hat. She leaned forward, taking hold of her cup, then settled back again. "Tell me," she said, her countenance turning quizzical, "what would you have done if I had been a real witch?"

Kate grinned. "Passed out, probably."

"Why such a fear of witches?"

"I don't even *believe* in green witches. We agreed it was the context, remember?"

Allegra rubbed her chin between her thumb and finger, peering wisely at Kate but saying nothing.

Kate felt she was expected to expound, to make a point. "For instance," she said, thinking an analogy might satisfy Allegra, "During the summer I used to see the farmer down the road checking on his corn late at night. He wore overalls and I didn't think anything of it. But if I had seen a man in a black suit in that same corn field...well, I'd have had my windows bolted and my rifle loaded in no time. Context..." Kate said, gesturing with one hand to indicate that no further explanation was necessary.

Allegra sighed facetiously. "Nonetheless, I'm sorry to hear you don't believe in witches."

"Why?" Kate asked, sipping her coffee.

"Well, since I'm more or less representing a witch today, I was about to offer to assist you...."

"Assist me? With my fear of witches?"

"Sometimes the best way to overcome our fears is to adopt them, spend some time with them. I thought I could help you."

Kate had a feeling she was being teased. "I'm sure you could."

"I know I could. But you don't believe in witches."

Kate regarded her playfully. "I will if you want me to."

"But you'd only be pretending."

"I wouldn't mind. Really."

"I'm afraid that wouldn't do."

Kate looked at her sideways. "Well, I believe in other things."

"Such as?" Allegra's eyes were calculating.

"Oh, I don't know..." Kate said, feigning nonchalance, "Friendship, romance...love."

"Oh? Then maybe you could help me with *my* fear?"

"Of love, you mean?"

"Maybe. But first you'd have to make me believe in it." Allegra lowered her head, still petting Merlin, then raised her eyes half way.

Kate cast her a sideways glance. "I'm not sure if you're teasing or seducing me."

"Neither," Allegra said, "I don't even know you, Dr. Gallagher."

Kate looked quickly away, blushing and grinning with embarrassment. When their eyes met again they both broke into laughter, and it was a minute before they laughed themselves out. It seemed to do them both some good. As exhausting as laughing could be, there was always something liberating about it. And as for Kate, she felt as though she had just run up and down a hill and lost the jitters along the way. Now rid of them, she was suddenly aware of an underlying comfort, a naturalness, in being with Allegra.

"You know," Kate said, thinking she ought to steer clear of the seduction piece for a while, "When I was young I did have one experience with a witch."

Allegra raised an eyebrow, looking as though she had just gotten a lead on some very important information. "Tell me more," she said.

"Well, there was this old witch who was hot and heavy on my trail for years. Every Halloween she followed me around the neighborhood." Kate leaned forward to light a cigarette, then settled back again. "The light was always fading by the time my friends and I got home from school and into costumes, so it was difficult to see clearly at a distance.

"We were trick-or-treating the first time it happened, and I suddenly got this weird feeling of being followed. I didn't want to turn around, but I did...and there she was, half a block away, hunched over and wearing this long black kerchief that blew up from the back of her head like a windsock. She always held her shawl closed with one hand, and in the other carried a big black sack which, we very well knew, could easily hold a couple of children." Kate let out a half-suppressed laugh through her nose, remembering those magical memories. "That witch was as awe-inspiring as she was frightening."

"Awe-inspiring?" Allegra's eyes were questioning.

"Some old, mystical woman sneaking around the ordinary world? Sure." Kate finished her coffee in one gulp. "Looking back, I guess it had to do with the whole notion of feminine powers, you know? Powers which seemed all the more thrilling because they were cloaked in darkness, hidden beneath all those black clothes." She gestured with her chin toward Allegra's black hat and smiled.

Kate's green-eyed guest settled deeper into the sofa. "Do you have any idea who the woman might have been?"

Allegra's voice, Kate thought, was a trifle too serious for a light-hearted childhood story such as this. "The witch was my grandmother!" she said. "At the age of six, trick-or-treating with adults was not the grown-up thing to do. I guess it was her way of keeping an eye on us and giving us a fun scare at the same time."

Allegra pursed her lips, then smiled. "You had me fooled for a moment."

"I didn't mean to..." Kate looked at her oddly. "She sure fooled us, though. I knew it was her—at least after the first Halloween—and the following year I expected to see her again. But then when she did appear, when I turned and saw her moving toward us in the shadows...I began to doubt it was her. I thought that maybe my grandmother couldn't make it, and a *real* witch had taken her place." Kate looked down and shook her head. "I'll never forget those Halloweens."

"Your grandmother was a special person," Allegra said, a certain tenderness in her voice.

"Yes...she still is."

Allegra gestured toward the bookshelves. "She writes children's books?"

"You don't miss a thing, do you?" Kate smiled. "My grandfather was an editor of children's books before he retired—that's how they met. In a way, they were responsible for my decision to become a vet. They introduced me to Dr. Doolittle books when I was four, and I thought all vets were like him. Needless to say, I grew to be sadly disillusioned. None of the vets we ever used had the same rapport with animals as Doolittle did. My grandparents told me that was all the more reason to become a Doolittle-type doctor.

"You'd be surprised how many vets don't even own a dog or cat...I can't understand it." Just then, Gandalf jumped from the window, strutting between her chair and the coffee table to find a comfortable spot by Allegra's feet. Then he grinned at Kate with a slightly protruding tongue, and for a fleeting moment Kate did understand it.

"Where are your grandparents now?" The witch asked.

Kate felt as though she was being interviewed. She was the one who typically asked questions, did most of the listening. Being the focal point of any discussion for too long made her feel somewhat exposed. "More coffee?" she asked.

"No...thank you. So?"

"Long Island. They've lived in a beach house in Montauk for as long as I can remember. My father would prefer to see them living closer to him, to other people, but they say that when they start missing people the summer season begins, and when they've had all they can stand of people, the season ends."

Kate shrugged. "They're creative types. They enjoy spending winters quietly, reading children's stories to each other by the fire...listening to the ocean, walking the beach with their dogs. My parents think they're weird, but they have their own opinion of my parents."

Allegra smiled. "I should think their lives are blessed. Too often we wait for the grand things in life to bring us happiness. But grand things are few and far between, and to wait only for them is to spend most of our time unhappy. It's when we learn to find pleasure in the simple things, in life's more humble miracles, that grace and happiness are likely to visit us all of our days."

Kate couldn't have agreed more. That was her philosophy, exactly—she just never tried to put it into words. And here she had been letting people convince her she was too much of a leisure sort; wanting to go home after work to play with the cats, take in a sunset, enjoy fine food, and a good book. She wasn't laid back at all—she was blessed. It was merely a question of semantics. "What a wonderful thought," Kate said.

Allegra leaned forward, resting her chin in her hand. "You're a wonderful woman."

Kate shrugged, feeling both humble and puffed with pride. "The way I've always figured it, is that every time I do something good to score a cosmic brownie point, I do something else, make a mistake, and lose a point, so that in the end, I can only hope to break even."

Allegra pondered Kate's theory for a moment. "I have a feeling you'll do more than break even. You're too kind."

"You don't know that about me."

"Oh, but I do, Kate...I see it." Allegra studied her. "Your heart shines in your eyes."

Kate had a sudden pang of guilt just then, because she was sure it was lust, and not her heart shining in her eyes. Her thoughts were not entirely kind at the moment, either; she had been sitting there warding off obsessional thoughts of what it would be like to kiss the witch across from her; to breathe the sweet and private essence of her skin; to know her the way only lovers know one another.

"Thank you," Kate said, running her hand over her mouth and thinking she would like to steer the conversation away from herself. "What about you?" she asked. "Do you have any memorable Halloween experiences to share?"

Allegra glanced at her watch. "There will be plenty of time for a Halloween experience tonight. I don't want to keep you from your patients."

"I have a few minutes."

"Then maybe we should spend them planning for tonight."

Kate moistened her lips and set her cup down, admiring the artistry of the celery-colored makeup that faded into the collar of Allegra's dress, only to resurface on her arms and hands and fade again into her palms. "It's incredibly realistic," Kate said.

"What's that?" Allegra asked, her thoughts seeming to have gone astray.

"Your skin...the color. It's flawless. How'd you do it?"

"Theatrical make-up." Allegra spread her fingers and casually inspected her hands, turning them palms-up, then back over again. "It's a liquid application. You paint it on, let it dry, then buff it to a desired tone."

"It must have taken hours."

"Not at all," Allegra intoned, her voice as casual as her inspection of her green hands. "Not nearly as long as it takes to get off."

"With what?"

"Water." Allegra gave a wink. "It's as good an excuse as any to take a long, hot bubble bath."

Kate clicked her tongue in jest. "Then you *can't* be a real witch."

"How so?"

"Witches and water don't mix."

"Who told you that?"

"It's a fictional fact. Wooden stakes kill vampires, silver bullets kill werewolves...water melts witches."

"Ah...well, personally speaking?" Allegra paused to cross her legs, then draped her arm across her knee. "It takes more than water to melt me. Of course, it *would* make an interesting experiment. You might try it sometime...just to prove your case in point."

"Try what?"

"Taking a bubble bath with a witch."

Kate's mouth twisted itself into a parody of challenge and intrigue. *Someone* was going to melt tonight, but it clearly wasn't going to be the witch. And water, Kate decided, probably wouldn't even figure into it. She sat there chewing thoughtfully on her lip until a grin slowly broke on her face. "Where on earth did you come from, anyway?"

"The top of the mountain."

Kate gave a surprised look. "That's it? That's all you're going to tell me? You live on the mountain, study folklore, deal in spices—*and the like*—don't forget, and fly to England for lavender cigarettes?"

"Maybe you'd like to fly there with me sometime. I bet you've never had a ride on a broom before...."

Patchy sunlight filtered through the windows, collecting in the witch's eyes like sunshine flickering in a lush, green forest. And all Kate could do for the moment was gaze into their kaleidoscopic beauty, feeling them pulling her, desirously urging her, into the tangled mysteries of their hypnotic depths.

~ *3* ~

*K*ate turned her black Jeep onto Route 45 and sped to work with only half an hour to spare before her first appointment. The animal hospital was just four miles away, but Kate enjoyed a little alone-time with her charges; serving breakfast, checking on healing wounds and stroking wounded egos before patients and their people arrived. And then, of course, there was Igor, her fifteen pound humpbacked leopard tortoise, who had free run of the office and, like any good creature of habit, would be hungry and waiting at the door for his usual fruit salad.

Reaching into her handbag, Kate pulled out a Halloween cassette and popped it in the dash. She had finished making it the previous night, and was relatively proud of her amateur attempt at mixing songs with lyrics to fit the festivities—club and house music, classic rock and jazz, all interspersed with spooky sound effects: groaning ghosts, laughing vampires, creaking doors...cackling witches.

Witches. Kate glanced at the expanse of land on her left. Further down she could see the sloping banks and the end of the kettle pond trickling off in between clumps of cattails and reeds and marsh grasses. Everywhere, herons and egrets now stood, skillfully spying the water for fish. This morning's encounter down there suddenly seemed surreal. But surreal, or real, or not, Kate was decidedly in an exceptionally good mood. Exhilarated, in fact, like someone who had just won a lottery and had yet to claim her prize.

Kate turned up the volume as she passed the Rockwell dairy farm on her right. Black and white cows moseyed about the voluminous hills that rolled out into the distance like a patchwork quilt spread beneath the clear, blue sky. A few cows stood at the edge of the road, watching cars drive by from behind a wire fence which seemed to amount to no more than a bakery string. Kate smiled sympathetically at them, as she always did when she passed, thinking how a brighter species—Gandalf, say—would have simply walked over, under, or bolted through that boundary line, then looked back and laughed. But for those cows, that thin wire was as strong as any iron gate. It was funny, in a sad sort of way, she thought, how some prisons were merely a state of mind.

Up ahead a truck carrying bales of hay turned in front of Kate's jeep and she slowed down, approaching the village of Broome, and watching out for children who ran from one cobblestone corner to the next in pursuit of a yellow school bus. Century-old houses stood on either side of the road; renovated Victorians and three-story colonials with huge wraparound porches that set the stage for carved pumpkins and straw-stuffed scarecrows sporting flannel shirts and worn out blue jeans. In several yards, homemade sheet-ghosts dangled from bare birch trees, blowing and flashing their goblin grins, seeming to wave at passersby as if they had taken on a life all their own. Smiling, Kate waved back at them. Then she quickly peeked in her rear view mirror to make sure no one had seen her. News traveled fast, and she didn't need anyone spreading ugly rumors about the new town vet being half out of her mind.

The town itself was small, and if you blinked your eyes for too long it was quite possible to pass right through it without ever having known. A bank, video store and curiosity shop were on one side; on the other, the post office, convenience store, and Mrs. O's Country Kitchen, a quaint diner-type place where Kate's neighbors gathered for breakfast on Sundays. Mrs. O could not have cared less about cooking, but the people didn't seem to mind. They really came to see her, and to fill their socialization quota for the week. All in all, they were a good lot, most having relocated from the city. And the friendships which had developed among them seemed to stem from their common love of the country. Age, race, sexual-orientation—none of it much mattered. It was precisely this general climate of acceptance that had relieved Kate's initial fear of moving to a dangerously homogeneous town, where threatened locals might have taken to burning a cross smack in front of her house when they caught wind of her whereabouts and, well...her howabouts.

At the end of town, Kate made a right onto Blueberry Road, then a quick left into the long, hidden driveway of the animal hospital. A new red Mustang was parked out front, and sitting behind the wheel was none other than Gabriella Giovanni, better known as Gigi. She had one of those cherubic, rosy-cheeked faces that always looked so happy—in a devilish sort of way—with wildly loose curls and a virgin white smile to match. Her brown eyes always seemed to smile, too, except that they were usually hidden, as they were now, behind a pair of black shades.

"You're late." Gigi said annoyed.

"That's right," Kate answered back, jumping down from her Jeep and walking over to the Mustang. "And it was worth every minute of it." She leaned into the open window, and with both hands slid Gigi's sunglasses from her face.

"Eh! What are you doing?" Gigi squinted, shielding her eyes from the morning sun.

"Late night?" Kate asked.

"An early morning is what it is! I didn't leave the restaurant until almost two." She looked at Kate and smiled. "And then I went on a panty raid over at Grover College."

Kate folded the sunglasses and handed them back to her. "In your dreams you did."

Gigi laughed and held up a bag. "I brought breakfast if you're interested. Bacon and egg on roll. But I'm pressed for time. I have to run around for last minute party stuff."

"Sounds good. I was just going to grab a donut inside." Kate fumbled for her keys and Gigi got out, slamming the car door behind her.

"You eat too much sugar," she said, following Kate inside, then walking past the reception area and straight into Kate's office. "They say sugar rots you from the inside out."

"Who's *they?*"

"You know. *They.* I read it someplace. One of my culinary magazines, I think." Gigi sat behind Kate's desk, taking the sandwiches and two containers of coffee from the bag. "You know what sugar does to children's teeth? It'll do the same thing to your insides."

"Geez...." Kate said, more to herself than Gigi. And here she had been thinking about quitting smoking. Maybe she'd do well to concentrate on giving up the cake and candy first. The problem with being able to eat anything without gaining an ounce was that there was no reason to keep track of good and bad foods.

Kate's attention momentarily shifted to the tappety-tap-tapping of Igor coming in from the examination room. "Morning, sweetie," she said, bending down to rub his black and yellow shell and tickle him under the chin. He tilted his round, egg-sized head and peered up at her with peaceful but hungry eyes, then followed her over to the small refrigerator. Kate pulled out a head of escarole, grabbed a banana and peach from a wicker basket on her desk and sat down, wondering how her tortoise could eat fructose all day long and still plan on outliving her by a hundred years or so.

Gigi leaned back, rocking herself from side to side in Kate's plush, swivel chair. "Why were you so late?" she said in between bites.

Kate didn't hear her. She was frowning at the fruit, still trying to fathom this business of rotting. It was a horrible notion, really, whether she believed it or not. But a woman needed her chocolate now and again, and if sugar-rot was her predestined way to go, then she'd much prefer it happened from the inside out, rather than the other way around. At least this way, the effects wouldn't become visible until the very end. And when she finally did disintegrate one day, people would throw their arms up in the air and say, "Who would have known? She looked so good only yesterday—"

"Hey, Doc!"

Kate shook away her sugar thoughts and looked up. "Huh?"

"What's with you, anyway?" Gigi glanced at her suspiciously. "I said, why were you late?"

Kate looked at Gigi, chewing the corner of her lip, then broke into an ear-to-ear smile. "I was busy meeting the woman of my dreams."

"You met someone? Tell me more," she said eagerly.

"I'm bringing her to the party tonight."

Gigi stopped swiveling and leaned forward, as if about to whisper something. Then she made a face and waved her hand at Kate. "You're kidding me, right?"

"Do I look like I'm kidding?" Kate set a plate in front of the tortoise, then took a sip of her coffee. "She's beautiful, Gigi...and she makes me nervous. No woman's ever made me this nervous." Kate took a bite of her sandwich.

"What do you mean? Who?" She was getting impatient for answers, and Kate had the feeling Gigi was about to get up and start pacing like she tended to do when growing restless.

"Her name is Allegra. I don't think you know her. *I've* never seen her before."

"Allegra...that's Italian, you know. It means lively, happy."

Kate smiled again. "I know." Thanks to Gigi's passion for the opera, Kate was reasonably familiar with musical terms.

"So where did you meet this *happy* woman?"

"By the pond. She was on her way to speak at the Stepping Stone in a witch's costume."

"What? I can't believe this!" Gigi slapped her own thigh and started swiveling again. "Here I am, introducing you to women all summer long— women who are eligible and more than interested— and you have to go meet a freaking witch in the woods!"

It was Gigi's style to be saucy, to come across as restless and dramatic and sometimes irritable. But, for the most part, it was all pretend. Deep down she was a hopeless romantic with a heart of gold; and if you pressed her, she'd easily admit to it all.

Gigi listened with undivided attention, as Kate blurted out the pond story in what appeared to be one amazingly long breath. When she was finished, Gigi sighed, smacking her lips in a parental manner. "A witch in the woods...I don't know, Doc. I think you're spending too much time hanging around cats and dogs and...*wolves*. Gigi nodded toward a black animal that watched her from an open room which housed the kennels. "She gives me the creeps."

Kate looked behind her and caught the creature's silent gaze. She had saved its life last week, in what she considered the most spiritual experience of her professional life. "Her name is Lycos. And she's a dog."

"You think so? I'm no zoologist, but I'll tell you, that dog has as much wolf in its blood as I have Sicilian in mine—one hundred percent, if you ask me."

She did look like a wolf, Kate admitted secretly, with her lanky legs and long, soulful face. Her coat was midnight black, thick and silky; her eyes a pale, green—so pale, that looking at them in the dim light was like staring into smoke. I told you she belongs to Mr. Hebron. He's picking her up today. And I doubt he'd keep a wolf."

"Never believe anything an elf tells you."

"The Hebrons are *dwarves*, Gigi."

"Same difference."

"It's not. Elves don't exist, they're mythical creatures. Dwarves are real people."

"Then why are their ears so pointy?"

Kate made a face. "I don't know why you're so down on dwarves today...you sure buy enough of their cheeses."

The Hebrons were a reclusive but friendly family who owned a sizable portion of land in the county. It was common knowledge that the family continued to inhabit ancestral homes built nearly two hundred years ago by relatives from Wales. A few of the older Hebrons were jewelers, and what with dwarves and the Welsh both having historically been known to fancy mining and other underground activities, hearsay had it that their cellars led to secret grottoes filled with a fabulous supply of heavenly gems and other exotic treasures from distant lands. More likely, their cellars were like anyone else's.

Most of the Hebron descendants were in the goat business—goat cheese, that is. Wonderfully flavorful cheeses made with dill and nuts and fruits and other tasty morsels that were hard to put a finger on, and which were considered true epicurean delights by chefs near and far. Gigi included.

"I'm not in the mood for cheese today," Gigi said grumpily, stuffing her garbage in the paper bag and leaning back to finish her coffee.

Kate got up, grabbed the other half of her sandwich, and turned on the kennel lights. As if on signal, Lycos carefully rose to her feet, her face tightening and betraying the soreness throughout her body. "A little stiff, are we?" Kate put her sandwich in between her teeth as she squatted and unlatched the cage door. Then she took it back in her hands, tore it, and offered half to the dog.

"Oh, that's great," Gigi commented, giving an exaggerated frown. "Save the wolf's life, then pump her full of bacon and cholesterol."

The dog looked over at Gigi. "It's okay," Kate said, urging Lycos to take it. "Dog's don't have to worry about cholesterol."

"No kidding...." Gigi came up behind Kate and extended her hand to the dog. "You're such a beautiful wolf," she said in a baby voice.

Lycos sniffed Gigi's hand in a somewhat suspicious fashion before acknowledging Kate kindly and accepting the food from her hand.

"She knows you saved her life, Kate. I can tell just by the way she stares at you." Gigi shook her head in admiration. "It's like something straight out of a Jack London story. She still gives me the creeps, though.... It's like she knows what we're saying."

And Gigi was right. There was a strange, imposing intelligence in those smoky eyes; an undeniable and unspoken bond between patient and doctor that began the night Kate battled to pull Lycos from the shadow of death. It was late Friday evening, a week ago to the day, to be exact, that the Hebrons had come screeching into Kate's driveway in a pickup. Mrs. Hebron, whose eyes barely cleared the steering wheel, climbed down and ran to Kate's door, pounding in a wild fury. The dog, she explained in between sobs of breath, had wandered off and been shot by poachers. Kate grabbed her jacket and keys, took Mr. Hebron's place in back of the truck so she could be with the dog, and had him follow behind in her Jeep.

When they got her to the hospital, the semiconscious dog was in critical condition; more from blood loss than organ damage, and Kate spent three hours in surgery with Lycos on a respirator before sending the Hebrons home to get some rest. She herself stayed at the hospital throughout the night, keeping a watchful and bloodshot eye on the sleeping animal. Kate was the kind of woman who relied on a good night's sleep, and watching the dreaming Lycos only contributed to her grogginess. By morning, the capillaries in her heavy eyes were so dilated that she remembered having scared herself when she looked in the mirror.

The following night she decided to sleep at the office to be close to her recovering patient, but ended up doing nothing more than tossing and turning on what had to be the world's most uncomfortable cot. By the time the third night rolled around Kate was seriously exhausted and, feeling the dog was pretty much out of danger, decided to have her assistant Annie, an animal husbandry student at a local agricultural college, put in evening hours for the rest of the week. Kate went home the next day and slept for twelve hours. But it had all been worth it; Lycos lived against all odds, and today she was going home.

"Yep, you done good, Doc," Gigi said, patting Kate on the back, and walking over to a cabinet mirror. "Maybe some higher power sent this happy witch in recognition of your good deed. I just hope she likes animals."

Kate opened the back door and let Lycos out. "She's a natural with them," Kate said, smiling at the thought of Allegra. "The cats are wild about her."

"The cats, too, huh?" Kate caught Gigi's reflection in the mirror and they started laughing. Then Gigi winked at her. "I was waiting for something to develop with Annie."

"Annie? She's in her second year of college. She's just a babe, Gigi."

"So? She's adorable and she has a crush on you."

"I'm thirty-four years old. What am I going to do with a nineteen-year-old besides get in trouble?"

"If my memory serves me right, we were hot for older women when we were Annie's age. How would you have felt if none of them took you seriously?"

Kate shrugged. "They didn't then, and they don't now. And I still like older women."

Gigi looked at Kate, then returned to her own reflection in the mirror, continuing to scrutinize her ever so subtly—what were they called?—character lines. "I don't know, Kate. I'm not a bad looking woman. I'm sensitive, caring, passionate...and I cook! So why is it I don't have a date for my own party? Huh? This is getting serious, you know. And I'll tell you one thing, if I'm not married by the time I'm forty, I'm going to Italy to find myself a wife."

Kate chuckled, walked over, and hugged Gigi from behind. "Don't give up," she said, jokingly. "You have to keep expecting the unexpected."

"You think I'm kidding? I'm getting tired of all these women who don't know what they want. Five more years and I'm leaving for Italy—the land of romance. You'll see."

Poor Gigi. She really was all those things—sensitive, caring, passionate, potentially monogamous—a good catch for the right woman. But she seemed to have the continuous misfortune of stumbling, head over heels, for the wrong ones; women who were fine for a few days, until they disclosed some dark and terrible secret about their lives, then departed in search of a personal resolution in which, Gigi was told, she could play no part. More often, there were those who, after a weekend of wonderful romance, decided they didn't know who they were or what they wanted. They, too, ran off to find themselves or their sexuality or some other indefinable thing. In short, Gigi dated a lot.

She turned around and hugged Kate. "I have to run. I'll see you and your witch at seven, okay? And don't be late. Is your cat costume all set?"

"Of course. I almost changed my mind, but stuck with the cat idea just to insult Gandalf. The cassette is finished, too. Take it out of the Jeep on your way."

"Great. I'll listen to it on my way home." Gigi smacked her lips. "It's going to be a *spooktacular* Halloween. By the way," she said as an afterthought, "did you get a Halloween card from your Grandmother?"

"I haven't gotten the mail yet."

"I got *mine* from her yesterday," Gigi said. "Did you send her one?"

Kate shook her head. "I meant to, but—"

"Well *I* did. How can you expect to get cards, when you don't send them, Doc?" Gigi smirked. "See you later," she said, quickly kissing Kate, then heading out. In the doorway she stopped for a moment and turned back. "Just trust me on one thing, okay?"

"What's that?"

"The Hebrons are elves, and that there dog is their pet wolf."

Before Kate could retort, Gigi was out the door, and Kate could hear her giggling all the way to the car.

$\mathcal{T}$he gabled house nestled high on the mountain peak. So high was it, that the meadows and valleys and labyrinth of endless hills below—even the mountain itself—seemed far away. It was an angel's view. Allegra gazed out the window, feeling as though she were looking down upon the entire world.

A great star shone like a distant jewel in the late afternoon light, and somewhere just beyond the fading sun there rose the promising outline of a full and waxing moon. A few more hours, and the black of night would bring the translucent sphere its rightful glory. And when its time came, so her time, too, would come.

"The two of you have finally met?" came a voice from behind her.

Everything in the room sat in moving shadows, save for a grand piano which borrowed the unsteady light of a fireplace. Allegra turned to face the silhouette of a woman who sat content, swaying back and forth in her rocking chair. There was no real need to turn on a lamp—not just yet. Such a thing would have only denied the woman the pleasure of savoring the pending twilight.

"Yes...we did," Allegra answered in a low voice. She bowed her head, as if to hide her eyes. "You know?"

Nothing could be seen of the other woman's face, but her raspy voice, wise and tired, betrayed her golden age. "You need not hide from me, Allegra. You *cannot* hide. My blood courses through your veins and tells me all I need to know. And if it did not, I would still know. This new-found joy is written all over your face, it covers your body like an aura. And when you turn away from me, I see it there on the back of your head, too."

Allegra smiled faintly, then turned back to the window and sighed. "If it's all the same to you, then, please converse with the back of my head. It makes me feel more easy." She crossed her arms, rubbing her shoulders with her hands. "It's getting chilly in here."

"The fire is roaring, my dear. I believe your chills are coming from inside."

Allegra was quiet for a moment, and then she said in a rather stately voice, "I want the driver tonight."

"A chauffeur...hmm...." The old woman lifted a lazy brow, her lips pursed in consideration of the request. "You will be joining her, I presume?"

"Yes."

"In costume?"

"I'm accompanying her to a Halloween party."

The woman nodded thoughtfully. "As you wish, then...and so you will learn," she said, her voice mysteriously raspy.

"What else am I to do? You don't know how I struggle to fight this cruel desire." Allegra's arms lifted, then fell heavily at her sides. "But I...I do believe I love her."

The woman's laugh was low and burdened. "I know your struggle all too well, and I am foolish to have ever thought I could save you from that pain...that you could ever learn from *my* mistakes. You must make your own. Such is human nature, that we make the same mistakes a hundred times before learning our lessons. And even then, we tend to foolishly make them over again." When Allegra said nothing, the old woman spoke with careful gentleness. "I will not argue her worthiness, nor yours.... No one has ever captured your affections like this. Dr. Gallagher must, no doubt, be a fine and worthy woman. But is she strong enough, Allegra, to know and keep the love of which you speak?"

"I don't know—I don't know much of anything at the moment."

"And you certainly don't know much about her. You have done nothing more than watch her from afar, Allegra." The old woman sighed. "You cannot take chances. You know our history, our legacy...you've heard the stories. Look what happened with that..."

"I know all that has happened!" Allegra's voice mounted with agitation. Then she bowed her head again and was silent. "I...I'm sorry, grandmother...."

"No, no, no," she said, her tone growing weary as she gave a half-hearted wave of her hand. "You need never apologize for loving." With a doleful smile, the woman reached out her arm to Allegra. "There is nothing more I can say or do, my darling...so before you go, you may as well come sit by the fire and play a song for this lover who so haunts your heart."

Allegra left the window and squeezed the woman's hand before she passed behind the chair. Quietly then, she sat on the piano bench, wiping her nervous palms, stretching her skillful fingers. And as they gracefully came to rest upon the glowing ivory keys, she began Beethoven's"Moonlight Sonata."

"Sonata quasi una Fantasia..." the old woman mused, keeping the soft tempo in her rocker. "He wrote it for Countess Giulietta Guicciardi. Did you know?"

"Mmm..." Allegra's music echoed softly throughout the room.

"Of all the things on this earth, I believe it is your music I will miss the most. And today you play it more beautifully than ever. I suppose the magic of love makes its own music...and hears nothing else." The woman's voice began to dwindle, the sonata soothing her like a sweet lullaby. "I can only pray..." she said with her last wakeful breath, "that pain and sorrow do not wait in the shadows of your joy."

"I will meet the sorrow that is mine. I know what can and cannot be." Allegra's green eyes grew teary and she blinked to free the sadness within them. "But I must see this through," she said, "...if it only lasts one night."

A tear streamed down Allegra's cheek, its wet trail glistening in the firelight, as she turned once more to the window and, through glassy eyes, stared at the translucent moon.

5

$\mathcal{D}$usk settled upon the village of Broome as Mrs. Banks and Barney, the basset hound, left the office. Kate normally didn't keep late afternoon hours, but today she had doubled up on appointments and juggled her schedule in order to take tomorrow off. And it was a lucky thing for Barney Banks, who had unexpectedly arrived at three-thirty with a bundle of porcupine quills about his nose. It was his third such incident this month, and having obviously failed to learn his lesson, Kate was beginning to think that maybe Barney was a little on the stupid side.

"He just can't help himself," Mrs. Banks had said. And Barney, feeling sorry for himself, hung his head and nodded in agreement. He knew the medical procedure by now, and had crept straight into the examination room, his long shiny ears hanging forward to hide his woeful face. In the space of an hour he was quill-free, and Kate handed him a strip of rawhide to soothe him on the way home. Barney knew it was more a consolation prize than a Halloween treat, but he readily took it and seemed instantly to forget his tender nose and injured pride. But Kate suspected he wasn't as apt to forget the porcupine. As the hound and his mistress got in the car, Barney climbed onto the passenger seat, staring through the windshield with a faraway look that suggested he was going home to even up the score. Kate shook her head at the slow-to-learn dog, knowing instinctively that he'd be back in a few days.

No sooner had Kate started to close the door, than she heard the high-pitched screeching of children's laughter. She waited in the doorway as a group of tiny witches passed Mrs. Banks' car, first waving at Barney, then stopping to ooh and ahh over the lit jack-o'-lantern on the step. Kate grabbed her plastic skeleton bowl of candy and waited as they approached.

"Trick-or-treat," they all screamed at once. Kate complimented them on their costumes and dropped two lollipops in each of their bags. "Thank you, Dr. Gallagher," they screamed again in unison, then traipsed away, dragging their too-tall bags behind them. The littlest witch began skipping behind the rest, trying to keep up with the older, and faster members of her coven.

Kate leaned in the doorway, lost in thought, until the girls' conical hats disappeared from view. She wondered what *her* witch was doing right now; where she was, and whether she was equally anticipating their evening together. Just the thought of Allegra made Kate's heart palpitate, and she unconsciously unwrapped a lollipop, sucking hard on it as she locked the door and went in the back room to wash Barney Banks off her hands.

Lycos had already finished dinner when the basset hound came in. Kate had closed her office door, leaving Lycos to relax in peace on a braided rug. For some unexplainable reason, she hadn't had the heart to cage the black dog during office hours. There really was no need to, she thought. Lycos wasn't at all interested in bothering with other dogs, and had formed a rather harmonious relationship with the tortoise.

Kate dried her hands, quickly checked on Igor, who was already fast asleep in his bedded, makeshift cave, then shut off the examination room lights. As she headed to her office, wanting to bid Lycos a private farewell, there came a sharp rap at the door. Kate walked over, peeking through the curtained pane of glass, but found no one there. Just as she turned away though, another knock sounded. This time Kate stood on her toes and, way below the level of glass, saw the curly tops of Mr. and Mrs. Hebron's heads.

"Ho! Happy Halloween," said Mr. Hebron, as Kate opened the door with a look of apology.

"A trick *and* a treat, please," added Mrs. Hebron in a most jolly tone.

Kate smiled down at them, thinking that on a dimly lit street she might very well mistake the two for one and the same person. Their physical identities were differentiated only by minor details; she had breasts, he had whiskers. Their weathered noses and sharp chins jutted out at equal distances, and their starry blue eyes, though set far too close together, were as piercing as sapphires. Both looked to be in prime condition, their bodies squat and robust; and even alone, Mrs. Hebron appeared quite capable of shoveling her way clear to the center of the earth.

"A trick and a treat?" Kate asked, returning Mrs. Hebron's humor. "How about a treat and a dog that does tricks?"

"A dog?" Mr. Hebron looked puzzled, as if he were about to scratch his head.

"A dog!" Mrs. Hebron repeated, elbowing her husband and squinting at him significantly from under bushy, threatening brows.

"A d—?" He looked at her dumbfounded—intellectually helpless, actually. Then suddenly a light bulb seemed to go on, and his eyes popped wide open. "Ho! A dog! Why yes, yes indeed. Our Lycos. Ha!" He held a meerschaum pipe in one hand, as did his wife, and with the back of the other wiped his forehead, as if expecting to find himself sweating. "Well then!" he said.

Kate held the door, gesturing for the Hebrons to come in. She had never towered over anyone before, and had always imagined that being a few heads taller would lend a sense of power. On the contrary, she now felt terribly lanky, and knew it had nothing at all to do with size. Both the pipe-smoking dwarves had an impressive air of majesty about them, although Mr. Hebron was, no doubt, the more easily unnerved of the two. Kate led them toward her office, the warm glow of her desk lamp spilling out from underneath the closed door, and was just taking hold of the doorknob when a low and eerie howl wafted in from inside. The three stopped, looking at one another in silence.

The corners of Mr. Hebron's mouth began twitching, as he let out a high-pitched tee-hee, and nervously shifted his weight from one foot to the other. "Ol' girl loves her moonshine," he said.

"Oh, Arba!" His wife pushed on his shoulder affectionately. "Such a romantic, you are." She winked at Kate. "He *always* looks to take the romantic view of things."

Kate regarded Mrs. Hebron with an understanding nod. "I think, Mr. Hebron, that—"

"Please," he interrupted, "call me Arba."

"And Teasel," Mrs. Hebron said.

"Arba...and Teasel..." Kate smiled politely at each of them, although she had the funny feeling they had deliberately sidetracked her. "As I was saying...*Arba*, I think Lycos is howling because she knows you're here. It's comparable to a... *wolf* howling to locate and gather with its pack, its family."

"By golly," said Mr. Hebron.

"Fascinating, I tell you," said Teasel to no one in particular. "If my memory serves me correctly, I once read something about each pack of wolves howling in a different key, so that if one calls out and is answered in another note, he knows the wolf is not one of his own."

Kate looked surprised. "I see someone's done their canine communication homework."

"By golly..." Mr. Hebron repeated himself, shaking his head in amazement as another howl drifted in. "Funny chaps, dogs are...always pretending to be so docile and—what would you say, evolved? But deep down, as you point out, Doc, their wild ancestors are busy prowling and lurking about those dark, recessive genes. Just waiting to burst out when the moon is—I mean, when the *time* is right." He wiped his brow again and looked at his wife with a constipated sort of grin. It seemed he would have liked nothing more, at the moment, than to be waiting outside while his wife finished taking care of business.

Something fishy was going on. Fibbing was not Arba Hebron's forte; in fact, he was an altogether lousy liar, and Teasel's crafty attempts to cover for him didn't fool Kate one bit. She looked at the dwarves askance, visions of Gigi's snickering face floating across her mind, mouthing warnings of dwarves and wolves and something about never trusting an elf. For a split second Kate was of two minds—the sensible, grown-up mind; and the other, more imaginative one, which had never reached full maturity, and which derived its pleasure from conjuring up fantastical explanations for late-night creaks and hanging clothes that most closely resemble monstrous intruders when the lights went out. It was this latter mind which suddenly reminded Kate of the grim fact that it was, after all, Halloween night, and here she was all alone with two shifty-eyed dwarves who were virtual strangers and who could, at any time now, subdue and rope her and carry her away to some hungry, red, scaly-skinned dragon that guarded the emeralds in their dank, clay-smelling grotto. And, to make matters worse, the howling wolf-dog she had saved from the clutches of death would probably sit by indifferently, serenading the whole ghastly crime beneath the moon. Spooking herself is what she was doing! And her grown-up mind, right then, thought to go ring Gigi's neck for helping to put the fear in her.

Teasel, seeming to pick up on Kate's sudden uneasiness, quickly broke the silence. "Well, Dr. Gallagher, we don't want to tie you up—"

Kate's eyes widened. "Tie me up...?"

"In case you have plans—being that it's Halloween and all. You just tell our Lycos that her *pack* has come to fetch her," and she chuckled.

Feeling rather silly for having let her imagination run wild, Kate cleared her throat in an authoritative manner and turned the doorknob, motioning for the Hebrons to have a peek at the howling Lycos. There she sat, facing the window in Kate's big chair, her front paws on the desk and her head thrown back. When she spotted them from the corner of her eye she stopped wailing, and with frozen O-shaped lips, turned and looked from Arba to Teasel in startled silence. Her lips relaxed then, and in one surprisingly graceful movement, the black dog leaped in the air, clearing the desk and landing in front of the open-armed dwarves.

"Haaa!" yelled Arba, as Lycos planted wet kisses all over their faces. And they returned every one, hugging her with a candid joy that Kate found truly touching. The dwarves, she concluded, were far more appealing, far less scary, when they were behaving freely and honestly and acting jolly, like good dwarves should.

Teasel looked up, a giant tear of gratitude hanging on for dear life in the corner of her eye. Kate watched the reunion, taking pride in her patient's recovery, and as she listened to the Hebrons sniffling, felt herself about to cry, too. But just then, Lycos stopped and sniffed and cocked her head, as though smelling an important message wafting on the wind. She wandered into the hallway and whimpered and sniffed again, expecting, perhaps, a third party to arrive, then trotted back in and bucked her doctor's hand. Kate bent down, hugging her gently, and kissed her on the nose.

Teasel straightened her woolen blazer and looked at Kate with something of a loving face. "It's hard to believe she was near death this time last Friday."

Arba's countenance turned suddenly serious. "We thought for sure we'd lost her."

Kate smiled lightheartedly. "I guess it just wasn't a good day to die, Mr. Hebron."

He studied her as if in judgment. "*You* didn't think so...that's what counts, Dr. Gallagher. Death, on the contrary, knows not the days, nor hours, nor even the seasons—only its own will."

"But the will of life was stronger last Friday...I'm glad Lycos won." With that, Kate went to her desk and handed Mrs. Hebron an envelope containing antibiotics, and an instruction sheet. "She's all yours for now. I'll see her in five days to remove the rest of her sutures." Kate glanced at her watch, then opened her arms, indicating they were free to go.

Arba patted his pocket. "If you have a moment we'd be happy to take care of the balance, and we have something—"

"No, no," Kate insisted, putting up a hand as if to stop him. "You've taken care of the surgery...I'd like her hotel bill to be on me."

The dwarves looked at one another in surprise. "You've been too kind," Teasel said. "You don't have to—"

That was the second person today to tell her she was too kind; maybe Allegra was right about the cosmic brownie points. "Actually," Kate broke in, "my reasons are rather selfish...I've had more of a stake in Lycos' recovery than you'll ever know."

Teasel gave a sagely squint which seemed to say she somehow understood all that Kate could not articulate. "Maybe someday you might tell us." And with a subtle nod she signaled Arba, who reached into his breast pocket, passing her a black velvet pouch which she, in turn, handed to Kate. "We want you to have this as a small token of our appreciation...and affection."

Reluctantly, Kate accepted the velvet pouch, still warm to the touch from lying pressed against the dwarf's chest. As she opened the strings and tilted it, what appeared to be a large and magnificent marble rolled into her hand. Milky white, it twinkled with pinks and blues and mint green speckles, like an opaque sky dotted with distant stars. And from the center there radiated a gentle splash of red which, like an ember, seemed to cause the whole marble to glow from within. Kate stared, mesmerized by its moving beauty.

"It's an opal," Teasel said, "taken many years ago from an Australian mine."

"It's wonderful," was all Kate could manage to say.

"Ahhh...and full of wonder, it is," added Arba. "The opal has long been held as a good luck amulet. Our ancestors in the Old World thought the gem to be alive because of its ability to change colors. But most of all, the stone is said to give one the power to see, and so has always been an emblem of faith—like that which you have given us these past few days. Keep it close, Dr. Gallagher, and if you *ever* get lost...look to it with hope. It will guide and give you the sight you need to find your way."

"I don't know what to say.... Thank you, thank you both." Kate let the spherical gem roll around the circumference of her palm, watching the colors changing and blending and sparkling.

With a quick slap of his hands, Arba then turned to the dog and whistled, causing Kate to jump. "Ho! Lycos! I believe I smell a juicy steak awaiting you." Kate dropped the opal into its pouch, as Mr. Hebron bowed graciously before her. Teasel came up, warmly extending her hands, and Kate took them both into her own and squeezed them tightly.

She left the office within minutes of the dwarves' departure, first running outside to extinguish her jack-o'-lantern and put it in the Jeep, then rushing back in to grab the refrigerated pecan pie and purple rose she had walked into town for during lunch. Kate had hoped to find a rose sprayed black for Halloween, but settled for the dark purple flower, figuring it would look black enough when she presented it to Allegra tonight.

It was a good thing she had run errands during lunch, for as she passed through town now, merchants were closing shop, and most of the stores were locked and dimly lit. High in the sky, above the outline of darkened mountains, a bone-white moon shone, illuminating floating wisps of black cloud-drift and casting its silver light upon the sidewalks and ornate lampposts. At each corner Kate glanced down the streets, where pumpkins burning soft and orange set every porch aglow, and masquerading monsters and mischief-makers busily paraded from house to house before the town's eight o'clock curfew rolled around. And as she coasted out of the village, she saw the dangling ghosts waving from their trees again; although, for some reason, their smiles didn't seem quite as friendly as they had this morning.

Anxious to get home, Kate picked up speed when she reached the long stretch of desolate farmland which lay ahead, and her mind had just begun drifting when what appeared to be a group of strange little animals ran in front of her headlights and she swerved to avoid hitting them. But it was just the wind, animating dried leaves and sending them skittering sideways across the road like fiddler crabs rushing off to some secret affair.

No sooner had she regained her bearings than a vehicle appeared in her rear view mirror, quickly gaining from behind. And as it sped up then slowed down alongside her, Kate realized it was the Hebron's truck. Teasel had a grocery bag on her lap, and the beautiful Lycos sat still as a statue between them, staring deeply at Kate with eyes that shone like the moon. Kate waved at them and Teasel, flashing a wide grin, rolled down her window. "Happy haunting!" the dwarf hollered in the wind, and then Arba stepped on the gas, honking twice as they whizzed past her.

It was All Hallow's Eve all right, and if Kate had to choose one word to sum up her day, it would have been just that— haunting. But it wasn't over yet; come to think of it, it was just beginning.

Suddenly, the reality of it all set in; a hauntingly beautiful woman in witch's clothing would be at her door in little over an hour. She fumbled for a cigarette, her thoughts racing to Allegra again...to those wanting eyes, that knowing smile. Funny sensations began filling Kate's stomach, making it sink and drop and flip as though she were a passenger on some dark and magical roller coaster, carrying her up and away into the starry night, to a place she had never been before.

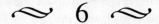

 *F*inally at home, with the work day behind and a promising night ahead, Kate found herself slipping into a romantic sort of mood. She placed a k.d. lang disc in her CD player, ground a handful of chocolate-raspberry coffee beans, and left half a pot of coffee to brew while she set about feeding the cats and running upstairs to shower. A spacious bathroom joined two rooms on the second floor, the largest having a tall, dome-shaped window and a wonderful southern exposure. The other, although it had a cathedral ceiling and a fairly new, dark green carpet, was considerably smaller. But having needed to settle into the house as soon as possible, she had chosen the carpeted one as her bedroom. Over the course of one weekend Kate and Gigi had painted the walls a warm peach, then driven thirty miles to the nearest mall to shop for curtains, throw pillows, a decorative duvet and other unnecessary but irresistible items with which to accessorize and tie in the two colors.

 In time, perhaps by Christmas, if her family decided to visit for the holidays, Kate would furnish the sunny room; convert it to a guest room that might double as a reading room, or just a nice sunny place to slip into a meditative stupor for a spell. For now, it was an utter mess, piled high with unpacked boxes. The cats were the only ones enjoying the sunny room these days. Early in the mornings Kate would often spy Merlin and Gandalf sunbathing side by side atop the boxes, decorating the place in their mind's eye and turning it into a feline bedroom with bunkbeds, scratching posts— solely for aesthetic purposes, of course—and planters full of catnip growing thick and lush and turning the whole room into an intoxicating paradise. Well, one thing was for sure; they'd never have their own room. Every cat owner has to draw the line somewhere. But if they enjoyed daydreaming, then she'd leave them to their fantasies; when cats weren't sleeping, eating or searching for something to kill, they were busy daydreaming about one thing or another, anyway.

By the time Kate stepped out of the shower, the rich smell of chocolate and raspberries was sneaking into the steamy bathroom. And as it teased her nose, as good smells tend to do, Kate decided she had no choice but to indulge in a cup at once. After briskly drying her hair with a towel, she wrapped it around her slender body and ran down to pour a cup, glancing at the kitchen clock on her way. The hands of time, it seemed, were moving much faster than Kate was managing to move. Fortunately, though, Allegra had offered to drive them to the party, insisting that with all Kate had to do she shouldn't have to worry about allowing extra time to find her way up the mountain.

With coffee in hand, Kate raced back upstairs, hurriedly fumbling for deodorant, lotion, powder and perfume. Her wedged hair, short as it was, could forfeit its five minutes of blow drying time, and so she ran a liberal amount of gel through it, pushing it to one side and leaving it to take care of itself. She then opened a tube of gray, Halloween face cream and smoothed it over her face and neck. The color complemented her hazel eyes the way the green had complemented Allegra's; of course, with supermarket-bought make-up, she hardly expected to compete with the professional results Allegra had achieved with theatrical cosmetics. She applied mascara and eyeliner heavier than usual, then used a black pencil to softly outline her lips and, with short, feathery strokes, drew whiskers. After wriggling into gray tights, Kate pulled on white slouch socks, stepped into a pair of white, ankle-high boots she had worn only once and would probably never wear again, then dashed to her closet for a white silk shirt ironed late last night. Around her neck she put a red bow tie, adorned with two tiny jingle bells from an old cat collar, and from her dresser drawer retrieved the highlights of her costume: a five-foot, gray and white striped tail, and a cat-eared hood, both of which had been sewn by the owner of a fabric store outside of town.

Standing in front of her full-length cheval mirror, Kate tucked her dark hair into the felt hood, tied it under her chin, then with a safety pin fastened the tail to the back of her tights. Last, but not least, she grabbed a charcoal gray bolero from its hanger, slipping into the short-waisted jacket and smoothing its fine satin lapels as she studied her reflection.

Kate was relieved to discover that the cat get-up she feared would look too cutesy was, indeed, rather elegant. Not bad at all, she thought, imagining that if she were from another world—a planet of cat women, say—she could have easily walked into any nightclub and turned a head or two; lifted a few tails, so to speak. With a feeling of new found-suavity, Kate collected her wallet, cigarettes and lighter, then strutted out of the room with a cocky sort of gait. But suavity and surefootedness, she learned, do not always mix. As she began her descent with one arm in the air and the other across her stomach—dancing as though she were starring in some feline rendition of *Zorba the Greek*—she stepped on her own tail, stopping herself short and nearly falling head-first down the stairs before catching hold of the banister and heroically saving her own life. And who else was sitting at the bottom of the stairs but Gandalf, entirely unimpressed by the whole scene. He stared at her with a look approaching that of disgust, as if suggesting that falling was fair punishment for her amateurish, tactless, and altogether blasphemous attempt at emulating one of God's finer creations.

"What are you staring at you little—" Kate cursed and scowled and hissed, though not so much out of anger as out of the fright she had just given herself. "You never could take a joke—never could laugh. That's your whole problem, Mr. Cat! *You* have a lousy attitude, and if you don't work on improving your sense of humor—"

Adding insult to injury, he turned his back and walked away, and Kate knew that if Gandalf had been blessed with index fingers he'd have one plugged in each ear by now, humming and singing to drown out her nonsense. Kate tugged on her lapels, straightening both her bolero and her pride, then continued down the stairs carrying the end of her tail safely in hand. The idea of falling and killing herself in a cat costume was positively humiliating. Imagine Allegra walking in and finding Dr. Gallagher sprawled beneath the stairs, her ears all bent, and the fatal tail still pinned to her buttocks and twisted about her body. And Gandalf, with an air of nonchalance, would simply shrug and say to the witch, "Oh well, what can you do?"

Kate certainly wasn't about to let some cheap cat ruin her good time. She poured a drop more coffee, lit a cigarette, and moved to the living room to find Merlin waking from a catnap. He stretched, responding to her costume with surprised delight. Merlin had been her prototype, after all, and his approval made her feel instantly better. She modeled for him, slowly reclaiming her sense of suavity, and practiced strutting with her new appendage—though on safer ground this time. Finally, she picked up a country magazine and, calm as a cucumber, settled into a chair. Kate glanced at her watch, crossed her legs, and flipped to a colorful article on preserving garden herbs and spices. But after an entire page, she realized she hadn't the slightest idea of what she'd just read and, under the circumstances, decided pacing was a far more natural activity.

During her travels around the room, Kate grabbed hold of the black velvet pouch on the coffee table, shook out the opal, and continued pacing. With one eye squinted, she held the stone in the air, rolling it between her fingers and examining its changing faces as it caught first the light of the lamps and then the light of the moon every time she passed the window. For a moment she could have sworn the opal was beginning to turn orange, to redden and glow. Then suddenly, in a spectacular display out of nowhere, a burst of white light shot across the gem's surface, disappearing as fast as it appeared. Kate's eyes widened, but then her heart sank with a thump and her eyes rounded even more, when she realized the shooting flash of white was the reflection of headlights pulling in the driveway.

Kate fumbled nervously with the opal and the pouch, and the pouch and the opal, before resigning herself to the fact that she wasn't capable of accomplishing the simple task of putting one into the other. With no time for a further struggle, she just plopped the gem atop the rumpled pouch, grabbed a mint from her candy dish and patted her pockets to be sure she had all she needed for the night. Kate felt the top of her head to be certain her ears were on straight, then exhaled with a *whoosh* and calmly opened the door to find, not the witch, but a tall man in a black suit. His hair was dark and slicked back, his complexion pale. No, pale wasn't the word for it—he was white, white as a ghost; in fact, he bore an uncanny resemblance to the imaginary man she had envisioned walking through the cornfield at night, and she thought to slam the door in his face right then.

"Dr. Gallagher," he addressed her formally, bowing with a quick jerking motion of his head, "Allegra is here for you...."

Kate regarded him with a poker face, not at all sure where this was leading. "Uh, yes...yes, thank you," she said, returning a sparing but equally gracious nod of the head.

As he turned to leave the porch, Kate dashed to the kitchen counter, scooped up the pecan pie and the rose, then shut the door behind her. To her amazement, waiting at the end of the driveway was a shiny black limousine. Kate looked on in confused delight as unseasonably warm winds, ghostly as they were, blew mysteriously about the Halloween air, setting leaves to rustling in the trees above, then sending them spiraling down to land atop the polished Lincoln.

Kate stepped off the porch, unable to see Allegra through the tinted windows. She knew, nonetheless, that the witch was watching her. The car's headlights became spotlights, and being on stage with ears and a tail made her feel a trifle awkward. As she approached the limousine, though, Allegra lowered the back window to reveal her face which, if it were at all possible, seemed greener and more beautiful than it had this morning.

The witch's sparkling eyes moved up and down Kate's body, "A cat..." she remarked in a low, ponderous voice.

"A limousine..." Kate retorted.

Allegra shrugged without pretense. "I thought I'd bring along a designated driver."

"You're just full of surprises, aren't you?"

"I try my best."

As Kate came up alongside the door, Allegra continued to eye her up and down, obviously pleased by the sight before her. "How appropriate," she said finally, referring to the costume.

Kate shrugged playfully. "What's a witch without a cat? I figured you might need a *familiar* for the evening."

"You can get *familiar* with me any time you like...Dr. Gallagher." She looked up with those shy and sexy eyes that had been on Kate's mind all day long.

The driver cleared his throat behind Kate, obviously uncomfortable with the dialogue. Allegra rolled her eyes in annoyance, as Kate stepped back to let him open the door. She handed Allegra the rose, then the pie and, as an afterthought, said, "Would you mind giving my friend Jack a ride to the party?"

"Jack?" Allegra's tone betrayed her disappointment at the mention of a third party.

Holding up one finger to indicate she'd be back in a moment, Kate acknowledged the chauffeur, then ran back to her Jeep, her tail dragging behind in the leaves. She returned momentarily with the carved pumpkin under one arm.

"A jack-o'-lantern," Allegra said with a smile of relief.

Kate pretended to cover the pumpkin's imaginary ears. "He's not well—been complaining of feelings of depersonalization all day," Kate whispered. "Says he can't feel his body. I didn't have the heart to make him walk to the party."

"I dare say!" Allegra played along, reaching for the pumpkin with enthusiastic arms. "Can we light him for the ride?"

"If you like," Kate said, climbing in the car. "Go ahead, set his head on fire—it makes him smile."

Allegra struck a match. "You make *me* smile." She lit the pumpkin, then sat him on the seat opposite them.

Kate grinned, relaxing suddenly, and as the driver got in the car, the witch and the cat sat side by side, leaning into one another and watching the glowing jack-o'-lantern. "You did a fine job," the witch commented. "It has the mark of a surgeon's hand."

"Comes with the territory," Kate said, stretching her fingers. "Except for those tricky teeth." It never failed; no matter how well you outlined the mouth, there was always a high probability of forgetting to carve around the teeth, and cutting straight through instead. This particular one was only missing two of the teeth it should have had. Kate looked with a critical eye. "The smile could have been more sinister, don't you think?"

"Oh, no... jack-o'-lanterns are supposed to be happy. They symbolize the sunshine. In days gone by they were carved and lit during Autumn feasts to pay tribute to the harvest sun."

"Really...?"

"Yes..." Allegra said, affectionately running her finger across Kate's gray chin. "...really."

Just then, Kate caught sight of the chauffeur staring at them in the rear view mirror, patiently waiting for a destination. Now *there* was a strange one, Kate thought. She nudged Allegra, gesturing toward the driver with her eyes.

"Where to?" he asked.

Allegra looked to Kate who decided it might be best to slide across to the seat nearest him, and sit beside the pumpkin while giving directions to La Zingara's Restaurant. But just as she set out to scoot across, something held her back.

A bit puzzled, Allegra looked behind Kate and inspected her tail. "Oh, goodness...!" She bit her lower lip which was, Kate was learning, something Allegra tended to do when trying to stifle a laugh. "I do believe Dewitt has caught your tail in the door."

Sure enough he had—a good three feet of it from the look of things. Kate was beginning to hate her tail, and for some unexplainable reason, had a compulsive urge to tear it loose from her tights and throw it out the window. "This tail nearly killed me once tonight," she said, shooting Dewitt a dirty look. But this only made the witch bite her lip harder.

As Kate opened the door, Allegra leaned across Kate's body, hoisting in what seemed an endless tail. "This certainly is an awfully long..." Allegra fell silent, and Kate looked down to watch the witch heaving with internal laughter.

"It's okay, laugh at me," Kate said with mock severity. "Strip me of my feline dignity." As though thankful for permission, Allegra laughed long and hard, her face practically in Kate's lap, her hands still gripping the striped monstrosity. And finally Kate gave in, thinking it best to laugh along—just to show she was big enough to poke fun at herself. But in truth, Allegra's laughter was contagious, and Kate was positively enjoying the fact of the witch lying in her lap. Of course, the man staring in the mirror she could have done without.

Using Kate's thigh to support herself, Allegra pushed herself up, her eyes wet with laughter, as Kate shut the car door and made a second attempt to switch seats.

"My apologies, Doctor," said Dewitt, although his tone was not at all convincing.

"No harm done," Kate lied, determined to be a good sport about the whole thing, just in case he did have leanings toward vampirism or, worse yet, ghoulish cannibalism. One could never be sure, especially on Halloween, and Kate couldn't think of one good reason why she'd want to get on his bad side—being he knew where she lived and all. "It wasn't a flesh and blood tail. Didn't hurt a bit," she added.

Kate could have sworn she saw the makings of a smile come and go on his white, strong-jawed face. They exchanged a few words and, as it turned out, he was quite familiar with La Zingara's and wouldn't need directions after all.

"La Zingara's..." Allegra repeated, "that's *The Gypsy's*, isn't it?"

Still sitting beside the pumpkin, Kate turned away from Dewitt to face Allegra. "Oh, boy...Gigi's going to adore you when she finds out you understand one word of Italian."

Allegra smiled. "How far?"

"About fifteen miles."

"Good...that gives us time to relax," she said.

Kate stared pensively at Allegra as the limousine pulled away, savoring the witch from head to toe; the black, flowing fabric of her dress melting into the velvet interior of the luxurious car. She didn't have her hat on, and the row of tiny white lights on either side of the ceiling seemed to bring out the strangest hint of auburn highlights in her otherwise black hair. "I must say I've never seen a more beautiful witch—you look greener than you did this morning, though."

"Perhaps I applied my makeup too heavily after I bathed."

"You've been in and out of costume twice today?" Kate was surprised. "That's a lot of work."

"Don't forget it was very early this morning that you last saw me. Staying in costume all this time would have been a bit uncomfortable." She stared at Kate for a silent moment, then took the rose that lay beside her, gently slipping it from its black paper and bringing it to her green nose. "A lavender rose?"

"I meant for it to look black."

"It does, but the scent betrays its true color. Lavender roses have a fragrance like no other...." She lowered the flower to her mouth, brushing her softly smiling lips against its petals. "This was very romantic of you," she whispered, "I will keep it always."

Allegra lifted the rose to her nose once more, penetrating Kate with her bewitching gaze as she deeply inhaled the flower's essence. "Come back here," she said, patting the seat beside her. "You're too far away...I miss you...." Although Kate was more than enjoying the view, she willingly switched seats, crossing over and settling beside the witch again.

"That will be all," Allegra said aloud for Dewitt's benefit.

He glanced at her in the mirror. "Do you want it closed?" he asked, referring to the partition.

"Please," she said. And when only the glass panel rose, she again said, louder this time, "Please, Dewitt!" He glanced at her sharply but, on cue, the solid panel rose, leaving the two women unseen and alone together at last.

Allegra looked at Kate sideways and rolled her eyes. "I borrowed his services from a family friend who's in town. He's really not such a bad fellow. I think he's a bit under the weather today."

It had nothing to do with the weather as far as Kate was concerned, and she felt like saying so. Dewitt needed to spend more time brushing up on his social skills and less time trudging through those cemeteries and cornfields and whatnot. Of course, suggesting anything of the sort would have been entirely inappropriate; sometimes it was best to keep your mouth shut.

Allegra opened a side compartment then pressed a button above her head, turning on and adjusting a small spotlight that came to shine upon an ice bucket. The light played upon the ice cubes in such a way that they sparkled like a bowl of diamonds, and in the middle of it all was a tall, slender bottle, its contents rich and clear and golden. "Care for some spirits?" she asked, gently propping her rose in the ice. A fine mist rose from the bucket, cloaking the dark rose, and making it appear as though it were growing from the mystical soil of a fairy's garden.

"Sure," Kate said. "What is it?"

"Dandelion wine." And then, as if anticipating the next question, she looked at Kate out of the corner of her eye and said, "Yes, I get it locally."

Kate smiled. "I've never seen wine that color. It's beautiful, really. If I didn't know better..." She paused.

"What?"

"I'd think you had worked your magic to capture and liquify the harvest sun itself."

In the midst of reaching for the bottle, Allegra stopped, seeming to change her mind about pouring the wine. Instead she turned to Kate, stretching and resting her arm along the length of the back seat. "The sun," she said musingly. "That's nice...I wonder what it *would* taste like."

Allegra looked at her adoringly, her eyes searching Kate's face; looking everywhere, yet nowhere in particular, until her eyes came to settle on an unruly wave that had freed itself from Kate's gray hood. The witch smiled to herself and with one gentle finger reached up, playfully brushing it from Kate's forehead, then tucked it back in with her fingers. "Is your hair still wet?"

"A little damp, maybe. I was in a hurry."

"That's not good. Why don't you take this thing off and give it time to dry?"

Before Kate could respond, Allegra was tugging at the strings beneath her chin, untying the hood and sliding it off the back of her head. "That's better." She smiled softly, then reached up again; this time running all her fingers through Kate's wavy hair, sending chill after chill along her scalp and down her spine and then to more dangerously sensitive parts of her body. It took Kate all of ten seconds to decide she was absolutely wild about the witch.

The whole idea of being touched by another person had always been a curious matter for Kate. She often wondered why stroking her own head, rubbing her own neck, never felt half as good as when someone else did it. It was sort of like being tickled; someone could poke you in the ribs and give you cause to die laughing, but try as you might, it was physically impossible to tickle yourself. Surely there was some kind of natural law explaining this phenomenon, although Kate was hardly inclined to figure it out at the moment.

As Allegra continued to stroke her hair, Kate tilted her head back, pressing it to Allegra's hand to receive her sensual touch. And with her own delicate hand—a surgeon's hand, as the witch had said—Kate found the nerve to reach back. She lifted her hand to Allegra's brow, trailing her fingers along the contour of her smooth, green face, then moved down to trace the outline of rosy lips she wanted so badly, but dared not kiss.

"Meeting you was so...so strange," Kate stammered. "What I mean to say, is that, well, we're virtual strangers, yet I feel like I've known you for a thousand years. Meanwhile, it's been only—how long?"

Allegra glanced at her watch. "Eleven hours. About forty minutes if you don't count the time we spent apart." The witch smiled, although there was a strange quality of seriousness about her. She covered Kate's hand with her own, closing her eyes and drawing in a quick, short breath, as though overwhelmed by the woman her eyes beheld. She turned away then, returning to the affair of the dandelion wine.

The full moon, strong and intrusive now, peered through the dark windows. It seemed to Kate as though it was following the limousine, racing with remarkable speed past shadowed branches of trees along the highway. And when Allegra pulled two crystal glasses from a hidden compartment, its light beamed off their many facets, casting tiny but brilliant splashes of color all around the velvet interior. Kate watched Allegra's every move as the witch prepared her potion, brewing what appeared to be bits of rainbow and drops of sunshine and a sprinkle of moonlight here and there until, finally, she turned back to Kate with two glasses of the golden elixir. "Shall we toast?" she asked, handing one crystal glass to Kate.

Kate nodded. "I've always been a lover of tradition."

"Well then..." Allegra raised her glass. "Here's to witches and their cats."

"And cats and their witches."

The witch winked. "And to hitchhiking jack-o'-lanterns," she said, acknowledging the smiling pumpkin.

"And to the pond..." Kate added. "I'm glad you were there." The musical clinking of their crystal glasses resounded throughout the limousine as they brought the wine to their lips. Of course, it took Kate two tries to find her own mouth, and as a bit of wine trickled down her chin, Allegra reached out, catching the drop on her finger tip.

Kate had finally managed to embarrass herself completely. She needed to find a mirror fast—give herself a good pep talk in it. "I'm not usually this clumsy," she pardoned herself.

"I rather like it." Allegra's smile was soft and sweet as she brought the drop of golden nectar back to Kate's mouth, prompting the cat to take it with the tip of her tongue. "It's nice to know that after a thousand years I can still unnerve you."

Kate returned the smile and gestured with her glass "A *thousand* years!"

"That's an awfully long time to wait for a kiss," Allegra said with a twinkle, sipping her wine, then taking Kate's glass and setting it down with her own.

Kate's throat tightened, her face turning suddenly serious, as Allegra tilted her head, moving forward to close the distance between them. But as Kate began to part her lips, Allegra pulled back; just long enough to tease her, to lovingly search her eyes, so that for a moment, only a breath of passion separated each woman from her desire.

Allegra moved forward again, now reaching Kate's mouth, taking one lip between her own to savor its supple moistness, the sweet traces of dandelion wine, before moving up to claim the other. Kate held her breath, opening her mouth, opening herself to the need she had never known before. Tenderly, almost hesitantly, Allegra touched the tip of her tongue to each corner of Kate's mouth, letting it finally slide in and down behind her lips and along the delicate roof of her mouth, then came out to find her wine-coated lips again. And when she suddenly stopped herself, she cupped Kate's face in her warm, trembling hands. "I didn't want to kiss you..." she said, her whispers barely audible beneath heavy breaths, "because I knew I'd never want to stop."

"And *now* look what you've gone and done," Kate teased. She smiled at Allegra, her hazel eyes partially closed, and slowly shook her head. "Don't..." Kate whispered, her smile evaporating. "Please don't stop...."

Suddenly there was no need for words, as Kate slid her hand around to the back of Allegra's head, touching for the first time, her silky raven hair. She pulled Allegra back to her, rubbing her mouth fervently across the witch's own, and with unrestrained hunger kissed her slowly, deeply, thoroughly.

Kate didn't want to stop kissing Allegra, either, and might never have if not for good ol' Dewitt. He lowered the partition a few inches just then to announce their approaching arrival.

Allegra took a long breath and closed her eyes for a spell, as if doing such a thing would help her re-orient, put the rest of the world back in perspective. She helped Kate on with the cat hood, and after giving her hand a tight squeeze, leaned across to extinguish the pumpkin's candle.

Watching the witch from behind, Kate lost herself in the aftermath of both a first kiss and a first taste of dandelions—to think people called those happy little flowers weeds! Kate wasn't much of a drinker, so half a glass of the golden wine seemed to have affected her in no time. But Kate knew the effects of the dandelions were nothing compared with the effects the witch was having on her senses. And as Kate entertained the prospect of knowing Allegra, knowing her intimately, she was almost certain she felt her tail and ears begin twitching just a bit. It was as though she were undergoing some sort of evolutionary regression; turning into a slinky cat set to playfully pounce on her new and wonderful mistress in a fit of feline madness. But Kate was too well bred a cat for such inappropriate behavior. She managed to mind her manners, and resigned herself to squirming with quiet desire as the Lincoln pulled up in front of La Zingara's.

*T*he Tudor-styled restaurant was situated just off the main road. It rested on a knoll bordered on three sides by a generous expanse of land. Beneath its slate roof and along the whitewashed stucco, a row of windows glowed with the amber light of rustic chandeliers within.

At the front of the cobbled walkway an iron torch blazed as it did every night, its high yellow flame bobbing and undulating in rhythm with the evening wind. The night itself was clear, well lit by the full moon, but the air had the feel of moisture about it. And from a quiet lake resting just behind La Zingara's a white fog had begun rolling in, its eerie tendrils creeping up through the parking lot and muffling the sounds of music and laughter coming from inside. All in all, it seemed like just the sort of place real Gypsies and other mysterious travelers might have taken a fancy to, wandering in during the wee hours to exchange strange tales over a frosted glass of bitter ale.

Kate waited beside the burning torch with the jack-o'-lantern in her arms, while Dewitt got back in the limousine. Allegra faced her holding the pie and a sealed bottle of wine she had brought along for Gigi. There in the thickening fog they stood, the witch and the cat, staring at one another as if a few words were in order; as if each had something she wanted to say to the other before the party swept their privacy away. But before either could speak, La Zingara's oak door, tall and heavy and fit for a giant, opened with a bang. Kate looked up, then winked at Allegra. "I think you're about to meet your hostess."

Wearing a Frankenstein costume, Gigi stood in the high, amber-lit doorway. Her attire was black and simple; turtleneck, pants, oversized blazer and elevated boots. But the mask she had obviously splurged on—its green, life-like skin and bushy black hair making quite an impression on the two spectators as she raised her head and outstretched arms to the sky and, in her best monster voice screamed, "La bella luna!"

"Our hostess?" Allegra asked amused. She followed Gigi's eyes and acknowledged the sky. "A beautiful moon it is," she cordially called out. In a dramatic display, Gigi clutched her chest. "Oh! Be still my heart!" she cried to the moon. "She's green like me and she speaks Italian, too!"

Kate looked at Allegra. "What did I tell you?" she said, shaking her head as Gigi, stiff-armed and stiff-legged, approached them.

"*Bella strega*," Gigi said, as Kate introduced the two. Then slipping out of character, she glanced at Kate. "That means *beautiful witch*."

Allegra smiled, shaking Gigi's hand warmly. "I like your friend already," she addressed Kate.

Gigi's face was hidden behind the mask, but judging from the sparkle emanating from her eye holes, Kate was pretty sure her face was beet-red and smiling ear to ear by now. Gigi accepted the bottle, thanking the witch as she read the label, then mentioned something about her Italian grandmother always picking dandelions along the parkway and steaming them for dinner. "Whose limo?" she finally asked.

Kate nodded with her chin toward Allegra.

"Your chauffeur's welcome to come in. There's plenty of seafood—a three course buffet," Gigi offered. "Besides, having a limo parked out front is good for business. People pass by, think we serve the rich and famous, and, come Friday, reservations are closed for the weekend. Go figure people."

Allegra went to the road and walked around to the driver's side. After a moment, she raised her head above the Lincoln's roof. "It's a generous invitation, Gigi, but he's planned to visit a nearby friend." Allegra bent down again, exchanging hushed words with Dewitt for another minute or so.

Kate listened to Gigi's labored breathing, her rubber cheeks making any number of rude and blubbering noises as she sucked in air, then forcefully blew it out the mouth hole. "You sound like you need a respirator," Kate said. "Are you okay in there?"

"Why? Can you tell I'm suffocating? Damned thing cost me over fifty dollars and I can't eat, drink, smoke or breathe with it on—can't see well either." She peered out at Kate with those dark, Sicilian eyes.

Kate turned back to the car and sighed. "So, what do you think so far?"

Gigi made a gesture with her hand, shaking it like someone who'd just burned her fingers. "Sexiest witch I've ever seen—she can play with my cauldron anytime. Do you think maybe she has someone for me? A sister? Cousin?" She shrugged. "Mother...?" Gigi seemed to get a kick out of her own joke, her silly laughter echoing from somewhere deep inside the caverns of her rubber face. "Where did she learn Italian, anyway?"

Kate didn't bother to answer. She just stared ahead dreamily. "I can't imagine what she looks like out of costume."

Gigi leaned into Kate with a whisper. "Who cares? Hell, I'd take her just the way she is."

Kate nudged Gigi with her shoulder. "She's mine...so keep your thoughts clean, Gabriella Giovanni."

The limousine pulled away about then, and as it coasted down the road, Allegra rejoined them.

"Come inside, come inside, my friends," Gigi said, offering each woman an elbow. "The goblins are getting restless."

"Goblins?" Allegra feigned surprise. "What ever happened to the Gypsies?"

"Las Zingaras?" Gigi laughed. "Who knows. I've been waiting for one with bangle bracelets and a crystal ball to walk in here one rainy night and tell me I'm going to fall in love with her. None so far. Only goblins tonight. And I'm sure they'd just love to have the two of you for dinner."

Kate glanced over at Allegra, not sure how the witch would take to Gigi's humor, but she appeared quite entertained by the suggestive bantering.

"I think I'll decline the *goblin* offer," the witch said. "I have my sights set on a cat tonight."

"Eh, You're better off," Gigi said, sneaking Kate a congratulatory pat on the back. "Goblins are a dime a dozen—believe me, I've been gobbled by a few in my time. It's not even worth getting into." Gigi sighed as they reached the door. "Speaking of goblins, though," she said to Kate, "I ended up using that recipe you had for goblin juice."

"Goblin juice..." Allegra looked at Kate. "You don't impress me as the type to concoct such things, Kate."

Kate started to smile, to think of something clever to say, but Gigi broke in first. "Doesn't look the type? Never trust the quiet ones—that's what my mother always told me." Gigi pointed to Kate with a sideways thumb. "Recipes for goblin juice are the least of the secrets this one keeps. And if she gets out of hand tonight you just let me know," Gigi warned. "I'll toss her out back with a bowl of milk." With that, Gigi held the door, using her thumb and middle finger to flick Kate's cat ear as she walked in. And even with the gray makeup, Kate's skin managed to achieve a reasonably pink tone for a moment.

Gigi led Kate and Allegra through the barroom, stopping now and again to introduce them to a few people, then stopping again in the archway of the small dining room to their right. The club music was loud, and small tables softly lit with oil lamps were lined against the walls, the center of the room having been cleared for dancing. A purple strobe light flickered and flashed over the bodies of masquerading dancers, and from steam kettles unobtrusively placed under tables, dry ice smoked and bubbled and spilled onto the floor, its wispy trails creeping forward like languid witches' fingers, wrapping themselves around moving legs so that the dancers appeared to be floating, their feet not quite touching the ground. It looked to Kate as though the fog coming off the lake had somehow found its way inside.

"You certainly outdid yourself," Kate said admiringly.

"Spooky, huh?" Gigi took the jack-o'-lantern from her, pulled out a lighter, and sat the glowing pumpkin on the nearest table.

"Quite!" Allegra commented, "Very sensual, too."

Gigi stepped back, nodding in agreement as she looked at the swirling fog. "It does have an erotic, kind of wild look—as good as any club you've been to, right?" She folded her arms with pride and pointed with her chin to a particular couple embraced and dancing.

As Allegra watched the two women, Kate watched Allegra, suddenly struck by the strong delicacy of her profile. Her eyes moved from the witch's face, to her hair, to her shoulders, following the line of her sleeve down to her cuff, then dropped to the sensual network of veins running beneath the pale green skin of her strong but slender hands.

Kate's own arms rested at her sides, and with one hand she inconspicuously reached over, pushing and slipping her fingers between the witch's fingers until they intertwined.

Allegra continued to look ahead, but responded quickly, gripping Kate's hand with an understood and silent passion. Together they looked on, watching the dancing lovers, until Gigi suggested they make their way to the dining room for appetizers and drinks. Kate, who now stood to the right of both Gigi and Allegra, thought to courteously release the witch's hand, so that they could turn and follow Gigi in single file. But just as Kate tried to let go, the witch strengthened her grip. "Perhaps I'd be remiss," she said, briefly turning to meet Kate's gaze, "In not asking whether my being seen with you tonight will present any difficulties."

"What do you mean?"

"Well...forgive me, but I don't know the nature of your relationship with any of these women. Someone's bound to conclude you have a new love interest."

"But I do..." Kate said with a charming honesty.

Allegra glanced down at their interwoven fingers. "Then don't let go...." She turned and extended her arm behind her, holding tight to Kate's hand as she followed Gigi.

With the good nature of a kitty-kat, Kate held on and walked behind, not really caring where Allegra led her; for the truth was that she would have followed the witch anywhere tonight: to the moon, the stars, the end of the earth...to bed, if that were Allegra's wish.

In the archway of the main dining room a pulsating ghost bobbed up and down, breaking into some electronic gibberish every time someone passed under it. Black and orange balloons, along with streamers and rubber snakes and paper bats and such, hung suspended from the rafters and oaken chandeliers. The room was deep and crowded. There must have been close to thirty women standing or sitting around the large, polished tables; some she knew, a few she had met once or twice, and there were still others with whom she was not at all acquainted. And in the spaces between all the people, Kate could make out the glow of logs burning cozily in a fireplace against the back wall.

In front of them, appetizers fit for the occasion decorated the buffet table. Atop a black linen tablecloth, mushrooms a la Grecque encircled a steaming cauldron of pumpkin soup. There were toast cut-outs topped with pumpkin-shaped salmon wearing caviar eyes and smiles, and a colorful Autumn salad full of artichoke hearts, butter leaf lettuce, and crisp yellow peppers blended with Gigi's green goddess dressing. And at the far end of the table, in between two bowls of the blood-red goblin juice, stood a Frankenstein figure made from boursin cheese dyed green with freshly ground parsley.

Gigi pointed to the punch bowls. "That one's spiked, the other isn't," she said. "And the bar is open if you'd rather have cocktails or something soft—I think I'll try the dandelion wine."

Kate smiled up at her green date. "What can I get you?"

"I couldn't very well pass up the chance to taste your goblin juice...now could I?" Kate regarded the witch for a moment, then wet her lips unconsciously and squeezed in to pour two glasses of the red punch. She could hear Allegra complimenting Gigi on her culinary talents, and listened as the two exchanged comments on the idea of chefs being fine artists who happened to work in an edible medium. Next thing Kate knew, Gigi was calling to her over someone's head, saying she had to check on the ravioli and wanted to show Allegra the kitchen. Stretching, Kate handed a drink to the witch and had meant to follow, but just as she turned, a tall woman dressed as the Queen of Hearts tapped her on the shoulder.

Kate grinned sheepishly as she recognized Mandy, a woman she had dated once during the summer. At the time, Kate's telephone hadn't yet been installed, and she had accepted Mandy's number, promising to call just as soon as her phone came. But by the time it did come, Kate had thrown her number away and blocked all memories of their date.

Mandy had taken her to a lesbian production of *Romeo and Juliet*— *Julie and Ramona* it was called. Stealthy as she was, Mandy first dashed away when it came time to buy the tickets, then dashed away again when the dinner check came later that same evening. It's not that Kate ever hesitated in treating anyone to anything—no one could accuse her of being tight—but she hated the idea of someone taking her for a pushover.

The play itself had been quite good, actually; the bittersweet emotions of Shakespearean irony lingering in Kate's heart throughout their sweet and sour dinner. To think of two lovers, two lives wasted all because of— what? Bad timing? A simple misunderstanding? Kate had hoped to toss around the poetic irony of love being so beautiful, even in its moment of tragedy. But Mandy didn't want to talk about irony. She rambled on and on, analyzing the whole play in terms of clinical depression and co-dependency. Kate cringed as she listened, and was pretty sure Shakespeare would have done the same thing. By the time dessert rolled around that summer evening, Mandy was off on an unbearable monologue about her capacity for unconditional love. Kate couldn't get a word in edgewise, and by the close of their date decided that Mandy was, without a doubt, unconditionally in love with herself.

"I've been waiting to hear from you," Mandy cooed, opening her arms, inviting Kate to hug her.

Kate made a gesture with her glass, indicating she couldn't hug her on account of the drink in her hand. But Mandy didn't catch on and came at her anyway, and Kate ended up giving her a one-armed, half-hearted hug. They exchanged pleasantries then, and Kate made a clever point of mentioning she was here with her *lover*, thinking that it might eliminate any discussion of future get-togethers. But the mention of a lover had little effect on Mandy; it went in one ear and out the other and, as luck would have it, straight into someone else's ear, as Kate felt that certain someone's arm slip around her waist from behind.

"Did someone say *lover*?" Allegra whispered so closely that Kate could feel the witch's lips tickling against her earlobe. "I just might hold you to it," the witch teased, her warm breath creating wonderful sensations in the cat's ear.

Kate was, as they say, in a pickle. She swallowed hard—gulped, really, and if not for the music being so loud, she thought the entire party would have turned around to see who had made the frog sound. What was she to do, now? Apologize to Allegra in front of Mandy for having lied, for having called the witch her lover? Or perhaps she might do better to qualify her statement by saying she meant *lover-to-be*, or...

"How do you do?" Allegra said to the Queen of Hearts. "I'm sorry to interrupt, but—"

Mandy batted her curled eyelashes, promptly offered her hand, wasting no time introducing herself, checking Allegra out as she did so. "And what line of work are *you* in?" she asked the witch.

"Why...magic, of course," Allegra replied curtly, then adjusted her black, conical hat. "I'm in the business of magic."

Mandy didn't stick around long after that. She chanted something through a tight smile, then politely pranced away in search of another audience.

Allegra raised her brow in mock surprise. "Was it something I said?" Then her face softened, her eyes narrowed. "I didn't mean to be rude, but it looked like you wanted to be saved. And what better woman to come to your rescue than your *lover*?"

"I can explain," Kate started, but then fell silent like any respectable woman who had just been caught with her pants down, so to speak, and knew there was little she could say to help herself. She changed the subject instead. "So you're in the business of magic, huh?"

"Why?" Allegra looked at her sideways. "Are you in the market for magic?"

"In the market?" Kate grinned. "You could very well be looking at your best customer yet."

"Hmmm..." Allegra twisted her mouth, thoughtful of the prospect. "I do believe that serving as both your proprietor and *lover* would present a conflict of interest."

"I see." Kate was thoughtful for a moment. She pawed her felt ear. "Well, just out of curiosity, how much would you normally charge for the type of magic you're making on me?"

Allegra pursed her lips, a glimmer coming to her eyes. "Oh...I don't know. How does payment in kind sound?"

"Sounds like it could lead anywhere."

"Mmm..." Allegra studied her. "One can only hope...."

Kate's heart picked up a little speed just then, and she wondered if the witch was at all aware of the workout she was giving Kate's nervous system. Lost for words, she glanced awkwardly at the buffet. "Are you hungry?"

Allegra smiled, her eyes narrowing again, as though she were entertaining a multitude of possible answers to this question as well.

They refilled their glasses, sampled the appetizers, and were carrying their plates into the dining room, when someone called Kate's name. She glanced around the room and spotted her friend Pat sitting at a fireside table with three other women, waving and crossing her hands over her head. "Over here," she called. "We saved seats."

Pat, a forest ranger—American as apple pie, as the saying goes—was one of the few, true locals Kate knew; a real woman's woman with a handshake that could bring a lumberjack to his knees. Just the ranger you'd want to see if a high-strung bear had you cornered up a tree. She always had a twinkle in her eyes; a strange, cheery, sort of twinkle which, Kate suspected, came from working outdoors and breathing in all that fresh, mountain air. In fact, it looked as though she had just wandered off one mountain or another, as she sat there in uniform with a plastic, Smokey the Bear mask pushed back and resting on top of her thick, auburn hair.

Beside Pat sat her lover, Maria, dressed as Mother Nature; a petite Latino woman whose feistiness made up for any difference in size. She had ventured upstate from Manhattan three years ago to complete a graduate internship in environmental conservation, and wound up falling in love with Pat and the country. Both had survived different, though equally difficult lives, but loving their work and loving each other somehow made everything else worthwhile. Currently, they were in the process of building a nursery onto their four-room log cabin, and all that remained to be decided now, was which of the two would have the baby.

Kate and Allegra made their way to the table where Maria and the other two women were laughing and mulling over photographs. Pat got up, opening her arms wide, and Kate welcomed one of her genuine and solid hugs which, for some reason, was always accompanied by a slap on the back. The more Pat liked you, the harder the slap, and Kate remembered having had the stuffing nearly hugged out of her the first time Pat ever embraced her. Since then, Kate had learned to prepare her body for those hugs, and would have gladly prepared Allegra, too, if she had known Pat would receive the witch with open arms. But Allegra held her own, handling the jolt like a real trooper.

A salt-and-pepper-haired woman in her late forties sat with her back to Kate, but quickly put down what appeared to be photos of Pat and Maria's land, and turned around in her seat. "Hello, stranger," she said, edging her bifocals to the tip of her nose and peering over them at Kate.

Kate gave the woman's shoulders a friendly squeeze. "Hi, Diane," she said. "How's Higgins?"

"Everything cleared up—the fur on her leg is back. But I need to bring her in again soon for her shots...unless you feel like coming out for dinner one night and doing it there. No offense, but she really dreads going to your office."

Kate smiled. "I won't take it personally."

Diane was a librarian in Waterswood, a well-populated town about ten miles north of Broome, and when they first met, Kate had felt the slightest hint of a crush coming on. There was something about her prim and proper style, or maybe her hair or her half-glasses, or a combination of the three that gave her enormous sex appeal, though perhaps in a scholarly sort of way. But Diane had been with Susan sixteen years, and that was reason enough for Kate to hold tight to her integrity—adulterous affairs were as much taboo as they were common in the community. Besides, Kate liked Susan, a horticulturist who just happened to own the best flower shop around. Rumor had it that during the warmer months Susan always came to visit with a colorful and heavenly fragrant bouquet of flowers for her hostess. And Kate had told herself, in no uncertain terms, that it was far better to keep the peace and the friendship and look forward to finding fresh flowers, rather than a dead fish on her doorstep. She leaned in and kissed Susan on the cheek.

The whole group was as warm and friendly as the fire that danced and reflected off the planked floors. Everyone greeted Allegra with hearty handshakes and an enthusiasm that made Kate wonder whether Gigi had tipped them off, or whether they simply took Kate's unusually smitten face as a sign that Allegra would be around for a long time to come.

With an easy social grace, Allegra greeted each woman in turn, and plates and glasses and ashtrays and such were quickly rearranged to make room for the two.

"You make a striking pair," Diane said, commenting on the cat and witch match.

"It wasn't planned—" Kate and Allegra began speaking at the same time, then paused to look at each other with apologetic smiles.

"Really? What a coincidence," Maria commented. "It must mean something. I'd take it to be a good omen if I were you," she said, pushing the photographs in their direction.

Kate liked the idea of a good omen, and playfully nudged Allegra's foot under the table as they sorted through pictures of Maria and Pat's log home in its various stages of construction. Three passersby in obviously rented costumes, slowed down en route to the dance floor. Taking notice of the pictures, they stopped to chat, and before long everyone was focused on septic problems and other joys of country living. Couples competitively recounted their home-owner horrors with, "you wouldn't believe what happened to us," and "you think yours was bad," and "ours was a nightmare," until they all were howling with laughter over stories which were, quite likely, not at all funny when they happened.

With warm reserve Allegra listened intently, choosing to speak little at first and seeming content to relax and observe the nature of the developing conversation which, after the three women continued to the dance floor, moved from septic tanks, to the biology of leach fields, to wells, to dowsing. To a recent city dweller like Kate, dowsing had always conjured up images of an ancient and esoteric art, but the term seemed common enough in rural vocabularies. When your well ran dry, or one needed to be dug for a new house, you called in a local dowser—simple as that. It was, Kate had learned, a money and time-saving alternative to having a well-digger taking trial and error stabs and poking around your land until a vein of water popped up.

"I'd like to try it," Maria said.

"Ahh..." Pat waved a cynical hand. "I don't believe in those water witches."

Maria glanced at her in disbelief. "This certainly is news to me, darling." Then to the others she said, "Pat hired one to dowse our land then, just to be sure, called in another for a second opinion, and..."

"*Water* witches?" Kate interrupted.

"Yeah, that's what people call them," Pat said, shrugging with disinterest.

Kate looked questioningly at the others, then looked across to Allegra for some sort of confirmation.

Allegra smiled as though finding Kate's rural naiveté truly endearing. "It's an affectionate name given them by Puritans who feared heresy."

Diane laughed. "Personally, *I've* always feared Puritans."

Allegra smiled with silent understanding.

"Anyway," Maria continued, "the first dowser spent two hours deciding on the best of four water sources she located. The second dowser had no idea the land had been dowsed and, wouldn't you know, he chooses the exact same spot as the first one." She challengingly turned to Pat. "And *you* don't believe?"

"I believe in dowsing," Pat answered with a smirk. "I just don't think there's anything mystical about it. Dowsers are skilled naturalists, detectives. They find signs of underground water by examining the soil, mineral deposits...the flora and fauna. There's nothing supernatural about it."

Just then, the flames in the fireplace grew tall, casting distorted, evil sorts of shadows on the wall; and for a moment the fire sputtered and crackled as though someone had tossed a handful of popping corn on the logs. Maria nearly jumped out of her seat; the rest of the women glanced at the fire, lifting their brows and turning to one another in respectful silence.

"I think you've just insulted the powers that be," Diane said to Pat.

"I'm not going home with *you*," Maria warned. "I'm sorry," she said to the others, "but I come from a superstitious family."

Pat broke into a hearty laugh. "Oh, come on," she teased, staring defiantly at the fire. "I just don't go in for all that occult stuff."

"Neither do dowsers," Allegra said. "It may simply be that things that seem supernatural to us, are nothing more than aspects of nature we don't yet understand. In fact, that was the foundation of medieval alchemy. Witches and warlocks were the ones who made a pact with the devil in exchange for magical powers. The alchemists were scientists, chemists, who generally opposed dealings with darkness. They believed magical powers could be cultivated through knowledge of nature's forces...the energy fields and physical properties of stones and metals and such—it's the same as people wearing crystals today because of their energy fields and supposed healing powers."

"Like *this* crystal?" Maria sarcastically asked, tugging on the chain around her neck. "The one that *Pat* gave me?"

Everyone snickered in Pat's direction.

Pat's mouth puckered as if she had just tasted something sour. "I bought it for you because it was *pretty*. That's *all*."

"Well, I believe in it," Susan said. "We've *done* it. Diane and I attended a dowsing workshop at the college a few years back." She touched her lover's hand as if recollecting a private joke. "Remember?"

Diane rolled her eyes. "Remember? That's how we spent our leisure time for the next month—dowsing and hiking and dowsing. I ordered books on the subject for the library and Susan bought us divining rods. One metal, and one made from—what is it? Hazel wood, I think. We were all set to moonlight as dowsers." She regarded her lover. "Where are those rods, anyway?"

"The attic, probably," Susan responded.

Diane frowned. "Along with all the other keepsakes from our would-be hobbies. That's our problem. We approach every new hobby with a gung-ho attitude, then the enthusiasm fizzles and the equipment gets put away. Our attic is piled sky-high with everything from cross-country skis to paint-by-numbers."

"And divining rods..." Allegra added.

"Yes...the rods." Diane laughed, but then her countenance grew serious again and she nodded at the witch. "I do agree with you, though. I think it's all a matter of attuning ourselves to forces that are a very real part of nature, even though they may seem to be out of our normal realm of perception."

"I guess it's like radio waves," Pat put in. "They're darting all around us but," she held out her hands, "if you don't turn on the radio, you can't hear the music."

Maria looked at her. "What a truly philosophical statement, Pat...I think it has bumper-sticker potential."

Kate grinned and gave the *thumbs up* sign to Pat, who grimaced and chuckled in a haughty sort of way.

"She's right, though," Allegra said. "In fact, one theory of dowsing is that our brains serve as receptors for electromagnetic waves emitted by water or, for that matter, any other object you choose to dowse for. The rod serves only as an intermediary between the object and the mind."

"So, theoretically," Pat added, "I should be able to use my metal detector without batteries. It doesn't make sense."

"Actually," Kate began, thinking she ought to make some intelligent contribution to a subject she knew zip about, "it's probably similar to magnetic resonance imaging of medical scanners."

"How does that work?" Maria asked.

"Well, I don't know too much about physics," Kate confessed, "but basically, the scanner activates the protons in your body. Movement excites them, and as the excitement builds, they produce an internal magnetic field. When another magnetic field is applied from outside the body, all the protons begin spinning together. Then, when the external magnetic field is finally taken away, your protons relax and return to their normal positions. And as they come to rest, they sort of glow and release electromagnetic radiation. *That's* what the scanner picks up, interprets, and turns into visual images."

Pat's glass came down hard on the table, as she tried to swallow a mouthful of goblin juice before she choked on laughter. "Now that's the best description of an orgasm I've *ever* heard." She returned the *thumbs up* sign to Kate.

Everyone laughed at Kate's expense, and as Allegra acknowledged her with shy, but humorous eyes, it crossed Kate's mind that she ought to crawl under the table.

Sensing Kate's embarrassment, Diane winked and promptly came to her rescue. "Have *you* ever dowsed?" she asked Allegra.

"I've...dabbled....." Allegra's words were drawn out as she slowly smiled with reserved admission.

Kate had a feeling Allegra had done more than dabbled; that she knew a lot more about a lot of things than she cared to let on. And it wouldn't have surprised Kate one bit to see the witch pull out her wallet and flash a membership card to the American Society of Dowsers. Not that Kate had ever heard of such a society, but societies existed for everything else, didn't they?

Pat got up then, collecting the empty glasses on a wicker tray, and went to fetch another round of goblin juice. She stubbornly refused to give up her theory of dowsers being skilled naturalists, and although Kate found such an explanation quite plausible, she went along with the more popular theory of unseen forces in the end. If nothing else, Kate liked to believe there were mysterious powers at work in the universe. And in Pat's absence, the conversation moved in just that direction, with Diane, Allegra and Maria focusing on more spiritual, cosmic matters. Of course, just how the conversation had originally gone from sewage to spirituality, no one could have said for sure.

Pat returned shortly, and soon after that the unmasked Gigi, her curls hanging damp from the high humidity inside the Frankenstein head, came to the table holding an adorable Peter Pan by the scruff of the neck. It was Annie.

"Look what just flew in," Gigi teased. "She's with two friends and none of them can produce identification. You think she's old enough? Should we let her stay, or what?" Gigi gave a vixenish flash of her pearl-white teeth, staring appraisingly into Annie's big blue eyes.

"Lay off, Gigi," Annie said, delivering a playful poke to Gigi's stomach. "I'm nineteen!"

"Poor baby...of course she can stay," Pat said sympathetically. She patted her lap. "Come to Smokey, Annie, I won't let that bad monster bother you."

"Oh, yeah, sure Smokey...!" Gigi winked at Maria, then nodded toward Pat's bear mask. "You just want to get your big bear paws on her." Gigi let go of the light hold she had on Annie's neck, squeezing her affectionately as she did.

Kate winked at Annie. "I think you should dress like that for work—it might enhance your rapport with the animals." Then to Allegra and Susan she said, "This is my assistant, Annie."

Annie waved to the group, a wide smile on her youthful and animated face, her short, sleek crop of blonde hair swishing from side to side with every turn of her head. Pat and Maria knew Annie well—they had recommended her to Kate—and Diane had met her the time she brought her terrier to Kate's office.

Gigi set a glass of dandelion wine on the table, and pulled up a chair by Maria. "Ahh...nineteen..." she mumbled to herself, "I was nineteen when I came out to my parents?"

"And...were they okay with it?" Annie stopped half way around the table with a sudden interest that suggested she was, perhaps, grappling with just such an issue.

"Okay with it? They took me to a shrink!" Gigi snorted a laugh, took a gulp of her dandelion elixir, and glanced at her cat-friend. "The doctor, as it turned out, was a colleague of Kate's father, although it wasn't until a few months later that Kate and I met. So my mother told this Freud-guy that I was having an *adjustment* problem. But I told him I was *perfectly* adjusted—that my parents were the ones who needed help adjusting." Gigi grinned. "I suggested he start seeing them on a weekly basis until they got a grip. Then, a couple of nights later, I was coming home late from a date with my first lover—this hot, phys-ed teacher—and my Pop saw us necking in her car. He told me I had to either stop seeing her or move out. *Ciao*, I said—and moved in with her."

Gigi smiled and waved a nonchalant hand. "Eventually they came around. Most do. But it took a while. *And*...wouldn't you know, four years later—right after one of my sister's got married—my youngest sister, Lynn, came out. And my parents accepted it!" Gigi slapped the table. "See? It's true what they say about the oldest kid having to break the ice, take the brunt of everything."

Diane smiled. "I admire the fact that your self-concept was that strong at such a young age. A lot of women wouldn't have been be so comfortable with their sexual orientation at nineteen."

"Nineteen? Hell..." Gigi waved her hand again at the group. "I was comfortable with it when I was six."

Maria's eyes opened in surprise, and Kate and Allegra smiled. "Six years old?" Maria asked, skeptically.

"Sure. First grade. I had a terrible crush on my teacher." Gigi slowly shook her head, looking down and sucking her teeth in fond reminiscence. "Mrs. Vinicola....I'll never forget those black lace bras she wore. I used to peek down her blouse when she bent over to check my homework." Gigi brought a fist to her mouth and bit her knuckle hard. "Oh...*God*...did that woman have beautiful breasts."

Allegra propped her elbow on the table, leaning her temple against two fingers, as she studied Gigi with amusement. "A real *true blue*, hmm?"

Gigi gave a wide smile. "Yep! Me and my best friend here." She glanced at Kate.

Maria laughed. "You know, Gigi, for some reason I can picture you cruising women when you were six. I bet you looked the same as you do now." She reached over and squeezed Gigi's flushed cheeks with one hand. "Look at this baby face...I *love it*." Then she let go and pressed the back of her hand to Gigi's skin. "You're so hot. Why?"

"Why? Because I've been wearing a hot mask and slaving over a hot stove for all you people." Gigi's voice dropped with a hint of exhaustion. "My girls are bringing out the chafing dishes."

"Your *girls*?" Pat inquired.

"*Women*," Gigi corrected. "I kept two of my waitresses to help out with dinner. You didn't see them?"

Pat scanned the crowd in the amber lit room. "You mean those two in the French maid costumes?"

Gigi held her head back slyly and peered down at Pat with half closed eyes. "They're *uniforms*."

"Well, excuse me," Pat teased. "No wonder you've been hiding in the kitchen—was that a hot stove or hot women you said you've been slaving over?"

"I've been slaving...let's just leave it at that. *You* tell *me* what I slaved over when you taste the food."

"What's on the menu, anyway?" Pat asked.

Allegra lifted a menu card from the table and passed it across to Pat.

Gigi smiled sweetly. "Thank you *bella strega*—at least someone around here noticed the menu."

"Steamed mussels with butter and wine sauce...mmm..." Pat read aloud, "And black ravioli stuffed with lobster and shrimp in orange cream sauce."

"How'd you make them black?" Annie asked.

"*Squid ink*," Gigi said absently.

"Oh, geez, Gigi." Pat held her throat, making that sour face again. "Squid ink? That's disgusting!"

"Eh!" Gigi defensively flailed her arms, though in a good natured sort of way. "You can't get black ravioli just anywhere, you know—only the finest restaurants. You know how much I pay for my ink?"

"Don't worry," Kate said. "It's tasteless and odorless—might stain your teeth, though," she joked.

Pat looked at them. "What ever happened to artificial coloring?"

Gigi's eyes opened wide and she pounded her fingers against her chest. "What kind of chef do you think I am, huh? I use only natural dyes— only the best. If I thought I'd have to contend with a meat-and-potatoes guest, I would have set aside some fresh pasta and melted a black crayon in it for you." Gigi shook her fist at Pat playfully.

"Okay, okay," Pat laughed, holding her arms up in surrender, "I'll try it." But then she turned away, mumbling something inaudible to Maria about squid and octopuses and poison ink.

Annie had made her way around the table by then, shaking hands with both Susan and Allegra, then glancing curiously at the witch as she passed behind Allegra's chair. Finally she squatted beside Kate, resting her hand on her boss's thigh to keep her balance. "How's Lycos?" she asked with a note of enthusiasm. "Did Mr. Hebron come?"

Allegra turned with sharp interest, and Diane, too, looked across the table questioningly.

"Mr. *and* Mrs. Hebron." Kate smiled gently. "I'm going to miss that dog terribly. It was quite a reunion, though. They said they had a steak waiting for her at home."

"Aw...they're *so* nice!" Annie cooed.

"The Hebrons?" Diane asked, as if trying to place the name.

"Yeah, you know," Gigi said, smiling at Kate, "the elves I buy my cheese from. They live in Broome."

"Oh...the dwarves." Diane nodded thoughtfully. "Yes. I didn't know their name. It's a very interesting one, actually."

"How so?" Kate questioned.

"Well, it's from the Old Testament, the name of an ancient city ruled by the race of giants. It's uncommon—and a bit funny that dwarves should have a name associated with giants."

Pat looked at Maria, then at Diane. "We go to church, read the Bible—how come we've never heard the dwarves' name mentioned?"

"I suppose it's just an unpopular piece of biblical trivia." Diane smiled. "Something only a minister's daughter would know."

"Maria looked up with surprise. "Really? Your dad was a minister? Sounds kind of oppressive...considering your lifestyle and all."

"It was for a while...." Diane looked down for a moment.

"But you've made your peace," Allegra commented. It was more a statement than a question, and Diane quickly looked up, locking eyes with the witch.

"Yes..." Diane smiled. "Yes, I have." She brought a thumb and finger to her eyeglasses. "History and culture have always been important to me in terms of understanding the way people perceive their world. Maybe I'm rationalizing, but even though the writing of the Bible was divinely inspired, the writers were *still* products of their cultures, of the historical periods in which they lived."

Allegra nodded thoughtfully, an understanding smile coming and going on her face, as she waited for Diane to continue.

"The fact of the matter is that in biblical times, homosexual acts were associated with pagan orgies or, as in the case of ancient Greece, with men and boys—what we would no doubt consider child molestation today. No one ever acknowledged same-sex relationships within the more loving context of monogamy."

"Hmm..." Kate reflected, secretly finding her way to Allegra's lap and squeezing her hand in memory of their early-morning conversation. "*Context* is everything, isn't it?"

"Absolutely," Diane continued, unaware of the private joke beneath the table. "For instance, the Bible tells us not to put up fences, lest we keep the hungry and poor from eating our crops." Diane held out her hands. "So what does that mean today? That everyone who locks their front door at night to keep out the hungry and poor is going to hell?" Diane looked to Susan, then Allegra, and they both chuckled.

"Amen!" Maria said loudly.

Kate shrugged. "I guess the Bible is somewhat like our legal system. All the laws are clearly printed in black and white, but the better the lawyer, the better the interpretation."

"That's exactly it," Diane agreed.

"Well," Gigi frowned. "I can't imagine being raised by a minister any more than I can imagine growing up with two shrinks," she said, pointing sideways to Kate.

"*Both* parents?" Everyone asked in unison.

Allegra was clearly amused as Kate hunched her shoulders and raised contorted fingers. "How do you think I got to be so normal?" she asked, widening her eyes in a crazy sort of stare.

"Wow..." Maria started, "Two years with a therapist was enough for me. They must have analyzed the hell out of you."

Kate shrugged with a grin. "Until I came out to them—they stopped analyzing me after that."

"Good heavens," Diane laughed. "I guess they figured they'd lost the battle over your *id*."

"No *id*. My parents aren't Freudians, they're devout Jungians. We had the *shadow* in my family. Same difference, though."

Susan, a fan of public radio, raised her arms and wiggled her fingers above her head, setting elongated shadows scurrying across the ceiling. "The *shaa-doww* knows." She spoke the way a ghost would if it were intent on scaring you out of your house.

"The id, the shadow..." Diane mused. "Either way, it represents the dark, uncivilized side of each of us, right?"

"Oooh..." Susan looked at Diane seductively. "Maybe your id and my shadow—or your shadow and my id—can get together and bring Halloween to a close with a rendezvous."

Diane lifted one eyebrow and smiled. "Sounds risky...I have a feeling my ego might never re-gain control of itself."

Kate smirked. "That's the chance you take. The shadow's like the proverbial monster in the closet...only *you're* the closet."

All the women looked at her strangely. "Well, that's how I understood it as a child. I overheard my parents discussing it with colleagues one night at a party. I was only four at the time, so you can imagine the scare I had the next day when I was playing outside and saw my shadow following me. I took off, tried to out-run it, but that darned thing stuck to me like glue. I don't think I've ever moved faster than I did that day."

"How awful for you," Diane said in between chuckles.

"A frightening experience for a child," Allegra added, although she, too, was laughing along with Diane.

Kate hung her head in jest, accepting their condolences with a smile. "I still haven't gotten over it. I think one day I'll start an A.C.O.T. group—Adult Children of Therapists."

Allegra slipped her arm around the back of Kate's chair, letting her hand rest lightly on Kate's shoulder. "So it seems you and your family share a lot in common."

"Pardon me?" Kate looked insulted. "Are you suggesting I'm anything like my parents?"

Pat let out a hoot. "Face it, Kate, you're in your thirties now. You know it's just a matter of time before you wake up one morning and look in the mirror and say, *'Mom? Dad? Is that you?'* "

"Happens to the best of us," Diane agreed solemnly.

Gigi laughed. "It's called heredity." With that, she got up and motioned for Pat to come with her. "Time to change the music—enough *hip hop* for a while."

Kate turned back to Allegra with an inquisitive smile. "Just what did you mean when you said I have a lot in common with my folks?"

"I was referring to your professional interests." Allegra thought for a moment. "They're very...*primal.*"

"*Primal*?" Kate asked, rapidly batting her eyelashes up and down.

"Seriously. Your grandparents are professionally involved with fairy tales, fantastical beings, which certainly tap into a very intrinsic and primal aspects of the human imagination—no one teaches a child to fear the dark, to believe in magic, to conjure up superhuman monsters and tricksters and heroes—it comes naturally. And doesn't the Jungian psychology your parents practice deal with similar, primal images...the origins of which precede our personal histories?"

Gazing into Allegra eyes, taken for a moment by the firelight washing across her soft, green face, Kate conceded. "The collective unconscious, yes. It contains archetypes or, as you say, primal images thought to be universal in nature."

"And tell me..." Allegra began to smile in acknowledgement of Kate's searching eyes. "How would you explain an animal's instinct?"

Kate considered the question carefully, suddenly feeling as though she were a playing piece on a checker board, about to be cornered by her opponent. "It's a form of knowledge, I suppose. Knowledge that's, well..." Kate paused to smile, "that's universal to a particular species. A type of memory, maybe, passed on through the genes—it eliminates the need for certain knowledge having to be re-learned by each new generation."

Diane, who had been quietly listening, took Allegra's point well. "So we're back to primal images, the notion of both humans and animals inheriting primal knowledge from ancestors," she said.

Kate sat thoughtfully, rubbing her chin with her fingers. She had been cornered, all right. "And as a vet," Allegra continued, "or any person who relates well with animals, you must be capable of communicating on a primal level, of understanding instincts and all basic emotions—fear, trust, love, humor, jealousy—"

"It's a matter of being aware...subconsciously aware," Diane pointed out, "of our own primal aspects."

"Makes sense to me," Maria said, leaning over the table with folded arms. Susan agreed. Rumbling thunder sounded over the speakers just then, along with a laughing witch whose high-pitched cackling faded into the song "Strange Brew."

Kate pursed her lips, smiling and slowly nodding at the women, then leaned over to Allegra. "Speaking of *primal*," she said in a teasing voice, "could I interest you in a dance?"

Annie, who was beginning to look a bit bored, suddenly lit up. "Yeah, come on. My friends are up there."

"See, it's a good thing we let them stay," Maria said. "Gigi needs some young blood to keep her dance floor alive."

"Oh, is that so?" Diane spoke, looking deeply wounded,. "I think we still have *some* life left in us." She took off her glasses and winked at Susan. "Grab our canes, darling. We'll show these kids how to boogie."

The sultry cajun music of the Neville Brothers played "Voodoo" then "Yellow Moon." And in the darkness of the foggy dance floor, the cat and witch came together. Allegra immediately matched Kate's rhythm, her hands resting on the cat's moving hips until she slowly ran them up under Kate's bolero and against the silk of her white shirt now glowing purple in the pulsating strobe light.

Kate had once heard it said that you could tell what kind of lover a person would make by the way they ate food. Kate assumed there must be a similar connection between sex and dancing, and decided right then and there, that she and Allegra would one day make wonderful love together.

Kate pulled the witch close, felt the heat rising from her warm skin; the moist and wild scent of fresh lavender filling her lungs, filling her senses. And as she buried her face in the witch's neck, in the silky tangles of raven hair, she could feel Allegra's wanting, pounding pulse; a pulse that seemed to pound its way into Kate and find its own secret place between her thighs.

"I've been thinking about you all day," Kate whispered.

Allegra breathed heavily. "I know," she said.

"Oh, *really?*" Kate laughed low under her breath, pulling back just far enough to gaze into Allegra's eyes. "Now, just *how* would you know that?"

Allegra smiled with partially closed eyes, the purple light throbbing between them. "You bought me a rose..." she whispered back, using her palm to rub Kate's chest just above her breasts, "...so you had to have thought about me *at least* once today."

Kate pulled her close again. "At least once..." she murmured.

"I'll confess..." Allegra whispered as they danced, "You've been on my mind, too. I kept thinking about what it would be like to hold you close to me...like this."

Kate wanted to speak, to say something more, but she couldn't find one good reason to interrupt the fine and private conversation in which their bodies were now engaged.

She sensed Allegra's arousal and grew acutely aware of her own, as the witch pressed her breasts, then her stomach into Kate, her body gyrating almost imperceptibly beneath the slipping and sliding fabric of her black dress. For a moment, the party, the voices, the people ceased to exist; only the music was left, the rhythm of the woman in her arms, and the secret promise of a love to come. The jack-o'-lantern, grinning as if it were in on the secret, stared happily at them from the dark table; and Kate had the feeling that if the pumpkin had been able to, it would have winked a triangular eye at her.

They danced like that for what seemed an eternity, although it wasn't nearly that long before the music changed, the tempo picked up, and Gigi came in pulling on her mask. It seemed to Kate as though the Frankenstein head might have been a size too big, but Gigi handled it well, letting it instantly transform her personality as masks will tend to do. That was the reason humans had created the silly things in the first place, wasn't it?

A few other women stopped in for a quick dance, and before they knew it, partners were being exchanged and Kate and Allegra were exchanging commiserating looks. Kate danced with Diane, Susan with Allegra; others danced alone or in threes until, finally, they all made a large circle around Gigi and Maria who had just struck up a mean and altogether sexy mambo.

None of them had eaten yet, and as the crowd around the dinner buffet lightened, they stopped dancing one by one, and followed the delectable smell of lobster and mussels and freshly baked bread. Against her will, Kate was soon separated from Allegra by a woman who stopped to introduce herself, saying she had heard of Kate and was shopping around for a new vet. By the time Kate finished talking, Allegra was caught up in conversation with someone else, and Kate could only gesture with her plate to say she would meet the witch back at their fireside table.

Pat, who thought she'd find the black ravioli so repulsive, was already on her way up for a second helping. As Kate sat down with the others, she was suddenly aware of an unpleasant sound—a nagging voice—that hadn't been in the dining room before.

"Doesn't she ever shut up?" Diane asked, referring to the clipped, grating speech of a new arrival—the only woman not in costume.

Kate turned to see Mildred Lutz, her short, mousey-brown curls wound and clinging so tightly to her head that it seemed they might, at any moment now, spring themselves loose and pop off her head. Her purse jiggled violently on the back of her chair, her arms flailing about in the air, as she pursued a political argument with some unsuspecting victims. Mildred ate and debated, ate and debated, probably not even tasting her food and, most likely, not even caring about what it was she was putting in her mouth. Kate wondered what those sex-and-food theorists would have to say about Lutz's eating habits.

Mildred was the county's tax assessor. A rather abrasive type, in kind terms. She never laughed, never so much as smiled; in fact, the only time she was known to show emotion was when she was involved in a heated debate such as this one, jumping at the chance to criticize any opinion which opposed her own.

Everyone agreed that Mildred wouldn't have been such a bad looking woman if not for her nastiness. But her disposition, awful as it was, seemed to have permanently etched itself in her face over the years; giving her beady eyes a suspicious, squinted look, and causing the corners of her mouth to droop way down in the manner of a bullfrog so that, all in all, she had an amphibious sort of look about her.

According to Pat, Mrs. Lutz's disposition had grown steadily worse since her automobile accident a few years ago. Mildred, as the story was told, had been peacefully cruising along the thruway—although it was hard for Kate to imagine Mildred doing anything peacefully—when suddenly, from out of nowhere, two large and very hairy spiders raced up the front of her pant leg. The critters were apparently a bit edgy, what with being trapped in a moving vehicle and all, and as they made an agitated dash for her face, Mildred panicked, lost control of her Volkswagen, and took a twenty foot plunge into a ravine. It was a wonder it didn't kill her.

People were naturally sympathetic about the accident, but to this day no one who knew Mildred could tell the story—at least not the part about the spiders—without bursting into laughter. Of course, Kate suspected their laughter came from the irony of knowing that, given a choice between plunging twenty feet into a ravine or being bitten by a nervous spider, most people wouldn't have thought twice about opting for the plunge.

"I don't know why she bothers showing up at parties," Diane remarked. "She never has a good time."

"Sure she does." Susan said. "She has a great time. It's the people she yells at that don't."

"How could she have a good time when she's always so miserable?" Pat asked, before stuffing another mussel in her mouth.

Maria paused and poked at a ravioli with her fork. "If she had nothing to complain about she wouldn't be happy. Some people like being miserable."

"Or making others miserable," Susan said. "Face it, she's been through two husbands and three wives—she abused all five of them."

"Hey," Pat whispered to Maria, pointing to the ceiling with a hint of mischief in her eyes, "Pull me down one of those rubber spiders there. I'll sneak over and sit it on her shoulder."

"Oh, stop!" Maria elbowed her lover. "You'll give the poor woman a heart attack."

Kate glanced toward the buffet just then, catching Allegra's gaze as the witch finally excused herself from the woman talking to her. Even from across the room, the magnetic locking of their eyes psychologically closed the space between them. She watched Allegra walking toward her, enjoying the chance to glimpse a full length view, to admire her from a distance as she came down the aisle with such natural grace. Kate could not tear her eyes away; if she had, though, she would have missed the unsettling interplay between Mildred and the witch.

Mildred looked up, did a double-take, then fell silent, her eyes growing wide and round as plums as the witch passed her table. Allegra stopped short, sudden worry washing over her face. She glanced at Kate, quickly shifting her eyes to the left and then the right, like a wild animal contemplating a fast getaway. But in the end it was Mildred who made the getaway.

In less than an instant, uncertainty disappeared from the witch's face, replaced now by a sudden and fierce confidence which seemed capable of burning holes through the otherwise fearless Mildred Lutz. Mildred was so visibly shaken for the moment, that the muscles in her hand went limp, and her fork slipped right out from between her fingers and bounced to the floor.

Allegra, very much the lady, kindly bent down, balancing her plate in one hand, and graciously retrieved the fork. With a stolid, almost imperceptible nod, the witch placed the fork beside Mildred, then continued on her way.

Kate glanced at the others, but they were busy eating and talking about what they were eating, and the incident had gone unnoticed. But Gigi, making table rounds, hadn't missed a thing. From across the amber-lit room she gave a questioning nod, a perplexed crease in her forehead.

Kate's tone grew concerned. "Is everything all right?" she whispered, as Allegra approached their table.

"Yes, I—" Allegra stopped, setting her plate down and gestured to indicate she had no explanation—that she was just as puzzled by the incident as Kate.

Kate kept her voice low. "Do you *know* Mildred?"

"Is that her name?" Allegra shook her head. "No, I don't know her...I don't think I want to, either."

"Hmm...*that's* funny." Kate glanced over to find Mildred blindly groping for the purse on the back of her chair. A moment later she was gone. "Don't take it personally. Mildred isn't the most pleasant of people."

The two women whose table Mildred had invaded were all the better for her hasty retreat. They appeared relieved by her departure, and carried on as though nothing had happened. Allegra, too, seemed to forget the incident in a matter of minutes, and conversation picked up again, waxing and waning throughout an enjoyable and, everyone agreed, scrumptious dinner.

Gigi had decided against a contest for best costume. She did have gifts for everyone—pumpkin-scented candles with little bags of cinnamon potpourri tied with orange ribbon—but no individual prizes. The purpose of a party was to have fun, she said, not to compete and be judged when it was all a matter of opinion, anyway. So instead, she had decided on bobbing for apples; a far more sportive activity.

During Allegra's earlier tour of the kitchen, Gigi had apparently pointed out the sack of apples, the soup kettle she had set aside for the game, and then, somewhere along the line, had appointed the witch her folklore consultant.

Bobbing for apples, Allegra told her, was traditionally a game of divination. On Halloween, the fruits were inscribed with names and, it was believed, you would later marry the person whose apple you caught. It was a wonderfully romantic idea, Gigi thought, and now had a few volunteers back in the kitchen, personalizing apples with waterproof markers.

"Who ever chose the *apple* to represent evil?" Maria wondered aloud.

Diane smiled thoughtfully. "We associate apples with evil, but they really symbolize knowledge. That's why we give them to teachers."

"But eating from the tree of knowledge awakened desire," Allegra added. "And so the forbidden fruit symbolizes desire, also...the *consciousness* of desire." Kate looked slyly at the witch.

Maria frowned. "I doubt apples even grew there."

"Where?" Gigi asked.

"The garden."

"Of *Eden*? Are you *serious*? You know why no one's found that place yet?"

Maria shook her head.

"Because it doesn't exist. Never did." Gigi waved her hand. Her feelings about religion were apparently as strong as Pat's were about dowsing.

"Maybe it just wasn't here. Maybe it was on another planet," Pat suggested. "Did you ever think of that?"

"Personally? I think the whole story was written on another planet." Gigi waved her hand again. "*Please*... don't get me started on organized religion. That stuff is too sexist for me."

"Well, wherever Eden was supposed to have been," Maria remarked, "you wouldn't have found *apples* growing there. I can think of at least a dozen fruits that are juicier and sweeter and a hell of a lot more sensuous than apples. Ask Pat. When I took her to my country we spent hours climbing trees, just sitting in the branches picking and eating fruits she had never seen before."

"Where?" Allegra asked.

"Ecuador."

The witch nodded. "It must have been a paradise. And I do think most people would agree with you about the apple. Some say the fruit of original sin was most likely a fig, or perhaps a date."

Maria and Diane both nodded meditatively. "A fig..." Maria repeated.

"I like figs better than apples, anyway," Gigi said. "They're...more womanly, more sensual...more fun to eat, if you catch my drift." With a devilish smile, Gigi excused herself to round up apple bobbers for her game, and began directing all the women toward a large circle of orange crepe paper placed around the apple-filled cauldron. This "witches' circle" was another one of Allegra's contributions. She told them that although wizards and magicians were said to remain within their protective magic circles to *keep out* the evil forces they called up, witches stood inside to *keep in* the magical powers thought to emanate from the feminine body. And of course Gigi, loving anything to do with female powers and feminine bodies, was instantly sold on the idea of the *witches' circle.*

Bobbing proved highly entertaining as each woman, laughing but determined, attempted to sloppily snatch the apple bearing the name of her true love. Less than half were successful, though; most ending up with someone else's lover's apple in their mouths.

When Allegra's turn came, Kate stood observing her from outside the witches' circle, her unruly eyes leaving the apples and roaming the contour of Allegra's black-stockinged legs. It seemed Gigi and several other women couldn't help but do the same, as the witch bent over, slowly lowering her face to the water.

One side of Gigi's mouth turned up in a crooked smile. "I don't know where you found her, Doc, but I'll tell you one thing..." Gigi shook her head and sighed. "*Allegra* sure has great *legras.*"

Kate smiled knowingly at Gigi, feeling the slightest, strangest pang of possessiveness and thinking that maybe everyone should be keeping their eyes on the apples, not on Allegra's *legras.*

The witch turned out to be one of the victorious bobbers, setting her sights on Kate's red apple, and dipping her mouth with the skill of a true markswoman. Water splashed and dripped from her chin as she probed and pushed and pinned the apple, then daintily caught the stem between her teeth. Those participating in the game began applauding as the witch straightened, holding in her mouth the dripping wet fruit of her desire.

Allegra looked at Kate, then letting the apple drop into her hand, turned to Gigi and teasingly said, "My prize, please."

"Her name is written on your apple—here she is," Gigi said, giving Kate a playful shove in the witch's direction.

In the end, everyone except Kate managed to snatch an apple. She was the last to bob and, try as she might, couldn't capture the damned thing. The apple simply refused to cooperate with her mouth. The stem broke off for starters, and after that the fruit just seemed too big or too hard or maybe too free to float about without its sister apples to crowd and keep it steady. Kate wondered if Maria was changing her mind about that good omen. She shrugged at Allegra apologetically, watching the witch's defiant apple riding the waves in its lonely sea of love. If only they had bobbed for figs, Kate thought.

By the time the bobbers had all dried their mouths, Gigi had seen to it that the dessert buffet was prepared. There was an ice carving of a witch's cauldron garnished inside and out with seasonal gourds, apple birds, D'Anjou and red Bartlett pears. A pumpkin-hazelnut cobbler with Wild

Turkey bourbon sauce awaited the guests, along with fresh brewed hazelnut coffee and an assortment of teas.

It was bad enough Kate had failed at bobbing, but to make matters worse, she was the only one with more than a wet chin. She was soaked right up to her cat ears, in fact, and decided to make a dash for the ladies room before dessert. On her way back to the dining room, though, her attention drifted to the moonlight spilling into the lake below. On impulse, she slid open the glass door and walked onto the deck, leaning over and resting her elbows on the wooden railing.

The fog had lifted, or at least crawled off the water and gone somewhere else, and the moon had turned the lake to a cauldron of liquid silver. Starlight twinkled amidst the quiet ripples, and two small fishing boats, tied to the pier of a small jutting dock, gently slapped the water and bobbed like those elusive apples in the kettle.

On a good day Gigi could always be found out there, drifting and sunning and competing with the water birds for her share of fish. Kate didn't have the patience for fishing—nor the heart, particularly—but Gigi often dragged her along, anyway. Toting a thermos and a book, Kate was content just to settle back in the boat, reading and enjoying the scenery—until Gigi reeled in a fish. Then Kate was up and about, shouting instructions on humanely removing the hook. Of course, once Kate had made eye contact with the fish, let alone handled the poor creature, it was hard for her to look at it as anything less than a friend and, well, everyone knows you can't very well go around eating your friends. So Kate would always make up some story about the fish being ill or diseased or gravid and ready to spawn. For a moment, Gigi would stare blankly at both of them, perhaps trying to determine whether Kate and the fish were in collusion. But in the end she conceded—releasing the fish with just the slightest hint of aggravation—and Kate would then happily return to her business of reading and relaxing. Until the next fish was caught. Come to think of it, though, Gigi hadn't invited her fishing in almost two weeks now.

Kate stared ahead at the boats, thinking it might be nice to take Allegra out one afternoon before the weather changed. She drew in one last breath of night air, and was just about to turn to go inside, when a sultry voice spoke from behind.

"Would you care to bob again?"

Kate swiveled to meet the smiling witch, silver moonlight reflecting in her forest green eyes. In her outstretched palm Allegra held the apple bearing her own name. "I'll make it easy for you this time," she said.

A smile came to Kate's face and she leaned back, putting one foot up behind her against the rail. "I suppose there comes a time in every woman's life when pride must succumb to desire." But as she reached to accept the apple, Allegra withdrew it.

"Not with your *hand*," the witch teased. "That would be cheating."

Kate hesitated, giving a sideways glance, then put her hands behind her back and leaned forward to take the apple with her mouth. It proved easy enough this time, and as she held the fruit between her teeth, not quite sure what to do with it, Allegra's hand came up to help hold the apple so Kate could take a bite.

"And where's *my* namesake?" Kate asked, after she had swallowed her juicy bite.

"I ate it." Allegra smiled. "Slowly...and with great pleasure, I might add."

Kate felt the heat rising in her cheeks. She laughed softly and opened her arms, and Allegra moved in to hug her.

"The water is so beautiful," Allegra said dreamily, as she rested her head on Kate's shoulder.

"Isn't it? Look at the moon...the whole night is beautiful."

Allegra's eyes scanned the sky as if she were tracking the hands of a clock. "It must be close to midnight," she guessed.

Kate straightened her left arm behind the witch's back to expose the watch beneath her cuff. "Just about."

"Will there be time left for the walk I promised you?"

"I wouldn't miss it for the world—that's how this date got started, isn't it?" Kate tilted her head back far enough to focus on Allegra's eyes. "What about Dewitt?"

"He's waiting for my call."

Kate took Allegra's hand, leading her inside to the phone, where she left the witch to make her call in privacy.

They enjoyed dessert with Gigi and the others before Dewitt arrived, and Diane took the opportunity to further pursue Allegra's knowledge of folklore. All the women listened attentively, as the modest, almost evasive storyteller enchanted them with mythological tidbits.

With her back to the fireplace, Allegra sat across from Kate. And as the fire roared and burned to the music of *Two Nice Girls*, then slowed to the classic "Rhiannon"—a song which was, according to Diane, about a legendary Welsh witch—Kate felt her attention waning. It's not that she had lost interest; on the contrary, Kate imagined the subject at hand had the makings of good pillow talk over the course of the next ten years or so. Maybe that's why her thoughts were straying; she was jumping ahead, caught up in the anticipation of—what? Pillow talk, most likely, and the fact that it necessarily involved the fact of lying in bed with Allegra. The more Kate told herself to keep focused on the conversation, the harder it was to do just that until, finally, she wasn't paying the slightest bit of attention to what the witch was saying. Allegra's low and melodic voice seemed to fade into the background, becoming part of the music, part of the atmosphere, as Kate watched her moving lips, the expressions on her voiceless, green face changing in time with the backdrop of flames, which rose and fell and rose behind her again.

Kate couldn't have said for sure how much time had passed, but when she suddenly came back to earth, someone was announcing that a limousine was waiting; Gigi was off preparing a take-out order of black ravioli and mussels for Dewitt; everyone was telling Allegra what a pleasure it was to have met her, and Diane was inviting the two of them for dinner one night soon. Kate smiled, trying to compensate for her rude, mental wandering, and only hoped she hadn't missed anything important.

Allegra carried Dewitt's bag of seafood, as Kate walked ahead to open La Zingara's heavy door. Before reaching it, though, the witch stepped hard and, it seemed, purposely on her tail. It stopped Kate short, and she slowly turned around, eyeing Allegra suspiciously.

"Sorry," the witch said, "I didn't mean to—"

"Sure you did." Kate peered wisely at her.

A smile broke on Allegra's face. "I just wanted to get your attention...you seemed a million miles away back there."

Kate couldn't help but smile, either. "That far away? No..." she said, turning back again and opening the door for Allegra. "I was much closer than that. Closer than you know." The witch didn't say another word; she simply acknowledged Kate with calculating eyes, then nodded with thanks at the open door.

Kate followed behind, making sure her entire tail was out before the heavy door banged shut. It trailed behind her now, imprinted with the mark of a dusty witch's boot. But Kate hadn't bothered to notice.

8

$\mathcal{B}$eneath the open sky of a meadow, a short way from the pond where they had met, the cat and witch sat stargazing on a carpet of velvety moss, their heads lifted to the infinite points of light that twitched and twinkled and bounced across the heavens. Black cloud-drift which had passed the moon earlier, was long gone now, and the midnight sky beyond the stars hung like a curtain of indigo blue.

"Sometimes things become clearer when you don't look at them directly," Allegra suggested. She had one arm around Kate, and with the other led her eyes to catch a glimpse of the shooting stars. "Don't stare too hard...let them come within your peripheral vision."

Kate took her lessons from the witch, pleased to discover that the celestial show in the corner of her eye was, indeed, far grander than the activity in her direct line of vision. Within minutes she was tracing lines of elusive stars as they shot themselves into cosmic oblivion.

The two were still in costume, Allegra having pointed out that nature walks could be enjoyed every day or night, but the fun of taking one in costume came only once a year. Hats and ears and tails had been left behind, though, along with two high-powered flashlights Kate had proudly taken from her rural-survival-closet. The grace and light of the full moon, Allegra told her, would guide them where they wished to go. And she was right; moonshine flooded the open meadow, lighting everything in its path, although the hedgerow up ahead and the stand of hemlocks beyond that, seemed a bit too spooky for Kate's liking.

"Have you ever seen the aurora borealis?" Allegra asked.

"The northern lights? Only in pictures. But I'd love to go to Alaska someday."

"I wish I could take you..." Allegra glanced over at Kate then pondered the sky again. "...someday."

The idea instantly appealed to Kate. And who knew, maybe in a year or two they would settle down together; get a dog, a horse, a couple of goats. Why, they could even get a Winnebago, pack up the whole family and drive to the aurora. Better yet, they'd get a house-sitter and leave the family home; travel north, just the two of them, and spend a few nights making love and camping out beneath the northern lights. "People say it's like seeing a rainbow at night," Kate said. "Are they stars?"

"Sun dust, really," the witch said. "Blown to earth by solar winds. I believe it has something to do with electro-magnetic energy." She patted a respectfully low portion of Kate's thigh. "Something comparable to that *wonderful* description of a medical scanner you gave Pat tonight."

Kate rolled her eyes. "I sure set myself up for that one," she said, leaning back on her elbows and laughing a little. "Magnetism...." She looked over at Allegra. "It seems to be explaining a lot of things tonight."

"Well, after all, the earth itself is a magnet. And aren't we too? Don't all animals have metals in their bodies?"

"Trace metals, yes," Kate answered in a doctor-like manner. "Iron, copper, calcium...magnesium. Some are ionized and so able to attract things to them. I never thought of it that way."

Kate studied Allegra, pushing wisps of black hair away from the witch's face. "Is it safe to assume, then, that magnetism might even explain love at first sight?"

Allegra stared with knowing eyes, a smile coming to her moonlit face. "Could be, but I rather like the way the Greeks explained it—that each of us is part of someone else from whom we're separated at birth. When and if the two natural halves ever meet during their earthly lives, they instantly recognize each other. "And *that*," she said, playfully pushing Kate over, "would be love at first sight."

Kate lay on her back, her knees bent, and she smiled at Allegra. "So that's how it happened."

Allegra stood up then, extending her hands to help pull Kate up. "How what happened?"

"How *we* happened." She clasped Allegra's hands, about ready to lift herself, then had a sudden change of heart and pulled the witch down on top of her instead.

Kate felt her senses heighten as they kissed beneath the stars, the light breeze caressing their hair like the hands of ghostly fairies. Suddenly, the thought that maybe the breeze wasn't the breeze at all gave Kate the willies. She slyly opened one eye as she kissed Allegra, half expecting to see a bunch of nymphs or pixies or wood sprites sneaking about and sprinkling star dust in prophecy of a coming wedding of two brides. It was, for argument's sake, still Halloween; the one night when all doors to all dimensions opened, and Kate supposed that rush hour traffic between dimensions would be getting pretty heavy right about now. The coast was clear, though. There was nothing about but the witch, the moon and the breeze.

Allegra suddenly pulled her mouth away and looked at Kate suspiciously. "Tell me, Kate Gallagher," she said in a soft but calculating tone, "Do you sleep with many women?"

Kate was taken aback by the question. "Allegra, I..."

The witch smiled. "That's the first time you've said my name. I like the way you say it," she whispered.

"Allegra..." Kate paused self-consciously, then smiled as she said her name again. "Do you have a last name?"

Allegra hesitated. "Netherland," she said, looking down.

"Allegra Netherland...." Kate lifted the witch's chin. "No, I don't *sleep* with many women. Why would you even think that of me?"

"Well, you're single, interesting, pretty much established...a little on the cute side, I'd say." Allegra looked with teasing, affectionate eyes. "Besides," she added, "Your best friend called you a heartbreaker."

"*What*? Gigi said that?" Kate was astounded. "I think those dandelions went to her head. You can't always take her seriously, you know. She kids a lot. Anyway," Kate paused and shook her head, "I haven't been with anyone since I left Long Island."

"Is that why you left?" Kate detected a note of sadness in Allegra's voice as she got up and offered Kate a hand again. "Were you running away from a broken heart?"

Kate thought about that while they walked hand in hand through the leaves and meadow grasses, as memories of summer and hints of winter laced the midnight air; a season past, a season promised, merging to give the autumn night a sweet, raw smell all its own.

"My heart's never been broken," Kate finally said. "Maybe that's the whole problem...I've never been in love."

"You've never loved a woman?" Allegra asked. "Now *that* surprises me."

"Well of course I've loved *women*. I love women. There's just never been anyone special...." Kate's voice trailed off. What she wanted to say was that she had never felt the longing, the desire, nor the sweet passion that was filling her now. "I guess I've read too many fairy tales in my time. Thought that when real love came it would be, well...magical."

Allegra stopped in her tracks and looked at Kate pensively. Actually it was more than a look, Kate thought. It was an optical touch that seemed to reach in and disrobe her soul. "And if you found that magic, Kate...would you run from it?"

Kate stared in silence, not even thinking to answer. She figured it was a rhetorical question. A ridiculous one at that. Why ever would anyone search to find something, then run when they had found it at last? It didn't make a bit of sense.

Allegra's eyes relinquished their grip, and she tenderly took Kate's hand again, sighing as though in resignation of having to put some important matter aside. They walked across the meadow with the breeze on their faces, and as their legs brushed against a dwindling patch of heather, Allegra's hand swooped down. With the innocence of a school girl she smiled and placed a sprig of the little purple flowers in Kate's shirt pocket. But before Kate could look down to acknowledge the gift, the witch's attention had shifted. Now she stood pointing to a solitary apple tree ahead; a legacy, it seemed, of an orchard long ago. The shiny skins of golden apples glistened on the leafless tree, its splayed and eccentrically bent branches giving it the look of a many-armed creature, lonely and all too happy to welcome any visitors to its meadow.

"Come on," Allegra said, a hint of adrenalin in her voice. She picked up speed then, excitedly urging Kate alongside her, and before long they were laughing and racing toward the apple tree. Kate wasn't quite sure why she was running, but it didn't much matter; running with Allegra was fun, the sensation of racing through the breeze unequivocally delightful.

No sooner had they reached the tree, than the witch had one foot raised to a notch, using it as a stirrup with which to boost herself and grab hold of the lower branches. "Watch out," she said as she shook the tree with what seemed unusual strength.

Kate stepped back, ducking and sheltering her head with one arm, as a barrage of ripe fruit thumped to the ground.

"There's always something for the deer to eat," Allegra said, lowering herself onto one foot then jumping back from the tree and brushing her hands. "But they can't eat what they can't reach—it's called the *browse line*." The witch threw an apple to Kate, then picked up two more, which she stuffed into the side pockets of her black dress. "Worse than not seeing food, is seeing it and knowing you can't partake of it."

Kate gestured toward the two bulges at the witch's sides. "What are we going to do with..."

"Shh!" Allegra held her finger to Kate's lips, slowly cocking her head this way and that way, like a wolf listening to the night. "Do you hear the breathing?" she whispered.

Now that, Kate thought, was a silly question to ask a city person standing alone in the middle of the woods at night. Why, such a question was bound to conjure up images of some asthmatic sociopath hiding behind a tree, just waiting for the chance to go mad. Kate's internal alarm went off immediately. "Hear *who* breathing?" she asked.

Allegra smiled and kissed Kate on the cheek, quickly putting her at ease. "The deer," she said. "Do you hear them breathing?"

Kate's eyes lit up and she wondered at the witch. "No...where?"

"Come," Allegra whispered, taking her by the hand. "Just walk calmly—it's not the sound, but the *mood* of your footsteps that alerts the animals." Kate, always the game but careful playmate, nodded and followed her past the edge of the wood and into the darkness.

The land before them inclined just a bit then, and they made their way among the textured trunks of ancient hemlocks, their gnarled roots covered over with needles, their canopies overhead swaying like metronomes and shading the moon and stars in such a way that the whole forest became a shifting tapestry of light and shadow. As they walked deeper and deeper, the air grew steadily damper, its moisture awakening a mixture of pungent forest smells: old oak and fresh pine and a musky odor which had a strange smell of life about it. Allegra stopped and held up her hand just then, silently gesturing toward a small moonlit clearing. And there, nestled and watching, were a doe and her fawn sitting as still as statues.

"This is my Halloween gift to you," Allegra whispered. Kate began to speak, but the witch placed a finger on her lips again. "Wait here," she said, then gracefully approached the resting animals.

The wary fawn grew fidgety, rising half way and nervously shifting its eyes to its mother as if ready to dash at the slightest confirmation of danger. But the doe did not move. She remained calm and peaceful, entranced somehow, and the fawn, having the utmost confidence in its mother's judgement, lowered itself and relaxed again beside her.

Kate looked on in silent amazement. It was all she could do to contain her happiness over this unexpected sight. Allegra had an apple out now, the palm of her other hand held up to the animals. Whether she was hypnotizing or reassuring them, Kate couldn't tell, but a few steps later Allegra was kneeling with the deer and motioning for Kate to join her. The ground was thick, cushioned with years of pine needles that made the forest floor feel like a feather bed. Kate's boots sank, sprang up and sank again as she tiptoed into the clearing where the witch patted a spot for her.

"They're a bit leery of being touched," Allegra said softly. "Use the food to gain their trust...it's a universal language."

The doe and fawn's ears flickered with each whispered word, and Kate hesitated, taking a moment to listen to the precious breathing Allegra had heard earlier. Two wet and runny noses, one bigger than the next, crinkled and twitched, their nostrils flaring and sending breath after steamy breath *whooshing* into the night. Their brown eyes, so alive and untainted, stayed patiently fixed on the apple as though they were wondering when the awe-struck Kate would come to her senses and fork up the fruit.

Allegra smiled, adding both her apples to the one already in Kate's hand, then sat and watched with deep affection as Kate fed the deer. There was an undercurrent of excitement in the witch's eyes; a clear and unmistakable joy which came not so much from being with the deer herself, as from witnessing Kate's joy in being there.

Kate sat still while the deer slurped and licked the last traces of apple juice from her fingers. She looked at the witch then, so beautiful in the forest light, and was struck with an instinctive feeling that Allegra was destined to become the true love of her life.

A short while later they were off again, leaving the deer undisturbed, and quietly making their way back through the hemlocks and hedgerow and across the moonlit meadow again.

"What a privilege..." Kate said, when she could finally speak. "Thank you...really, thank you."

"It was *my* privilege to bring you there," Allegra said.

They walked on in silence for a while, eventually winding up on the dirt road again, with Allegra stopping now and then to identify the flowering oddities that Kate pointed out. Wild rose hips waited for the morning blackbirds, and there were teasels and pokeweed and white woodland asters about, and a scattering of soft yellow flowers over the fall-blooming witch hazel. Here and there Allegra snapped a twig or crumbled a leaf or picked a berry, so that Kate would know all the wonders in this moonlit garden by more than just a name. In between Kate's questions, Allegra took the liberty of popping a lemony sumac berry into Kate's eager mouth—the nonpoisonous variety she carefully pointed out—then laughed at Kate's expression as she took first a whiff of the astringent but fleeting smell of sassafras, then sniffed natural cyanide from a twig off a cherry tree.

As they reached the white house, Kate pointed one last time to her left. "What are those pods? They're all over my property."

"Milkweed. You'd recognize it in summer. It doesn't look at all like it does in season. It's quite toxic, actually—and equally delicious if you happen to be a monarch butterfly. That's all the caterpillar eats...." Allegra paused, arching one eyebrow, "...and to unassuming predators, turns into a butterfly as deadly as it is beautiful." The witch broke off a swollen, woody pod the size of her palm and spread it open to expose its silky substance. "Make a wish," she said.

Kate smiled. "You, too."

They each took a generous pinch of the white, wispy seeds, and stood watching as both the wind and the lunar light caught their shiny trailers and sent them floating like tiny sailboats over the chimney and into the chilly night.

Back inside they freshened up, and Kate left Allegra to choose the music while she set some hot cider to mull. The witch wasted no time selecting Tchaikovsky's *"Dance of the Sugar Plum Fairy,"* and strolled to the window then, listening to the music as sudden gusts of wind moved in, whistling and howling and using the trees as an instrument through which to play its own song of romance. Allegra smiled in recognition of its song; smiled at the moon as though it were her sister. And then, as if requesting a favor from the wind and moon and their powers, she tightly closed her eyes. Tensed fingers slowly rose to her temples, and she began pressing, rubbing them in time with the music. Even tighter now she shut her eyes with concentrated effort; then, suddenly, there was no music—not a single light— and the satisfied witch opened her eyes to the dimly moonlit room.

"Allegra? Guess we just lost power." A wooden bowl of fruit crashed to the kitchen floor, and then what sounded like a can and a spoon fell with a clang, as Kate fumbled to locate a candle on the counter. She used the fire under the pot to light it, then cupped and carefully followed the flame inside. "Are you okay?"

The witch turned her head from the window, and glanced backwards at Kate. "I'm *fine*...how are *you*?"

Kate furrowed her brow, but then she smiled. "Okay...I just knocked some things over. Let me check the circuit breaker."

"No...don't bother," Allegra said quickly. "The lights will be back on soon enough." She gave a casual, backwards glance from the window. "Weather is always strange in the mountains, you know."

"I guess." Kate shrugged. "This isn't the first time I've lost my power."

"Then we may as well enjoy the moonbeams." Allegra turned and went to her. "I'll help you," she offered.

Allegra held the candle while Kate poured the mulled cider, then led their way out of the kitchen and back to the living room. Kate gestured toward the floor, at the open door of the potbelly stove. "Would you rather sit down here by the fire?"

"I'd love to." Allegra smiled, taking the cider from her, and after she had set the cups on the floor, ran her fingers along the stem of a withered cactus. "What happened to this poor plant?"

"Negligence," Kate confessed, grabbing from the sofa a cotton throw, which she then spread over the carpet. "I'll have to remember to water it in the morning," she said, tossing a heap of upholstered pillows to the floor.

The witch knelt, and just as Kate looked around the dark room, thinking to light a second candle, Allegra blew out the first one. The log Kate had thrown in the stove before their walk, had since burned itself out and only embers now softly lit the stove. "How about another log? It'll give us more light," Kate proposed. She pardoned herself and was just about to step across Allegra for wood, when the witch tugged on her sleeve. "It's very warm in here, already...stop making such a fuss."

Kate took off her bolero and crouched, resigning herself to relaxing beside the witch, then picked up her cider and toasted. "I suppose a blackout *is* a perfect way to end a Halloween," she said. A gust of wind rattled the windows just then, and the light of the full moon streamed in, absorbing colors and turning everything in the room to varying shades of gray, so that it seemed to Kate they were actresses in a black and white movie.

"I couldn't agree more." Allegra's smile was mischievous, her eyes tantalizing. "There must be a *magnetic* storm brewing somewhere out *there*. It will pass, though."

Kate set her cup down and crawled on her knees to Allegra. "It won't be passing anytime soon...and I don't think it's out there. I think you've got a storm brewing in me."

"Likewise," Allegra whispered, as she played with Kate's hair. Kate stayed on her knees and closed her eyes as a chill swept over her scalp, then moved forward for a deep and teasing kiss. Shifting her weight to free one arm, she ran her hand along the contour of Allegra's torso, along the side of her breast, feeling the witch shudder as she grazed her nipple, responsive and hardening beneath her black dress.

Kate normally had a rule about sex on the first date, but then some saying about rules being made to be broken came to mind and she decided to put the whole matter to rest. It was impossible, Kate decided, to lose control and obey rules at the same time.

Slowly, she fiddled with Allegra's buttons, opening one and then the next, amidst the sounds of wet kisses and autumn leaves blowing about in the outside breeze. But no sooner had she opened the last button, than Allegra gasped slightly, pulling back a bit.

Kate swallowed hard and looked at the witch with worry; afraid that maybe she had overstepped her boundaries—broken the rules after all, so to speak. "I'm sorry," Kate whispered. "I didn't mean to—"

"Oh, Kate...no, it's not that." Allegra took and kissed the hand that had been touching her, her eyes moving nervously from the moon to the wall clock and back to Kate. "I...I haven't been with..." She sighed deeply. "It's been a while for me."

Kate lifted Allegra's chin. "Allegra, we don't have to make love." Kate's tone was tender and she smiled with deep affection; an affection that surprised even *her*. "I could spend the whole night just kissing you, just...just getting over the initial shock of ever having *met* you."

Allegra brought her trembling fingers to Kate's lips. "I do want you, Kate...you'll never know how much."

"Not unless you'd like to show me...."

Allegra regarded Kate with silent deliberation. But then as if deciding, perhaps, that there was no sense wasting time with such decisions, her mouth impulsively replaced her fingers. She kissed Kate hungrily, then stopped as abruptly as she had started, sitting back on her heels to willingly open the last of her buttons. And as they both faced one another on their knees, Allegra smiled thinly and guided her waiting lover's hands to her body.

Kate spread open the front of the black dress, taking time to tenderly bite and taste Allegra's shoulders before pushing it off and down to reveal a black lace bra. She paused to feast her eyes on the beauty she had uncovered; all the beauty yet to be uncovered. And as she did, the witch took her turn with Kate. Stripping her of the silk shirt, she trailed a teasing tongue along the line of Kate's white camisole, using her teeth to gently lift the thin straps so that they fell from Kate's shoulders.

In the deepening hours of the night they shared the slow pleasure of undressing one another. And when they had, Kate pulled the witch to her and lay back under the naked weight of Allegra's needful body. Perspiration laced with lavender slipped between their stomachs, their breasts, as Kate moved beneath the witch, luxuriating in the wonderful sensations of her skin merging with the new and naked desire of another.

With strands of dark hair tickling Kate's breasts, Allegra—almost a shadow now in the changing moonlight—smiled down at her. Her smile quickly vanished, though, and a wild glimmer blazed in her blackened eyes.

"You're making me very excited right now," she whispered, then softly bit Kate's lip, and then bit it again. "I've been aching for you all night."

Kate pulled her down, kissing her lips, her eyes, then rubbed an open mouth across her ear. "Let me take that ache away."

And with that she slid her hands around to Allegra's buttocks, separating the soft mounds and reaching between her moist thighs to find the source of desire that now dripped from her like honey. Allegra gasped as Kate found her sex, her mouth opening in breathless pleasure as Kate explored the swollen, cavernous delights of the witch's femininity. "You're very wet," Kate murmured.

"It's all for you," Allegra moaned in between heavy breaths. Then, "Love me," she pleaded, "...make love to me."

All too willing to oblige her, Kate turned over, feeling desire rush from her own body, and rolled Allegra onto her back. She traveled the length of her body—a body silhouetted against the silver moonshine—first taking Allegra's firm breasts in her hungry mouth, then taking hold of her own breast and moving down to run an erect nipple through the witch's wetness. She spread her lover's legs wide then, letting her eyes settle on the urgent invitation before her. And Allegra, seeing her own wetness glistening on Kate's shadowed breast, suddenly gasped with anticipation—cried for relief—lifting her pelvis, her sex, in offering. Kate grabbed blindly for a pillow, slid it underneath her lover, then lowered herself, taking Allegra in her mouth with a passion fierce and new, matched only by a sensitivity to her open, wanting lover.

As Allegra's uttered pleasures pierced the night, Kate held tightly to her hips, feeling the witch's muscles tense and contract, her body ready to explode and overflow with pleasure. And just as it did, Allegra gripped Kate's hand, and with the other grabbed and clutched a corner of the blanket. Suddenly then, her body arched and shuddered, her thighs constricting around Kate's shoulders.

Kate rocked with her, moved with her, accepting and drinking all the love that Allegra had to give. And when she had, she moved up with force, sinking and curling her fingers deep inside to stimulate the witch's darkly kept secret. Allegra, it seemed, could do nothing to stop herself from coming again. She engulfed Kate's fingers inside her body, holding them there and not letting go for a very long time.

Kate had never felt so close to a woman in all her life. She lay with her cheek pressed against her lover's breast, listening to Allegra's slowing heartbeat, feeling the residual spasms that issued from her responsive body.

Allegra pulled her close, kissing her again and again, whispering sweet and wonderful things in her ear, and when her strength seemed to have returned said, "Come up here to me." Desire shone in her face, and with directive hands she urged Kate to straddle her.

Barely able to speak, Kate brought herself to a sitting position over Allegra's shoulders. And beneath her buttocks, she felt Allegra's heartbeat quicken as she exposed herself to those waiting, glimmering eyes.

"Oh...sweetheart," the witch whispered, as she opened and explored Kate with her fingers. "I think you need some attention right here."

Kate was not one to argue. Helplessly, she knelt over Allegra, completely dependent on this bewitching stranger to take away a desire that now burned itself into an unbearable ache.

"Let go..." Allegra coaxed, " give me all of you...I want every drop."

Kate looked down at herself, then looked into the sparkling eyes of a face partially masked in darkness, catching her breath as she lowered her sex to the witch's waiting lips. Almost spontaneously Kate lost control of herself, delivering an orgasm, wonderfully long and hard, into Allegra's accepting mouth. From somewhere outside herself, she could hear the resonance of her own cries, though they seemed, somehow, to be coming from some other place, some other person.

The lights never came back on, and after an interlude of kissing and laughing and making impressive shadow animals on the wall, Kate got up and made her way to the kitchen in the fading traces of a waning moon. She was back in no time, though, ever so carefully balancing the pot of mulled cider and a plate of homemade cookies.

Allegra had already pulled down a second cotton throw from the sofa, and had two lavender cigarettes lit. They snuggled up and savored them then, listening to the wind knocking incessantly as tree branches scratched and tapped on the window like a long-fingered sentinel who had come bearing a secret message.

Allegra spoke musingly as she slowly ran her fingers along Kate's face and neck. "Do you think you'll stay here—in the country?"

"Considering I just bought a house and a practice...? I'd say I'm pretty much settled. It's been a dream for many years. I've always wanted to live some place where I could look out my window and not see another house, you know? And I want animals," she said, staring at the ceiling and thinking of Merlin and Gandalf, who were probably fast asleep in her bed by now. "I want pets who can contribute to the household...maybe a gaggle of geese, a couple of goats...so I never have to mow the grass. A pig, too. I'd really like a pet pig...." Kate put out her cigarette, then turned to Allegra in the dark and grinned. "...and a lover like you," she said, kissing her witch.

Allegra returned the kiss and smiled softly. "You like being sur-rounded by living things...by life, don't you?"

"Yes...I guess I do."

"And what about Dr. Barringer?" Allegra wondered aloud. "I hear he's still handling the farms."

"He's working out of his home...he stops in to see me, though." Kate ran her fingers up and down Allegra's arms, and along the sides of her breasts. "It's giving me time to adjust to the domestic practice. Come Spring, I'll start making cow calls with him. Then when he and his wife move to Florida—which should be by next year—I'll be ready to handle the farms as well. Hopefully, I'll be able to buy the rest of his property, maybe get relatives to financially back me if I can't afford it alone."

"You know you won't make the money you'd make in the city."

"True, but vets don't make all that much money working for someone else, anyway. It's very expensive to start a lucrative practice downstate. And houses? This place would have cost me triple what I paid for it here."

As they talked, Kate turned on her side, propping her head in her hand. But soon Allegra was roaming the length of Kate's naked body; her touch tender at first, then becoming heavier, more urgent, as she stared at Kate with returning desire. "I want you again..." she said, her pupils fully dilated in the fading lunar glow.

Kate smiled at the witch adoringly. "Then take me...."

Allegra got on her knees. "Stay the way you are," she instructed, holding onto Kate so that she remained on her side. She prompted Kate to bend one leg, slowly pushed it up with her hands, and moved in to straddle Kate's other, outstretched leg. Allegra slid up, one knee coming to rest in front of Kate's breasts, the other sliding in behind her back. And taking her lover by the waist then, she pulled Kate down to her, pushed herself firmly in, so that their open sexes met in a mixture of heat and wet softness, in the middle of which a hardness began to protrude and seek the hardness of the other.

"What are you *doing*?" Kate gasped, her voice growing shaky with surprised excitement.

Allegra smiled down at her. "Making you come again." Her hips began to slowly gyrate. "Do you feel me...?"

Kate nodded, struggling to see in the darkness, to watch the place where their bodies came together. She pressed her palms into the witch's stomach, reached and fondled her damp breasts, then wrapped her arms around her back to keep Allegra's rotating hips in place. Together they moved and swayed, their sexes meeting and parting and meeting again with increasing force and fervor. Allegra's tempo gradually built, then slowed with a teasing, thrusting rhythm that nearly drove Kate to madness.

"You're going to come soon..." Allegra told her. "I can feel you getting harder."

"Come with me—" was all Kate could manage to say.

"I am..." Allegra whispered, "I'm going to come all over you." Then she stopped and bent down, black strands of hair falling forward, to wildly cover her lover's mouth with kisses. The empty sensation of cool air touched Kate's thighs, but then Allegra sat up, the crosscurrents of their wet fevers meeting once again in the dimly moonlit room.

As their sexes slipped and swelled, Kate felt herself being sucked into Allegra's body and, at the same time, sucking Allegra into her own. She felt herself about to climax. "I can't hold back much..."

"Now...!" Allegra urged, as her own orgasm began to flow.

Like hot nectar, Kate felt Allegra's fluid spilling into her, filling her— mixing with her own before trickling down her leg. Their pleasure-cries filled the dark room, lingering with the sounds of their merging sexes.

Kate wasn't quite sure she'd live through it all. With what strength she had left, she pulled Allegra down, then kissed and hugged and held her tightly. She wanted to say so many things; on impulse, wanted to tell the witch she loved her—wanted to give away the words she had never given any woman before. It seemed as natural as it was premature.

"I love the way you love me," she said instead.

"And I...I love being with you," Allegra whispered reflectively. With that, she flipped Kate on to her stomach and began to massage her. "I could love you, Kate Gallagher. I could—" She stopped herself short.

"But you've only seen me at my best," Kate teased.

"Oh...I have a feeling I could handle the rest." Allegra leaned over, kissing and running her tongue across Kate's back. "I've learned a lot about you tonight."

"Certainly a lot more than I've learned about *you*." Kate said, her voice dwindling as Allegra skillfully kneaded her muscles. "Tell me more about you...I want to know..."

"Shh...it's not good to be so inquisitive at four in the morning.

Just relax...you've been on the go all day."

"We could go upstairs and get some sleep. You must be exhausted, too..." Kate mumbled, the witch's fine touch making her groggy. "How was your day, anyway? Did your...talk...go well...? "

"Shh..." Allegra laughed lowly, continuing to caress Kate's back...softly, sweetly.

Kate finally gave in and shut up, her satisfied body melting beneath Allegra's wonderful hands. Her eyelids grew heavy and she sucked air in through her lips, just before drifting off into a deep and peaceful sleep.

9

*A*s the limousine climbed and wound its way around the mountain, dawn broke the night like a hatching bird, chipping its shell and glimpsing, for the first time, the light of the world through a crack in the darkness. That's how Allegra imagined Kate would have seen it, and the thought of her still-sleeping lover brought a wave of joy to her face.

A single ray of sunlight turned the dirt road to dusty gold, although the forested land about them remained cloaked in nocturnal shadows. Allegra stared ahead, then glanced at the young woman who had taken Dewitt's place in the driver's seat beside her. Her hair was the color of wheat—almost the color of the gold-lit road—much longer and straighter than her own black hair. "Oh, Keziah..." Allegra said, collecting her thoughts just enough to respond to her cousin's many questions about the party. "To think Mildred was even *there*." Allegra released a burdened sigh. "I just *prayed* she wouldn't make a scene."

"Lady Lutz?" Keziah laughed impassively. "Be serious. She knows better." She turned to Allegra with violet eyes that twinkled with the vibrancy of unearthly treasures. "I just can't believe you saw her there."

"How do you think I felt?" Allegra rested her arm against the door, leaned her head in her hand. "From what I gather, women tolerate her socially to avoid getting on her bad side."

"I didn't know Mildred had a *good* side."

"Apparently, she's known for snooping around private property, always looking for something to report...illegal additions or improvements that might warrant a tax increase."

"Mildred's still snooping, is she? When will she ever learn her lesson." Keziah winked. "Personally, she's *far* too obstinate for my taste."

"Are you sure she won't *warn* Kate?"

"She's too self-serving a woman for goodwill," Keziah remarked with cold confidence. "She'd never jeopardize her safety in the name of altruism. How well does Kate know her, anyway?"

"They've only met once or twice. Kate can't stand her."

"Your Dr. Gallagher sounds like my kind of woman."

Allegra sighed again as she gazed out the window, watching the land grow higher, the mountain whisking her away from the woman in whose arms she longed to be. "Now what do I do?"

"Just what you said you'd be content to do...you hold on to the gift of a memory." Keziah patted her knee sympathetically, "It's all you *can* do."

"I suppose..." Allegra let her head bounce back against the upholstery. "Thank you for meeting me."

"What are cousins for? Besides, Dewitt couldn't stay awake. He was a nervous wreck waiting for your call—you know how fidgety he gets near sun up. Keziah gave a sympathetic smile. "So how did you leave things?"

"With Kate? I didn't. I waited until she was sound asleep before I called Dewitt—I didn't want to chance her offering to drive me home." Allegra squirmed and repositioned herself, as if she could still feel Kate between her legs. "I watched her for a while, then left a note.... I would have given anything to have stayed, Keziah...anything."

The Lincoln leveled off about then, and Keziah made a series of sharp turns, the evergreens becoming more lush and dense with each successive curve she took. "Do you want to have breakfast with your grandmother and me at the house or—"

"No." Allegra's voice was distant. "No, not today. Please...take me home. I need to be alone for just awhile."

"I *am* sorry, Allegra. I know how much this meant to you." She flung aside her wheaten hair, her gem-like eyes acknowledging Allegra with understanding. "I gather she was all you expected?"

"She was more. She was..." Allegra's voice cracked and she fell silent, turning to the window again and gazing at the dark evergreens which shadowed the rising sun. "Grandmother knew..." she said, absently playing with the ends of her hair. "Here I thought I could satiate my desire. But to feed it, Keziah...is only to make the hunger grow stronger. And now?" Allegra forced out a pained, almost rueful laugh. "Now I can feel that desire sprouting its carnal arms."

"Such as?"

"Jealousy...." Allegra let out a breath of frustration. "I cannot *bear* the thought of her with another woman."

"Ah...the sacred and profane...what vile roommates they are." Keziah quietly drove on, finally turning onto a tertiary road that had a lost and forgotten look about it. In between the tread marks, weeds and wild flowers grew high and vines crawled out from locust trees.

"Let me off here," Allegra said. And when the car slowed to a stop, she reached over and squeezed her cousin's hand.

Keziah smiled. "I needn't remind you that someone is anxiously anticipating your arrival...?"

"Did she sleep well?"

"Soundly. But for the last hour she's been pacing and whining for you. It's driving everyone crazy."

Allegra lowered her head and smiled, as she opened the limousine door. "Give me just a little time," she said. "I'll come for her within the hour."

The black Lincoln backed out of the overgrown road and drove away, leaving behind a looming cloud of dust in the early morning mist. Past the ivy-covered locust trees Allegra walked, then snaked her way through the huge hemlocks. Soon, the land ahead opened up, and a gray stone cottage came into view. It stood in the far corner of a wide field, a giant sun suspended and hanging behind it like an overripe tangerine. Allegra made her way to the distant cottage, a cool, lonely breeze whistling as it swept through the switch grass.

Her vision blurred for a moment, her forest green eyes growing as moist as the fine mist weighing the morning air. She fought back her tears, though, trying instead to focus on the sounds of the world around her. Pheasants tiptoed in the brush, cottontail rabbits hopped over crisp autumn leaves, and overhead the rhythmic thumping of long-winged birds sounded in the haze of dawn. Not too far off, she began to feel the percussive vibrations of a running buck, his hooves beating their ancient song against the hardening earth. It was a drumbeat, a heartbeat, as old as the earth itself. And Allegra dearly loved its music. Usually, the mornings would find her spirit dancing to this woodland concerto. But today she could not dance. She walked ahead steadily, her defiant arms outstretched to break the hollow winds of fate.

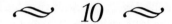

10

A semiconscious arm blindly patted the carpet, half expecting to find someone there. The space was empty, though, and the realization of Allegra's absence made Kate snap to with a start. The electricity had returned during the night, and Kate raised herself on her elbows, squinting her eyes against the brightness of both the lamplight and the sun.

Being on the floor gave her a sort of worm's eye view of the window. For a moment she blankly stared at the noisy chickadees, splashing seed and fluttering about on a feeder dangling from her birch tree, then glanced at the potted cactus in her line of vision. It was looking oddly well today; not at all shriveled as it had been when Allegra inspected it last night. In fact...Kate rubbed her eyes...it was sporting a pink and rather proud little bud this morning.

Kate rolled over and sat up. She had no idea when Allegra had left—couldn't even remember having fallen asleep—but got to her feet then, draping a blanket around herself and wandered into the kitchen. There was a note stuck to the coffee pot, and Kate smiled as she pulled it free. "My Beautiful and Darling Kate," it read. "I didn't have the heart to wake you. Please know I leave dreaming of the passion and promise of an everlasting love."

Kate leaned dreamily against the counter and brought the blanket to her face, burying herself in the lingering scent of lavender and love, and read the note over and over until the phone rang.

"Are you alone?" Gigi's voice was low and hushed, and in the background Kate could hear the swishing of passing cars.

"Yes, I'm alone—I just woke up. Why are you whispering?"

Gigi hesitated. "I don't know...."

"Where are you?"

"In town. In a phone booth. I didn't want to come over without calling...just in case."

"In case what?"

"You know....in case the witch was with you." Gigi paused. "Wanna take a ride? It's a gorgeous day."

Kate looked at the kitchen clock. "Have you eaten?"

"No, why? You making breakfast?"

"I'll take you out."

"It's a date. But we'll have to find a place to eat over in Cobblecreek. I have to make a stop there before noon—pick you up in fifteen minutes, okay?"

Kate skipped making coffee and went upstairs to find Merlin and Gandalf curled up and sound asleep in the middle of her unmade bed. She would have much preferred not to shower just yet; there was something appealing about keeping the sweet, almost imperceptible traces of their lovemaking on her skin—of keeping Allegra secretly close to her all day long. Traces of gray cat makeup were still smudged about her face, however, and she decided she had no choice. But the steamy water only made Kate want Allegra more. It revived the smell of lavender, giving the night's lovemaking a haunting afterlife that left Kate longing and aching and wanting Allegra all over again.

After drying her hair, she dressed and called her office from the bedroom phone. She cradled the receiver in her neck while tucking a denim shirt into her khaki pants, and slipped Allegra's folded note into her breast pocket. Fortunately there were no messages, no emergencies with Lycos, and so she picked up the yawning cats and sat them, still yawning, on the porch to have their breakfast, then ran back inside to water her resurrected cactus.

Fifteen minutes later, Kate was donning a jacket and sunglasses and hopping into Gigi's topless, red Mustang. The night had carried the winds away with it, and the surface of the water they passed on their left was now as smooth as glass; the day as clear and still as a picture. Of course, moving sixty miles an hour with the top down created just the opposite impression. Wind beat against their sunglasses, whipped through their hair, and the noise of their flapping jackets competed with Gigi's sound system.

"So?" Gigi yelled over the noise.

Kate cracked a smile. "So *what?*"

"*So...?*" Gigi glanced at her through her dark shades, her curls blowing every which way in the wind. "Did you sleep with her, or what?"

The reflection of her own grinning face in Gigi's sunglasses made Kate grin even more. "None of your business."

"Wha—? None of my..." Gigi looked truly insulted. "Of *course* it's my business. I'm your best friend! I need to know these things."

Kate laughed. "Watch the road, will you please?"

"You *did*, didn't you? You've got that stupid, moonstruck look on your face. Son of a gun, Doc!" Gigi slapped the steering wheel. "I *knew* it! I just knew you'd spend the night with her."

Kate adjusted her sunglasses and slid down in the seat. "Is it *that* obvious, or is it just your woman's intuition?"

"It was the sexual tension between you and her. In sixteen years I've never seen you so intent on a woman. Of course, I don't know Allegra well, but I know she couldn't take her eyes off you. And she sure asked a lot of questions."

"Speaking of which..." Kate straightened up in her seat. "Why did you go and tell her I'm a heartbreaker?"

"Did I?" Gigi crinkled her eyebrows. "Maybe I did."

"Well, don't go around saying things like that. You had her thinking I'm some kind of womanizer."

Gigi laughed. "If I said anything, I only meant that most of the women you've been with would have liked to pursue a long-term relationship with you."

"Then you should have said exactly that. You made it sound like I sleep with every woman I meet."

"You mean like you did last night?" Gigi lowered her sunglasses and winked at Kate.

Kate made a face and stared ahead into the wind.

A few minutes later they were in Cobblecreek, and while Gigi took care of her business, Kate strolled across to a little country store. The Tree House, it was called. A sawed off white birch filled the window, and hanging from its branches were hand-crafted bird houses brightly painted with an assortment of flowers. One in the middle drew Kate's attention immediately; something wasn't quite right about it. Purple Nightshade delicately bordered its edges, and near the peak was the silhouette of a winged creature flying across a waning, yellow moon. But there was no door, and Kate wondered if perhaps it might be an eat-your-way-in woodpecker house. Upon closer inspection, however, she discovered it didn't have a floor, either, and when her curiosity got the best of her she moseyed inside. Soon she was coming out again, carrying three of the doorless, floorless houses; two bound together with string, the third tied separately.

Gigi sat waiting on the hood of her car as Kate approached.

Kate smiled and handed one to her. "I got one for you, me and Allegra."

"Wow...a bird house? Thanks, doc," Gigi said, turning the house around in her hands. "It's gorgeous, but...where's the hole?"

"It's not for birds—it's a *bat* house. "Turn it over," Kate enthusiastically instructed. "See?" She pointed to several slats inside. "They fly in through the bottom and hang from the compartments."

Gigi couldn't even pretend she liked it. Her face had the unmistakable look of someone who'd just gotten a fruit cake for Christmas.

"That's really sweet of you, baby...but, I..."

"What?"

"I don't want bats for neighbors."

"You know how much I just learned about bats from the old man who makes these houses? He says you can't beat them when it comes to biological control. Each bat eats up to five hundred mosquitoes an hour in the summer—the house comfortably sleeps seventy-five. That's almost forty thous..." Kate paused. Gigi was rubbing her stomach, as though the thought of that many bats at once was making her queasy. "You don't want it, do you?" Kate asked, the enthusiasm leaving her voice.

"I...I just couldn't! Really. It's a nice thought, Doc. But get your money back."

Kate smiled with resignation. "It's a present—I don't want my money back. Go exchange it for a bird house."

"Yeah?" Gigi's face lit up, and a few minutes later she came back smiling and swinging a bird house painted white with splashes of wild tiger lilies. "Thanks, Doc, it's just what I wanted." She sat it next to the bat houses in the back seat, then shook her head. "Why can't you just get a bug zapper like normal people?"

Kate considered the idea, but the more she thought about it the less normal it seemed. There was something incongruous about civilized people enjoying an outdoor party while listening to insects being electrocuted—especially the big ones that seemed to suffer an incredibly long *zap*. Bats were better.

"Are you sure *Allegra's* going to want a bat house?"

"Are you kidding? She'll absolutely love it."

Gigi rolled her eyes in disbelief as she pulled away from the curb. "Now there's a match made in heaven," she mumbled.

They passed a farm stand down the road, and Gigi suggested they stop for some fresh cider and Indian corn, so they did. There was a small cafe across the road, and they spent the morning discussing the party over breakfast, then talked some more over a second and a third cup of coffee.

"So what the hell went on with Mildred last night?"

Kate shrugged. "Allegra didn't even know who she was."

"I followed Mildred out to the parking lot," Gigi said. "She told me she had forgotten a prior engagement...but something wasn't right about it. Her voice sounded shaky." Gigi lit a cigarette and rubbed her chin like a detective. "All the color left her face, you know? I don't understand it. Mildred's a bully...I've never seen her submissive like that."

"Well, Mildred obviously mistook her for someone else. Allegra was in costume, after all." Kate lit one of her own cigarettes and sat back staring at Gigi, who still had that investigative, crime-solving look in her big, brown eyes. A far away look which, for an instant, reminded Kate of Barney Banks.

"Gigi?"

"Wha—?"

"Would you..." Kate paused as the waitress came by to fill their cups, then she smiled and leaned forward. "Would you *marry* a woman?" she whispered.

"Me? The right woman? Absolutely. You know I believe in taking vows. We're always complaining that we don't have the same benefits and legal rights as straight couples do, but half the time we don't even take our commitments seriously. *You're* the one who's always scoffed at the idea."

"Well, I've changed my mind." Kate cleared her throat. "I think I'm starting to like the thought of being with someone when I'm seventy...of sitting in matching rocking chairs on our porch and flipping through photo albums of twenty or thirty years of a life spent together."

"*Flipping* through photos? I think *you've* flipped. I've never known you to get sentimental about this stuff." Gigi folded her arms and smiled knowingly. "That sexy little witch sure put a sweet love spell on you, huh?" Gigi sipped her coffee. "It's about time *someone* did. I mean, no offense, but I was beginning to think you had some kind of intimacy issues, you know?" Gigi teased.

Kate smiled, then nodded with conviction. "I needed to meet the right woman. And she's it, Gigi. She's what I've been waiting for...I just never knew what it was I was waiting for until I found her."

Gigi's face turned serious. "I have a good feeling about the two of you. There was a—I don't know—a certain naturalness between the two of you." Then she smiled. "Besides, that silly, smitten face becomes you. You're glowing, Gallagher."

Gigi wasn't the only one who liked the way Kate looked. On their way home, Kate ran into the post office for stamps, while Gigi waited in the car. Both the Postmaster and a neighbor Kate recognized commented on how vibrant she was looking today. Of course, she couldn't very well tell them her vibrancy was the result of having had sex and falling in love the night before, so she politely thanked them instead, collected her stamps, and walked out thinking about Allegra and feeling as vibrant and smitten and silly-in-love as she looked.

Love was a strange business. Yes, indeed. It had a way of turning the whole world into one big, beautiful poem. She was finally beginning to understand what all the fuss was about. And for a split second she even understood why the initial intensity of new love had to eventually stabilize. It had to do with survival of the species, she was sure. Why, if the novelty never wore off, if the unfamiliar never became familiar, we'd all remain in a love-daze, sitting in our offices and classrooms, just staring out the window, fantasizing about our lovers. Nothing would ever get done. And then we'd get in our cars and drive home daydreaming until we all crashed into one another. It was a romantic notion, and as Kate headed back to the Mustang, thinking of Allegra and not watching where she was going, she bumped right into a pedestrian. Gigi rolled her eyes, as an apologetic and embarrassed Kate got back in the car.

There were no messages on Kate's answering machine, and while Gigi went about pouring cider, Kate hung her Indian corn on the front door and rearranged the pumpkins on the porch. Gigi was lying on the living room floor with the cats when she came back in. "Where'd you get this marble?" Gigi asked.

"Marble?" Kate took a closer look. "It's not a marble. It's my opal from the Hebrons. Where was it?"

"Under the sofa cushion. Merlin was trying to get at it." Gigi studied the gem, holding it more respectfully now that it wasn't just a marble anymore. "No kidding...? The *Hebrons* gave you this? Boy, with all the cheese I buy from them, you'd think they'd toss one my way."

Kate had meant to show Allegra the stone last night—it seemed the sort of thing she would have appreciated. But with their romantic agenda and the lights going out and the cat having knocked it off the table, well, it had simply slipped her mind.

"Your glass is on the counter," Gigi said, setting the opal on the table and following Kate into the kitchen. She took Kate's calendar off the wall and turned the page. "November first. We're driving downstate together for Thanksgiving, right? We better make plans now."

"Gigi... please. There's still shaving cream and eggs in the road. Why do we always have to rush? By the time we sit down to Thanksgiving dinner we'll be rushing out to shop for Christmas presents, and before we get to open presents, we'll be pressured to make plans for New Year's Eve." Kate shook her head. It seemed to be the way of the world. And when the holidays were over and she could finally look forward to settling down and enjoying the winter evenings and a few quiet snowfalls, the department stores would be putting out their new line of bathing suits. Someone should have banned the sale of such things until after the first official day of Spring.

"Thanksgiving will be here before we know it," Gigi pressed. "I'm closing for the holiday, but I need time to make arrangements with my manager for that weekend—so I can take a few days off. And so do you. So let's settle on some dates here, huh?" She impatiently tapped the calendar with her index finger.

They sat down together and made tentative plans. Kate figured Annie would jump at the chance to house-sit for Merlin and Gandalf. But her thoughts were still a long way off from Thanksgiving, and when Gigi left, Kate spent the rest of the day waiting for the phone to ring. Allegra never called, though.

Kate couldn't find a Netherland listed in the directory, and by the time night rolled around she regretted having fallen asleep before Dewitt came, before getting Allegra's phone number and address. By nine o'clock she was terribly fidgety, and once again opened the directory to find the Hebrons' number. They owned over nine hundred acres on the mountain, after all, and if there was anyone else living up there, the dwarves would certainly know about it.

Teasel answered the phone, jolly as usual, and wanted right away to know if Kate had a good Halloween. Kate focused on business at first, asking about Lycos, although she knew it was an unusual hour to pretend to be checking on patients. Lycos was just fine, Teasel told her.

"No..." Teasel responded to Kate's inquiry about any Netherlands living on the mountain. "...no, I don't believe I've ever heard the name, Dr. Gallagher. All the land up here is privately owned by us Hebrons," she said matter-of-factly. "There are a few acres of state land, but..." There was a pause. "Is this a family or *person* you're trying to locate?"

"A per...a woman," Kate said, feeling as though someone had just knocked the wind out of her. *No Netherland? No Allegra? No arcane witch flying around the mountain?* Kate's heart plummeted.

"Sorry I can't help," Teasel apologized, in a tone still too cheery to suit Kate's suddenly dark mood. "But if it's important you find this...*woman*...you might want to describe her and I'll keep a sharp eye out...if you know what I mean," the dwarf offered.

Oh sure, Kate thought to herself. *A description...well, let's see. Last time I saw her she was painted green and dressed like a witch—a very sexy witch, mind you, with extraordinary hands, and wonderful lips and...if you happen to see anyone fitting her description, please tell her I said hi, and ask if she'd be so sweet as to stop by and seduce me again next* Halloween.

"Thanks, but it's really not important," Kate said, with contrived casualness. "I was just curious, that's all," she added, then cringed on her end of the phone. "Give my regards to Arba, okay? And I'll see you and Lycos in the office next week."

That night only the cats got a good night's sleep. They slept soundly on the foot of the bed, curled up on either side of Kate's legs, while Kate herself lay wide awake in the middle, restlessly fondling her opal for lack of anything better to fondle.

A cool breeze blew through the partially opened window, setting the curtains to puffing and fluttering, as waves of moonlight washed softly, peacefully, across her bed. Kate was not at peace, though; it was some time before the stone's smooth, polished surface began to soothe her. Between her thumb and finger she made circles, thoughtlessly entertaining herself, and watching as the opal soaked in the moon like a sponge.

The colorful speckles were cool at first: soft purple, brilliant blue, a soothing green. Slowly, though, the colors seemed to collide and collapse on themselves, spiraling as they grew lighter. And in her groggy state, Kate imagined she was the earth, the stone her natural satellite—a magnificent lavender moon suspended above her. A lavender moon, she thought, about to fall from orbit and break her heart.

Kate yawned and blinked her eyes, sensitive to the bright, warming hues which seemed now to jump across the spectrum, swirling to a warm and golden yellow. Growing groggy, Kate wondered whether the stone's temperature was actually increasing, or if the warming colors simply created that illusion. Friction...that was it, she thought. Friction from all the fondling. Soon, the arm holding the opal in the air lost its strength. She turned, slipping the hand with the stone under her pillow, and curled up beneath the down comforter. It continued to soothe her like a pacifier of sorts, subliminally touching her with the dreamy notion that her witch was close by, wanting her, thinking of her. Tomorrow Allegra would call for sure.

But tomorrow turned into the next day, and the one after it, and the one after that, until, on the fourth day, Kate received a white wicker basket shipped from England; a basket filled with lavender pomanders, potpourri and satin sachets; lavender honey, tobacco, biscuits and tea—an assortment of things to tease and delight the senses, although Allegra herself, the most elusive tease of all, remained mysteriously absent. Inside the basket was a card which simply read: "There is so much I owe you in apology, in explanation, in gratitude. Forgive me."

Forgive you? Certainly not, Kate thought. *Never, never, ever.* There she sat, devastated by the card. She had never been rejected before. And now, the only woman to ever come along and steal her heart had done just that—*by mail*, no less—not even affording Kate a farewell rebuttal.

The weeks passed without so much as another word from Allegra, although the lavender pomander permeated the room so thoroughly, that every time Kate arrived home from work, she half expected to find the witch waiting in the next room. It nearly drove her crazy.

Tempestuous winds soon blew in the first frost of the coming season, and the days chilled their way into late November. Kate spent her free time lamenting, her heart heavy with confusion and frustration. But most of all, she just plain missed Allegra—missed her terribly. And for the first time in her life, it seemed, she understood the loneliness of yearning for a lost love.

Kate spent many evenings dining at La Zingara's. Occupying a corner table by the fireplace—just across from the table where she and Allegra had sat on Halloween—Kate ate alone, usually flipping thoughtlessly through a medical journal or, more often, re-reading Margery Williams' *The Velveteen Rabbit*. Kate told herself it was far healthier to focus on a rabbit made real by love, than on the wicked love of the witch who was fast becoming the bane of her existence. And on nights when business was slow, Gigi joined her, the two trying to make sense of Allegra's disappearance. Of course, Gigi, drawing on her own misfortunes in love, had nothing in the way of positive scenarios to offer.

"She's leading a double life," Gigi insisted one night while sitting opposite Kate. She wore her white chef's hat which, like a cloud, extended and puffed itself well over a foot above her head. "I hate to say this, Doc, but the way I see it, is that she either lives with another woman..." she paused, counting her suspicions on her fingers, "...or, she's married with ten kids somewhere. Or..." she flicked a third finger, " she couldn't deal with her feelings for you...homophobic stuff, maybe."

Kate was silent.

"Bottom line is that she lied. Lied about her last name, lied about where she lives, lied about the talk she—" Gigi stopped abruptly, her dark eyes rounding with guilt *"Whoops..."*

Kate looked at her askance. "Gigi...? *Tell me!*"

With a conceding huff, Gigi picked up her cigarettes, took one, then carelessly flung the pack on the table. "The Stepping Stone," she began, rubbing a thumb across the end of her nose. "I called there yesterday. You remember the benefit I catered for them? Well, I figured they'd help me out, give me Allegra's number, but..." she shrugged and let out a sigh. "There was never an *Allegra Netherland* there, Kate. No witch, no kid's show....The center was closed on Halloween."

Gigi's words pierced Kate like a needle. She swallowed, struggling to stay calm. "When were you going to tell me this?"

"Now. Just now. Tonight...I swear!" she defensively put a hand to her chest. "I was *crushed* when I found out. I knew you'd be *doubly* crushed."

"I'm *already* crushed, Gigi...I'm an emotional *wreck*. But I don't need to be protected, okay? I can deal with the truth. I'm a big girl now."

"A big girl...yeah, right." Gigi ran a hand over her mouth, muffling her voice. "Sure you're a big girl...just keep reading *The Velveteen Rabbit* there," she muttered.

Kate looked at her sneeringly. "Let's leave the *rabbit* out of this."

"Mama mia...!" Gigi smacked her forehead. "Kate! I'm just looking out for your heart, you know? I loved that *bella strega*. I loved you *with* her. But I don't have much faith in women these days. You know how it is with me and the singles scene—I've had it, Doc. I'm ready to throw in my towel, wave the white flag." She snuffed her half-finished cigarette, then helped herself to a swallow of Kate's red wine. "How's the food, by the way?"

Kate nodded. "Good. Wonderful...really. I just don't have much of an appetite," she confessed, looking down at her half eaten dinner—one of Gigi's new vegetarian delights.

"Anyway," Gigi went on, "the way I see it, is that if your witch wants you...she knows where to find you." She picked up a spare fork and speared a square of Kate's toasted tofu. "Never chase a woman. Look how much time I wasted...chasing nothing but illusions. I mean, I know people go around saying that we all have to be responsible for our own happiness. But that's hogwash, Doc." Gigi waved a disgusted hand. "As far as I'm concerned? It's a lover's *job* to make the woman she loves happy. I'm talking about the little things, you know? Like bringing home special gifts, listening, compromising, paying attention...."

Gigi held out her arms and shrugged. "You know *me*. I *love* making a woman happy. It's my nature! If a woman says she wants polka dotted roses? Well, dammit, I'll find out where they grow. And if it's sunsets she loves? I'll drive her a thousand miles to find the best damned sunset this side of the moon." Gigi was heating up now, starting to talk with her hands, her Sicilian eyes turning into reservoirs of earnest passion. "But do you think any woman has ever thought to do that for me?"

Gigi stared into space then, her countenance twisting itself into something approaching aggravation. "I've been with a lot of *bonzos* in my time, Kate. Only you, my best friend, have ever done things to make me happy. Like the opera. You hate it— and the fact that it's four hours long makes you hate it even more. But do you complain? No! Once a year you bite your tongue and accompany me...just because it makes me smile. I love you for that, Doc. I really love you for it."

Kate stared at her, suddenly thinking how ridiculous Gigi looked with that cloud-of-a-hat on her head. She made a face and sighed. "What are you trying to say?"

Gigi reached across the table and put her hand on Kate's. "What I'm saying, Gallagher, is that love is...well...have you ever seen an Italian rose garden?"

Kate shook her head, regarding both Gigi and the hat with a frown.

"Well, they're beautiful. And you know why they're beautiful? Because they're tended to and weeded and watered with love. That's how I treated each of my lovers—like freaking Italian rose gardens. I weeded and watered, and watered and weeded...but did any one of them take care of my garden? No. One day I said to myself, *why is it that their gardens always grow and bloom all over the place...and mine is always a dry and sorry sight? You* know...that's when I finally came to my senses and shut off the sprinkler."

Kate was getting antsy. She rolled her eyes, slouching way down in her seat. "What's your point, Gigi?"

"Point?" Gigi asked excitedly. "What? You think I'm sitting here dishing you out some tuttifrutti poetry? The point, *Gallagher*, is that if Allegra really cared about you, you'd be getting your garden watered!" With a huff, she leaned back, then reached forward again to take a sip of Kate's water. "Face it, Doc, you've been had." She shrugged. "*Literally.* You've been *had*!"

Kate grimaced. "Your candor is truly charming, ol' buddy."

"Thank you," Gigi said, missing Kate's sarcasm.

Kate trudged her way through the remaining days of November, her Italian rose garden growing thirstier and thirstier. Fortunately, work was uneventful; enough, at least, not to interfere with her misery. She took care of a few minor cat-inflicted injuries, spayed several dogs, neutered two cats and, as expected, saw porcupine-Barney, whose stubborn nose was beginning to resemble a pin cushion. And then there was Lycos. Seeing the black dog was the only thing that brought a genuine smile to Kate's face. Of course, by the time Thanksgiving arrived, her face needed more than a smile.

Kate discovered that as wonderful as love made you look, it also could have the reverse effect. All the people who had described Kate's appearance as vibrant only weeks ago, were now commenting on how tired she looked. And Kate knew that when people said you look tired, they were basically saying you looked like hell.

❧ *11* ❧

*A*utumn turned to winter in the few days Kate and Gigi had been gone. As they drove back home, forty, sixty, eighty miles north of New York city, December's arctic air began seeping in through the Jeep; enough, at least, to make them turn on the heat. They came off the Taconic Parkway well after dark, then pulled into an open diner for a bite to eat before continuing the rest of the way.

A light snow covered the ground, making the asphalt parking lot sparkle beneath a solitary streetlight. Everything beyond the lighted diner sat in shadows, and surrounding them was the faint outline of black mountains against a distant, starry sky.

"Sure is good to be back," Gigi said, first stretching then zipping her leather jacket. "I can feel the stress leaving my body already."

"It is," Kate answered. She watched the steam leaving her mouth as she spoke. "But, you know, driving downstate made me realize that since I've lived in the country, not one person has blown their horn at me."

"Everyone is always in an angry rush down there, always screaming and squawking and—did you see all those drivers flashing you the bird?"

Kate smiled. "No, but I saw you giving an awful lot of *them* the finger."

"That's because they were giving it to *us*—I was just taking care of business for you."

Smiling, Kate put her hand on Gigi's back. "What a buddy," she said, opening and holding the diner door for Gigi.

It *was* good to be back. Kate had hardly been in a festive mood, but under the circumstances, Thanksgiving had gone well. Pretending to be fine was a tiring matter, though; especially around grandparents who had an intuitive knack for seeing right through Kate's poker face. Gigi had spent the holiday with her family in Glen Cove, Kate with hers in Garden City, and the next night was spent visiting each other's family. On the weekend they met up with old friends and hopped from club to club between Long Island and Manhattan. Kate danced and drank a bit, and managed to muster up her social graces, but she was still preoccupied with Allegra and her mind wasn't on what she was doing.

At least being back in the country made Kate feel somehow closer to her elusive lover. An hour later they were ready to hit the road again for the final leg of the trip. Kate ordered a ham and cheese sandwich-to-go for the cats, along with two containers of coffee for the forty-minute drive ahead of them. "It's strange," Kate commented, as they drove along the winding, moonlit roads, "but I can almost *feel* her presence."

"You just feel her in your heart—her body's in England, babe." Gigi lit a cigarette and stretched her arm along the back of Kate's seat. "I don't know what to say that I haven't said already. I'm a woman, you know? And I still can't figure women out. I guess we can't always have our cake and eat it, too."

Kate frowned. She hated that expression. Always had. There was no logic in it. Why would anyone want their cake if they couldn't eat it? "Don't ever bake me a birthday cake and then tell me I can't have a piece, okay? If I can't eat it, I don't want it." Kate propped her coffee container between her thighs and rubbed her face with a free hand. "Oh, Gigi..." she shook her head. "What am I going to do? I just can't let go...."

"I know it hurts, Kate, but like I said before, she probably leads a double life. You know nothing about her—who knows what her motives were for seducing you. What I'd like to know... is what the hell she was doing hanging around a pond in the first place."

Kate took a deep breath and was silent for a moment. "When Allegra and I were talking... after we made love? She said she wanted us to enjoy *experiencing* each other...that there would be plenty of time to learn about each other later—except later never came, or hasn't come yet." Kate glanced over.

"Well? See? There you go!" Gigi slapped her thigh. "She didn't *want* you to know *too* much."

"If what you say were true...if what happened between us was purely physical and she cared nothing about me... then I could resolve things and move on. But I'm stuck, Gigi, because it just wasn't that way — she was feeling something very real. We both were. It was too passionate." Kate sighed heavily. "If I didn't have you to talk to about all this I think I would have exploded by now."

"Hey," Gigi said, making light of the situation, "you've gotten me through a romantic crisis or two."

"...or three or four," Kate smiled.

By eight o'clock, they were finally pulling into Kate's driveway, and Gigi, exhausted from the trip and needing to stop by her restaurant, threw her duffle bag in her car and went straight there.

No sooner had Kate gotten to the porch, than Annie was at the door with the guilty grin of an adolescent who'd been up to no good while her parents were away. "You're early," she said.

"Am I?" Kate looked at her with one suspiciously raised brow. Music played in the living room and a cozy fire burned. On the kitchen counter there sat a wine bottle and two half-empty glasses. "Don't tell me I missed a pajama party." Kate's voice was teasingly stern.

Annie smiled. "Yeah. I mean, no. Laura just left. You know her. She picked me up from work once. Remember?"

"No," Kate said, putting her keys and her bag down. She hung her jacket on a coat rack, then pushed up the sleeves of her striped turtleneck. "Laura stayed with you?"

"I didn't wanna sleep alone...I got spooked. All these weird things started happening." She paused for a second. "I washed the sheets." Then she looked up at Kate, her impossibly cute bangs hanging over her blue eyes. "You're not mad, are you?"

Kate smiled. "Should I be mad because you got lucky?"

The pitter-patter of cat feet sounded on the stairs, and Kate squatted down as a happy Merlin rushed to greet her. Even Gandalf failed to contain himself for a moment. Back and forth, they rubbed against her until she handed over the sandwich in her hand. Either cat would have killed for a piece of American cheese.

The tea kettle began whistling on the stove just then, and Annie rushed to turn it off. "I was gonna make hot chocolate."

"Sounds good," Kate said. "Mind if I join you for a cup?"

Annie seemed to relax then. "You got any whipped cream?" she asked, opening the refrigerator.

"Would I run out of whipped cream? There's a can in back."

"Go inside," Annie said as she fixed their cups. A delivery came for you."

"For me? Supplies?"

"No. It came here, to the house. Wednesday evening, right after you left." Annie's eyes sparkled with excitement. "It's on the table."

Kate looked at her oddly, then went to the doorway and peeked in the living room. Sitting there, taking up the better part of the coffee table, was a gingerbread house covered in cellophane—the biggest, most delicious piece of architecture Kate had ever seen. "Who sent it?"

Kate looked at her oddly, then went to the doorway and peeked in the living room. Sitting there, taking up the better part of the coffee table, was a gingerbread house covered in cellophane—the biggest, most delicious piece of architecture Kate had ever seen. "Who sent it?"

"I don't know. I guess someone who didn't know you were out of town for the holiday."

Turning on the lights, Kate walked over to inspect it. The top of the cellophane was stealthily torn, and a whole row of gumdrops had been stolen from the roof.

Kate squinted her eyes and looked back at Annie standing in the doorway. "Nibble, nibble little mouse, who's been nibbling at my—" Kate stopped when she heard herself, then again recited the words. "...who's that nibbling at my...house! The witch!" Kate exclaimed. "The *witch* lives in the gingerbread house."

"What witch?"

"*Hansel and Gretel?* Don't you remember the witch?"

Annie shook her head, obviously unfamiliar with the story. "It was before my time, I guess."

Kate looked at her in disbelief. "Before your time? It was before my time, too, Annie! It's a fairy tale. A classic." Kate frantically searched for a card attached to the cellophane. "Didn't anyone ever read you a bedtime— oh, *never mind,*" Kate said, shaking her head. I suppose you were too busy with computers and video games at the age of four to worry about literary deprivation. Are you sure there wasn't a card?"

"I'm positive."

"It's *got* to be from the witch—from Allegra, I mean." Excitedly, Kate peeked in the candy windows, poked her fingers down the chimney, wiggled them in the front door, hoping to feel or find a card hidden somewhere.

Instantly, Kate's mood improved drastically; the town vet who had moped around all month suddenly came to life again. She didn't know what the gingerbread house meant, or what would come of it, but at least it was a sign that she was still on Allegra's mind.

"Let's eat it from the back," Kate said. "I want to appreciate the front for a few days." Annie didn't care which end she ate from, and so they got a knife and sat on the sofa enjoying the edible architecture with their hot chocolate, while Annie updated her on business matters.

Kate got up and looked at the pad on her desk. "Rachel Hebron.... Do I know her?"

"I think she was the *queen bee* of the dwarves. I remember my parents and everyone always talking about her when I was little. She was in the papers all the time—even on the local news—because of all the money she poured into charities and whatnot. They treated her like a saint."

"Really...?" Kate tore off the page from the pad and sat down with it. "Should I go? Did it sound like Arba expected me?"

"Sort of, but he knows you were away, so don't worry about it."

"Well, I'm obviously too late for the wake...but the funeral's tomorrow at ten." Kate thought for a moment. "I could stop at the cemetery on my way to the office. What time is my first appointment?"

"One. Your only morning appointment was Lycos."

"You're coming to work right after classes?"

"By noon." Annie plucked a cherry off the house. "I hate funerals," she said.

"Is that why you were spooked about sleeping here alone? Because of the call?" Kate smiled inquisitively. "Or was it a ploy to get a woman over here to *protect* you?"

"She got spooked, too. We were eating dinner and watching a movie—right after the house came." She pointed to the gingerbread structure. "And I swear I saw someone peeking in the window. A little person, like a kid. So I went out on the porch and it smelled like someone was smoking a pipe out there. Really! You can ask Laura. She smelled it, too. Anyway, I thought maybe it was Mr. Hebron coming because of trouble with Lycos or something. I didn't know who else it could be. But then the phone rang and it was him. He couldn't have been outside and on the phone at the same time, right? So we forgot about it. Nothing else happened. But when we turned the lights out in the bedroom, Laura said she saw that stone on your dresser glowing." Annie looked at Kate defensively. "You don't believe me?"

Kate smiled. "I think you two have been watching too many bad movies."

"Oh yeah? And what's your excuse for spooking so easily?"

Kate looked at her with surprise and pointed to herself mockingly. "Me? I just have a virile imagination—and it comes from literature, not grade B movies. And before you leave," Kate said, walking over to the bookshelves and pulling out a Brothers Grimm collection, "I'm going to read you a bedtime story."

"In bed?" Annie asked hopefully.

Kate laughed. "No, not in *bed*...I don't need anything to further complicate my life, thank you."

"I only asked," Annie said, grinning crookedly and rolling her eyes. "You want more hot chocolate?"

They curled up on the sofa with piping hot cocoa and a roaring fire, and Kate read her "Hansel and Gretel." With mischief in her voice, she read, " 'Nibble, nibble little mouse, who's that nibbling at my house?' " And the children said, " 'Tis heaven's own child, the tempest wild.' "

Annie didn't make a peep throughout the story. She stuffed her mouth with gingerbread and listened with undivided attention as Kate read on and on. Kate only wished she could have been reading the story aloud to Allegra; of course, if it *had* been Allegra, they certainly would have read it in bed.

The fire had burned down to embers when she finally finished, and the room had grown cool. Although Annie wanted to linger and prolong the pleasure of the evening, Kate suddenly wanted to be alone.

When Annie left, she flopped in a chair with a pile of mail, skimming through bills and advertisements until she came upon a plain white envelope with no stamp, simply addressed to Dr. Gallagher. Kate opened and unfolded a letter written on high quality linen paper. The penmanship was exquisite and flowery, the mark of a finely trained hand—an old hand, however, growing unsteady with age. Kate's brows furrowed as she read.

"Fear not the fates who weave from above, lest you destroy a tapestry woven with love. Follow the moon rising high in the east, led by the stone and wit of the beast."

It was not signed, and Kate didn't know what to make of it. But as cryptic as the message seemed, she had an inexplicable feeling that it signified something larger than herself. Visions of a phantom sneaking past her window came to mind, and she deeply regretted not having paid full attention to Annie's talk about a pipe-smoking snoop. Actually, Kate now regretted Annie's departure, and it occurred to her that she should have asked both Annie and Laura—whoever she was—to come back and spend the night with her.

Kate crawled into bed with racing thoughts: first of witches and gingerbread houses, then of dwarves and funerals and mysterious pen pals. It was enough to keep a woman awake all night. Except that she was thoroughly exhausted. In the darkness of her room Kate intermittently opened one heavy eyelid to check on the status of the suspicious opal, suddenly recalling the warmth it had emitted the one night she had fondled it. For fear of spooking herself, she repressed the memory just as suddenly. Tonight it behaved like an ordinary opal, though, and soon she let her thoughts go and drifted into a deep but disturbing sleep.

☾ ☾ ☾

The morning sky was full of portent. Outside the kitchen window, the thermometer held at thirty-three degrees, and it seemed to Kate as though the weather couldn't decide to go ahead with winter, or jump ahead to spring and pound the sky with thunder. Either way, heavy precipitation was forecast and Kate, running a bit late, left the house wearing a black London Fog over a white sweater and straight black skirt. She carried along her supply of freshly laundered lab coats, thinking to wear one over her clothes when she later got to work.

It was a quarter past ten when she arrived at the cemetery. What looked like a reporter with a camera around his neck, was getting in his car, and a procession of limousines was parked along the quiet road. Through the iron-speared gates, out a ways on a grassy knoll, Kate spied a moderately sized congregation. She left the Jeep and approached the entrance where two finely dressed men stood quietly talking. Surprisingly, one requested her name while the other glanced inside a slim, leather-bound book, his finger moving down the page until it stopped at her name and he gestured for the other to permit her passage.

The service had already begun, and Kate stepped lightly to keep her pumps from clicking too loudly against the pavement. Once she reached the grass, however, she walked briskly and came up behind the people without calling attention to herself.

All heads were bowed as the minister officiating at the service read the twenty-third Psalm. Kate followed suit and lowered her head, while her eyes actively strained to spy any familiar faces. Some wore veils, others sunglasses; the purpose of which, Kate suspected, was to hide eyes puffy with grief on this sunless day.

A long line of dwarves stood in the front, although it was hard for Kate to determine who was who over the taller people standing behind them. But just as the minister finished, Teasel Hebron turned and caught her eye through the small crowd. She regarded Kate with a respectful, thankful nod, then turned back and discreetly jabbed Arba in the ribs with what seemed to Kate an undercurrent of excitement. Arba looked back acknowledging

Kate's presence with an appreciative smile, then quickly whispered something to his wife.

As the foreboding sky blackened overhead, several black umbrellas popped open in anticipation of the rain. Kate had not brought an umbrella, and only hoped the minister would see fit to hasten the eulogy before the sky opened up.

"Fair weather cometh out of the north," he said, addressing the sky with rehearsed solemnity. She missed what he said next. Then he stood before the casket. "Dearest Rachel, our beloved angel, loving guardian, it is in the flesh that we miss and mourn you today. Lo, our spirits rejoice in your ascent to freedom from the earthly bondage that is both the gift and the curse of our people."

Just about then, a spiraling wind whipped through the necropolis, lifting veils and stirring hats and causing people to clutch at their coats in its frigid wake. And just as it settled, a disturbingly fine scent wafted past Kate's nose. Her heart pounded at the smell of it, and she looked about in confused alarm, searching for the source of that unmistakable and hauntingly familiar scent. Lavender. A rush of adrenalin brought her senses to attention and caused her hands to tremble a bit. She stretched her neck, struggling to scan the crowd, and just as she looked to her left, she glimpsed out of the corner of her eye, the face of a woman watching her on her right. Kate's head spun to catch the spectator, but by then the woman had turned away.

She was of light complexion, her profile partially hidden now by a wide-brimmed hat. In a state of quiet alarm Kate inched her way forward, attempting to get a better view. Then her heart lunged again, as she recognized the finely sculpted nose and chin she had traced with her fingers, the sweet lips she had once kissed. For a split second Kate looked in the Hebrons' direction, part of her wanting to race up there, forget her etiquette and rudely inquire about the mysterious woman in the black hat. A second later, though, both the hat and the woman were gone.

In one desperate, pivoting movement Kate turned, and behind her, off to the right, spotted a dark, sultry figure disappearing into the cemetery. Kate followed in pursuit—walking calmly until she was off the knoll and well out of view of the service—then picked up speed to gain on the woman who was hurrying away. "Allegra...?" she called in a forceful whisper. "Allegra...." The woman only quickened her pace, edging past a mausoleum, whisking down a row of headstones, all the while holding the brim of her hat against the erratic winds of an impending storm.

"I know it's you, Allegra." And then, when Kate could no longer contain the hurt of having to chase her, she yelled, "Why are you *running* from me?"

Some twenty feet ahead of Kate, the woman suddenly stopped and stood with her back turned, seeming to gather both her thoughts and the courage to face her suitor.

"Look at me!" Kate demanded. Still, the woman stood motionless amidst the landscape of granite gravestones. Row after row, they extended toward the horizon, passing into eternity in fading shades of gray. And here and there, scattered about the grass, were giant pillars supporting white stone angels. They appeared to glow against the ominous sky. The vibrant grass glowed, too, defying winter and mysteriously tinting the atmosphere the way greenery does before a storm in Spring. But it wasn't Spring; the dead of winter was nearing, the day unnaturally dark and raw.

"Why can't you look at me?" Kate repeated, desperation and hurt in her voice.

Swiftly, angrily, Allegra finally spun around. And as she did, the tempestuous winds whirled again, this time sending her hat sailing in Kate's direction. Kate chased it several feet, stepped lightly on the brim with the toe of her pump, and bent down to retrieve it. She stood then, giving Allegra a sheepish shrug. But Allegra paid no mind to the fact of her hat flying off her head. She only pulled her collar higher, shoved her black-gloved hands deep inside her pockets, as the wind played with her raven hair; blowing, brushing it away from a fair-skinned face which looked somehow different than it had on Halloween.

Seeing Allegra's *real* face for the first time made Kate feel uncomfortable, even a bit inappropriate, as though she were confronting intimate issues with a virtual stranger.

Allegra only stared, her stolid eyes absorbing and reflecting the gray-green hues of the necropolis about her. But somewhere, buried deep beneath their stony surface, Kate saw the remnants of tender emotion; a trace of sadness, even a touch of shame. Well, *good*, Kate thought, she *should* be ashamed. But despite her sense of estrangement, despite her anger toward the lover who had so bafflingly rejected her, Kate wanted nothing more than to take that lover in her arms and revive the green eyes that had shown such warmth and affection weeks ago.

Thunder rumbled in the distance, and with it Allegra anxiously regarded the impending storm. "I *must* go," she said, her bottom lip quivering as she spoke. And then she bit her lip to stop the quivering; bit it the way she once bit it to keep from laughing.

"Dammit, Allegra," Kate choked, her tone mounting with desperation. "*Talk* to me. I deserve *that much* from you—it's only fair."

Allegra tilted her head back, regarding her with impassive, narrowing eyes. "Life is hardly fair, Kate, and we *don't* always get what we deserve."

"Obviously!" Kate exploded. Her cheeks flushed with frustration, and she imagined her own eyes had just turned as stone-cold as Allegra's. "What has *happened*? Where is the woman I met on Halloween? We made...we made *love*...!" Kate crinkled her brow, her eyes beginning to burn as they filled with angry tears. "You know something? I think I liked you better as a witch."

A bitter, rueful laugh issued from Allegra's throat. "A *witch*?"

"*Yes,* a witch."

"How very amusing. And in what way? My appearance or—"

"Your *attitude*," Kate snarled. "You were far more *likable* in costume. In fact...I think you liked *yourself* better in costume, too."

"Oh, really?" Allegra said bitterly, tugging on and yanking her collar higher as the first heavy drop of December rain plunked to the ground. "Well maybe *this* is my costume."

Kate wasn't in the mood for Allegra's droll humor. Not today. No sirree. She tried to speak calmly, but her volume only built. "Maybe you're right, Allegra. Maybe you were in costume then... and maybe you're in one now," she said, flashing a sarcastic grin. "Maybe every damned minute we spent together was one big masquerade! Huh?"

Pressured clouds about ready to burst rolled in overhead with visible speed, churning the threatening sky and hastening the coming of twilight. A sharp jag of lightning lit the cemetery, shaking the hallowed ground with thunder. Then, almost at once, the sky opened and the downpour came.

Panic struck Allegra's face. She reached nervously for her hat, but Kate, deciding everyone was entitled to an infantile outburst on occasion, held it up and out of reach, smirking like a vindictive little brat.

"Give me my hat," Allegra demanded.

"No...! You can't have it back."

"Don't be a *child*," Allegra hissed. She lunged for the black hat, missing it and almost stumbling forward as the spike of her heel caught and stabbed the sacred earth.

Kate stepped away and hid the hat behind her back. "You can't have it," she insisted, wiping freezing rain from her mouth.

"Give-me-my-*hat*!" Allegra said through clenched teeth, scowling.

Kate disdained a reply.

The muscles in Allegra's jaw tensed. "I *said*...give me my—"

"No! What for? So you can run away again? Give me an answer, and I'll give it back." Kate wiggled the hat in the air. She was too caught up in her own anger to see the agitated worry consuming Allegra's face.

"I *can't,*" Allegra pleaded. "I've *got* to go! Please, Kate. We *must* put our feelings to rest."

"Rest! *Rest?*" Kate was mortified—and nearly dripping wet. She shifted her weight onto one foot, put the hand that held the hat on her hip, oblivious to the frigid torrent the clouds poured upon her. "Is that really what you want to do? Put your feelings to rest? Put them to rest like the...like the..." She flailed her free arm at the myriad tombstones. "Like the *dead?*" Kate spoke with such force that the rain running off her nose and lips was sprayed outward. "Well that's just great!" she yelled. "Go live like the dead, Allegra...if it's more comfortable for you. But, personally? *I* think it's a damn crime."

Allegra, who was just starting to push past Kate, stopped dead in her tracks, and turned back with one furiously arched eyebrow. "A *crime?*" she asked, glaring at Kate.

"Yes, a crime..." Kate swung her arm again. "A crime against the *heart.*"

Allegra seemed suddenly to forget her urge to run. "I see..." she said, nodding and pretending to be pondering the concept. "That's awfully poetic, Kate, but I should think such a crime against the heart might best be called a *sin...?*"

Her hand still on her hip, Kate stared Allegra up and down, hastily tapping her wet foot against the ground. "A crime, a sin—call it what you will," she snapped.

Allegra eyes grew wide with rage. "Well *don't* you talk to me about *sin,* Kate Gallagher. I'm afraid you are not *equipped* to debate such a subject with me."

Kate's eyes narrowed. She pushed aside her ridiculously wet hair, trying to think of something cleverly nasty to say; her intelligence had just been insulted, after all. A lexicon of counterattacks raced through her head. But before she could snatch a suitable one, Allegra's face began to strangely change as the icy rain began to draw faint streaks of green down Allegra's cheeks.

The sight made Kate's mind go blank and her eyes popped open with horror. She staggered back, quickly shook her head, blinked her eyes, as if trying to shrug off a bad hallucination. Lightning struck again, followed by a crash of thunder, and the rain—indifferent to Allegra's plight, and having no apparent loyalties of its own—continued turning the fair-skinned maiden into an all-too-familiar witch.

All emotion drained from Allegra's melting face. "What's...wrong...?" she began, but then her eyes, as green as the marks forming on her skin, widened in sudden understanding of Kate's shock. Her own face froze in mirrored horror, as she brought trembling fingertips to her face and touched the flesh-toned make-up now oozing from her chin.

Fighting faintness, Kate woozily took another step back and, cupping a hand over her gaping mouth, watched with confusion and fear as the rain washed Allegra green—stripped her of her human mask. Kate saw the rain dripping from Allegra's hatless head—her unprotected face and hair; saw the witch's lips moving, pleading, but could not hear a word beyond the ringing in her ears. And just then, as Allegra reached out to grab and steady her with one black-gloved hand, Kate saw the strange luminescence of her covered fingertips. It was as though there were a green light beneath her gloves, charging her hand from within.

Kate shrieked, pulled back from the hand, then turned and stumbled and cracked her forehead on a granite pillar. She was up as fast as she fell, though, paying no attention to the blood trickling from a gash above her brow. Her only thought now was to flee this deserted graveyard; to run from her childhood shadow, from the monster who once lived in her closet...from the magic of a green witch who had once loved her. To think she had thought herself in love...*made* love...! Another zigzag of lightning ripped through the sky and Kate took off, almost flying.

"Wait!" Allegra screamed over the thunder. "Oh, Kate... Please! I beg you—"

Kate's knees were shaking so badly, it was a wonder she could stand at all. Breaking into a scampering run, her arms propelling her along, she scurried through a maze of graves, scrambled past the mausoleums that had hidden them from the service. Wiping rain and blood from her eye, she bounded up and over the sloping land; seeing no one, wanting nothing, but to reach the iron gates of this consecrated land.

Not until she was in the Jeep, fumbling with her keys, did she realize the crumpled brim of Allegra's hat was still tightly clutched in her fist. She screamed, flinging it out the window as if it were—what? A living entity, vested with the magical power that would set it to lunging at the telepathic command of its mistress. Quickly, she used an elbow to lock her door, and then with tires screeching, pulled out and swerved around one remaining limousine—Dewitt, no doubt.

❈ ❈ ❈

Kate sped down the lonely road, checking her rear-view mirror, as if half-expecting to be forced into a high-speed chase. But the black car did not follow. Through the raindrops on the back window, Kate watched the Lincoln's windshield wipers swishing back and forth, its beaming headlights cutting through the storm, until she swerved around a bend and watched it finally disappear from sight.

On a grassy knoll, Allegra stood alone; a dark figure with clothes tightly clinging to her wet body. She raised a violent arm to the mocking sky, screamed at the heavens for denying her the woman she so desired. Her pupils dilated with rage—her green irises luminescent like her fingers—and her hands shook. She regarded the necropolis wildly, searching for something on which to expend her dangerous reservoir of fury. From left to right, right to left, she rapidly scanned the stormy landscape until, in an instant, her eyes locked on a white stone angel. In the center of the cemetery it stood enormously tall, its chiseled body spread wide in winged ascendence.

Allegra's jaw tightened. Slowly, she raised one gloved and trembling finger, her green nostrils flaring as she pointed to target the angel. *"Curse you!"* she screamed. *"Curse* the day you *set foot* on this earth!"

Her arm came down with the swiftness, sharpness of a maestro. And as it did, another bolt of lightning coursed through the air, only this time the jagged line of electrical energy flew straight from her fingertip—a mere extension, a manifestation as it were, of all her power, regret and rage.

At once, the sound of a sharp crack resounded throughout the cemetery, and the giant pillar began rumbling, quaking, ripping itself free from the earth. High above it, the white and glowing angel gave way. Its stone wings shook and wavered and swayed, then across the ground it fell and shattered with a thunderous crash and a boom.

Allegra pushed a wet strand of raven hair from her mouth, her breaths now short and labored. And again, she screamed her fury at the strewn pieces of broken angel. Her screams became curses, her curses cries. But all were lost—drowned in the storm—so that her sounds became nothing more than tortured echoes heard by no one in this deafened city of the dead.

~ *12* ~

"*I* can't believe this, I just can't believe it...are you sure you're okay, Doc?" Gigi lit another cigarette and continued pacing back and forth between the bookshelves and the sofa on which Kate lay sprawled in a sweat suit. She stopped for a moment, bending over to peer so closely into Kate's face that her dangling curls tickled Kate's nose. Then she stood and checked her watch. "I don't know, Doc. Your eyes haven't blinked in almost eighteen minutes—you sure you're not going into shock?"

Kate groaned. "I'm trying to come *out* of shock...."

Gigi's eyebrows dropped a notch. "Oh...." Then she picked up her pace again, her cigarette held tightly between her fingers, her thumb pressed against her temple, as if it were somehow helping her to think better. "And you're sure you don't need a stitch?" she said as an afterthought.

Kate touched the bandage on her brow. "It's not that deep."

"I know you're a doctor, but I could take you to a...a *regular* doctor, you know?"

"I don't need a regular doctor. I need a *witch doctor,*" Kate grumbled. "Get the Yellow Pages. See if there's one listed in the area. And while you're at it, find me a hardware store that carries hex signs."

"You really think she put a love spell on you?"

"Of *course.... Some* sort of sexual enchantment." Kate stared blankly at the ceiling, her arm flung over her head, her leg dangling lifelessly from the sofa. "It's all starting to make sense, Gigi. I should have known I'd never fall that hard for a woman without the influence of magic." Her voice was weak, distant. "All the women I've been with put together couldn't do as much for me as she did in one night." Kate tried to ease herself up, then fell back with a grunt. "I'm thirsty."

"Stay still," Gigi said. She rushed to the kitchen and came back with a glass of ice water.

"Maybe it was something in the dandelion wine," Kate surmised, as she sipped the water.

Gigi twisted her lips thoughtfully. "Couldn't be. I drank it, too. Although, now that you mention it...I was taken by her... I think everyone at the party was...." Gigi made a fat smoke ring in the air, staring thoughtfully until it dissipated.

"You were just *impressed* by her. It's not the same thing." Kate frowned. "Besides, I drank from a different bottle—the one in the limousine... unless, maybe she used an aromatic potion." Kate pointed with a finger toward a laced, heart-shaped pomander hanging in the doorway, "...like the *lavender* all over this place." She let her arm flop down. "I need to air this house out, Gigi. I'm probably being intoxicated as we speak."

"Nah...I don't buy it. Your imagination is running wild."

"Running wild? After what I saw today?" Kate was still appalled. "She's green...it defies the laws of nature...!"

"Alright, alright, I'm sorry. We'll get to the bottom of all this." Gigi took a bottle from the liquor cabinet beneath the bookshelves, and with a shake of her head and an inaudible mumble, poured them each a shot of brandy.

Kate rubbed her head and pulled herself up. "I'm going to call Teasel Hebron, and find out who Allegra really is, and why she was even at the cemetery."

"No, Kate. Please. We don't want them involved in your personal life right now. Besides, I've already decided. Annie canceled your afternoon appointments, and I don't have to be at the restaurant until four, so we're going to pay Mildred a visit. I have this funny feeling..."

"Mildred? Why *her*? I *don't* want to see her," Kate complained. She had bad memories of her first social encounter with Mildred. Always the diplomat, Kate had pleasantly approached Mildred at a small gathering once, then made the mistake of saying she was a vet. It set Mildred to ranting and raving about vets not being *real* doctors, and how she would never permit a *filthy animal* in her home. She even confessed, with thoroughly morbid pride, Kate thought, to having poisoned a few stray cats in her time. Kate had wanted to pummel her on the spot, but instead she got up, toasted Mildred, and walked away, leaving Mildred in the middle of a sentence. From then on, Kate was convinced that the infamous spider attack was a fine example of nature's retribution; she was sure it had some significance within the larger scheme of things. "I'm not going," Kate protested.

"Hey! Do you want to find out what's going on here, or not? I'm going, and you're coming with me." Gigi frowned, but then her face softened. "Anyway," she said, "I want to keep an eye on you—make sure you're okay." Half an hour later they were pulling into Mildred Lutz's circular driveway. The house was enormous and looked to Kate as though it might very well have been a copy of the state Capitol. It sat on several acres of land, every tree having been felled in favor of an artificially landscaped lawn.

Gigi revved the engine before turning off the ignition, and just as she did, Kate caught sight of a white lace curtain moving in the downstairs window. No sooner had they gotten out of the car, than Mrs. Lutz, as she preferred to be called, was nervously edging her way out the front door and pulling it closed behind her. Mildred obviously had no intentions of entertaining company today. And it was just as well; Kate had no real interest in visiting her sterile, petless, heartless home, or sitting on a sofa probably covered in plastic—the kind your thighs stick to when you sit for too long.

Mildred regarded Kate's bandage with squinted eyes, looking her up and down as though she were assessing a measly piece of property. Then she shot her demanding eyes at Gigi. "What is the meaning of this?"

"No one's heard from you," Gigi began. "I was worried... concerned, really, about what happened with you the night of the party... you seemed to be having some trouble with that woman."

Mildred's eyes grew beady with suspicion. "What *woman*?"

"The witch," Kate pressed.

"Don't play games with me," Mildred warned. She pointed a crooked finger at Kate's nose, nearly causing Kate to go cross-eyed. "Did *they* send you here?"

"Eh, relax!" Gigi said defensively. She spread her arms and puffed her chest, so that she suddenly appeared a little bigger and tougher than life. "This isn't necessary, Mildred."

"Neither was my accident!"

Gigi gave Kate a quick glance, as if to say, *see*? Then to Mildred she said, "I don't know what you're talking about."

"You know damned well what I'm talking about. Do you think I'm stupid, Gabriella?" Mildred looked at Kate sharply. "Did your green *girlfriend* put you up to coming here? Is she afraid I'm going to talk?"

Kate's eyes widened with surprise. "What—"

"Well, let me tell you!" Mildred interrupted. "I know what those people are—you think I haven't seen their hang-out behind the quarry? You just tell your girlfriend—and Keziah, and all the rest of them—to leave me the hell alone. They have no right to harass me like this."

Kate stared at Mildred in disbelief, but then she felt her mouth begin to quiver and turn up in something of a smile. There was nothing funny about the situation, so naturally Kate couldn't explain her sudden impulse to burst out laughing. Nerves, probably. Maybe Mildred's froggish face. Or perhaps a combination of the two. Her lips twitched again. She wiped her face as a spray of spit hit her cheek—a byproduct of Mrs. Lutz's tirade—and suddenly pictured herself a fly about ready to be snapped up by a viciously sticky tongue. Of course, *knowing* you weren't supposed to laugh was always enough to compound a simple case of the giggles.

"You're laughing *now*," Mildred nodded. "But just you wait. When they've had their fun with you they'll *kill* you. Just like Keziah tried to kill me."

The word *kill* proved an instant cure for the giggles. Kate's eyes widened and she glanced over at Gigi.

"I think you're jumping the gun here, Mildred," Gigi said.

"You do, do you? Well, I've done my research." Mildred turned back to Kate. Do you know what type of spiders were found in my car? *Hmmm?* Do you? *Lycosidae!*" she exclaimed, pointing a long finger in the air like an amphibious schoolmarm giving a vocabulary lesson to tadpoles.

"I'm a veterinarian, not an entomologist, Mrs. Lu—" Kate stopped abruptly. "...*Lycos*?" she repeated weakly.

"Lycosidae. *Wolf spiders*. They're *highly* secretive animals, hate to be disturbed by people. They hide in very dark, isolated places—not in *cars*! They were *planted* there, *Doctor* Gallagher." With a humph and a huff, Mildred marched away. "*Don't* you come back here," she croaked. "I want no part in your follies. And you can tell *them* I said so." She slammed the front door then, leaving Kate and Gigi standing totally perplexed in the driveway.

They rode most of the way in silence, Gigi muttering and sighing and shaking her head every few minutes, as she tried to process the bits and pieces of information Mildred had unknowingly given them.

"The quarry..." Gigi wondered aloud, when they had reached Kate's house. "And who the hell is Keziah?"

"Beats me." Kate shook her head. "And that stuff about wolf spiders..." Kate added in a faraway voice, "it bothers me. I wonder where Lycos the dog got her name."

"I told you that dog was a wolf," Gigi said, turning into Kate's driveway and stopping to wearily rub the bridge of her nose. "Things are getting strange here. And Mildred obviously thinks we're part of it."

"You don't..." Kate paused and looked down at her nails. "You don't think she might really try to kill me, do you?"

"Allegra? No. I can't believe she'd want to harm you. I'd watch out for that Keziah, though — Allegra's compatriot, or whatever she is."

"Geez...Gigi." Kate puffed her cheeks. "If Allegra wanted to...*silence* me, she could have done it in the cemetery. I'm surprised she didn't, actually...I was terribly antagonistic. But I couldn't help it. I was so furious with her...and then so afraid." Kate put her head in her hands. "Why did I run from her? Maybe if I had stayed she would have given me some answers... removed whatever spell she's put on me."

"Kate..." Gigi started, reaching over to the passenger seat and gently massaging the back of her friend's neck. "Anyone would have gotten the hell out of there...come here," she said, pulling Kate close and hugging her with one arm. "Listen, we'll figure this out, okay? As soon as I get to work I'll call my purveyors and find out if anyone supplies any clubs or restaurants near the quarry. As far as I know, there's nothing back there but woods— all owned by the cement company. I'll check, though, and call you in a few hours."

Kate hugged her back. "I love you...you know?"

"Eh..." Gigi smiled. "Sometimes I think you're the only woman that ever will."

"No...one of these days you're going to meet the woman who deserves you. And you'll see..." Kate said, getting out of the car, then looking back in, "she'll have been well worth the wait. And you won't be finding her in Italy, either. I'd never let you go that far."

❨ ❨ ❨

The afternoon seemed to take forever to pass into evening. Kate tried napping, but her eyes refused to stay closed. Then she heated a slice of pizza Annie had left in the refrigerator, but she hardly had an appetite and ended up playing with the cheese, mostly. Gandalf offered to eat it, then kept her company in the living room, pawing clean his greasy lips while keeping a concerned and watchful eye on Kate.

After three hours of mulling over her harrowing morning, Kate realized her bottom lip was protruding and she was feeling a terrible sense of loss—that was the most ludicrous part of the whole thing; feeling loss over a truly green witch who had cast a spell, then seduced and dumped her all in one night. But Kate was sure her sadness was all part of the spell, so she purposely ignored her feelings, and began pulling out books, almost wishing she had made a trip to Diane's library to do a bit of research on spiders and witchcraft and potions for counteracting sexual enchantments.

Kate's encyclopedia was of no help, and she was just stuffing it back into place on the shelf, when the phone startled her. She picked it up and held the receiver silently, thinking it best to let the caller be the first to say hello.

"Kate? You there? Is everything alright?" It was only Gigi, her hushed voice muffled by the loud clinking and clanking of pots and pans in La Zingara's kitchen.

"Hi...I'm okay."

"You haven't talked to the elves or anyone, have you?"

"You told me not to."

"Whew! Good. Listen," Gigi said, her voice urgent and more hushed. "I spoke to my purveyors. My produce man delivers to a place in that area, but he said he couldn't disclose names or addresses. Then I called Tony, my meat man—he owes me a few favors." Kate could hear paper crinkling in the receiver. "I have the info jotted down here," Gigi whispered. "He says he delivers to a *private* club called the Widow's Peak. It's over on Wolf Road, behind the quarry. And guess what? Are you ready for this? He delivers to a man named Dewitt *Hebron*."

Goose bumps rose on Kate's arms. "The chauffeur...."

"That's Allegra's driver, the guy you said looked like a ghoul, right? Dewitt? Holy shit, Doc. I don't know *what's* going on, but I'll tell you one thing—you're cooked. Stewed. Your butt's in a pot of boiling water. All you have to do is add the carrots and potatoes...Kate? You still there?"

"Huh?" For a moment all Kate could hear was her own heartbeat pounding in her ear and vibrating against the receiver.

"Listen. Stay calm. It's Monday night. I don't expect to be serving past eight. I'll swing by as soon as I get out of here, and we'll head on up to the quarry." Gigi paused. "I, umm...I called your grandparents."

Kate frowned. "Oh...Gigi. Why?"

"They know *everything*. We can't tell people up here what's going on, and I thought someone should know...in case something happens to us.... Your grandmother's the only one who'd believe what happened. And— don't yell at me—I called your mother, too. All she knows is that you're having problems in the romance department. She's a psychiatrist, Kate," Gigi defended herself. "I was afraid you might bug out on me, you know?"

Without a word, Kate hung up the phone, sat in the chair with her head in her hands, and decided right then and there that her life had become a sideshow.

Twilight passed into night, stealing the safety of the day and making everything seem a little bit spookier. All Kate could think of was Dewitt breaking down the door and dragging her off to Allegra's lair. A *Hebron*...she tossed the matter over and over, remembering Diane's curious response to the name at the Halloween party. She decided to call Diane at home, make up a lie about being in the area and having a little time to vaccinate her dog. At least it would give her time to learn more about the Hebrons before Gigi came. And it seemed a wise alternative to staying home and listening for Dewitt's fatal knock.

Kate rehearsed first, making sure she could speak without her voice cracking. As luck would have it, Susan was conducting a workshop on dried flower arrangements, so Diane would be alone, and more than happy to hear Kate was in Waterswood.

Without a minute to spare, Kate changed into jeans and hiking boots, sped to the office to fill a syringe, capped and shoved it in her coat, then headed east. In the space of an hour she was standing in the amber light which burned outside the dome-shaped door of Diane and Susan's Tudor. Kate pocketed a dog biscuit she had taken from her supply in the glove compartment, then rapped the metal ring of the knocker. Higgins, the terrier began yapping and sniffing along the base of the door, and Kate took a deep, calming breath while waiting for it to open.

"What on earth happened to you?" Diane greeted her.

Kate grinned. "Just a fall in the woods. It's nothing."

Diane's face was sympathetic. "I have dinner for you. I'm keeping everything hot for Susan and there's plenty here."

Kate bent down to greet the eagerly waiting Westie.

"Thanks, Diane, but I'm not hungry."

"I made coffee..."

"That I'd love," Kate said, taking an opportune moment to give Higgins her shot. With one hand, she stealthily popped off the needle's cap in her pocket, then pulled up the skin between the dog's shoulders. By the time Higgins turned to see what pinched her, it was over. And before she could give it any more thought, Kate stuck a biscuit in her mouth and sent her trotting merrily into the living room.

I need to ask you something," Kate said, as they settled at the dining room table with their coffee cups. "Remember—at the party—I mentioned the dwarves, and you commented on the name *Hebron?*"

"Yes..."

"I'd like to know more about that."

"About the giants?"

"That, too," Kate nodded, trying her best to be nonchalant.

Diane looked at her askance. "Well, as for *giants*, many religions and mythologies give accounts which parallel the Judaic and Christian version. The Norse pagans...the Greeks. In fact, the Cyclops were one family of giants who were defeated by Hercules. What's interesting is that most stories of giants have this universal theme of origin—gods mating with humans. The result being a formidable race of powerful, often violent demigods—giants not always in size, but in their powers.

"The Hebrons, also?" Kate asked, starting to pick at her nails. "Do you mind if I smoke?" she added.

"Hebron was a city, not a people," Diane told her. Then she made a face. "I'll find you an ashtray." She brought one in from the kitchen, filled their cups again, then withdrew a book from her barrister shelves. "Look, it's snowing," Diane said, as she passed the window.

"Snowing?" Kate peeked out the curtain to see the large flakes silently falling to the ground.

"We're expecting a few inches. I hope Susan gets home before the roads get bad. You didn't hear the weather today?"

"Uh-uh."

Diane sat down again, put on those sexy bifocals, and folded her hands on the book. "What's going on, Kate? Are you having some sort of trouble with those dwarves?"

"Not particularly." Kate couldn't look Diane in the eye.

"I see. Is something wrong with you and Allegra?"

Kate shook her head yes.

Diane looked surprised. "You're still with her...."

Kate shook her head no.

"Oh, Kate, I'm sorry," she said. "We enjoyed her company so much at the party. I wanted the two of you to come for dinner. We left two messages on your machine."

"I know. I'm sorry I didn't call, but—" Kate stopped and sighed. "Diane, I wish I could explain, but I can't. Not yet. If I tried now you'd think I was crazy."

Diane studied her for a long moment. "Well whatever it is, I trust things will work themselves out." She took her glasses off and smiled. "There was something special between the two of you. In fact, Susan was saying how nice it was to see you so... romantically *connected*." She rested her chin on her hands. "You're a good catch, Kate. If I had been younger..."

"Younger?" Kate smiled. "What does that have to do with anything? How about if you had been single?"

Diane laughed. "Yes, that too." She put her glasses back on and patted the book. "As for the giants, Genesis 6:4 speaks of the sons of God, angels we assume, interbreeding with the daughters of men. Most people overlook the scripture because, well, they like to think of angels as asexual." Diane turned a few pages. "Nephilim, they were called; a mighty and destructive breed of superhumans, the first family having been known as the children of *Arba*."

Kate nearly choked on her cigarette, but Diane was busy skimming through her book and didn't notice. "They ruled the city of Hebron until they were conquered and driven into either the earth or the ocean. After that," she said, closing the book, they disappear from history without a trace."

Kate coughed and cleared her throat, trying to compose herself. "You...you really believe all this? I mean, I'm not criticizing...it's just that I didn't grow up with any of this stuff. In my house, *psychology* was the religion."

"And as a preacher's kid, I had as much religion as you had psychology. Yes, I believe, but believing wasn't always easy. I'm older than you, Kate, and for lesbians my age, accepting who we were meant losing our families, our government, and our God. I couldn't deny my sexuality, nor could I deny my religious convictions—they're part of me—so I had to work at integrating the two. My problem was that I was listening to the moral majority and not my own heart. Eventually, I decided that if I am to be judged for what I am, then it will be by the God who made me. Not by the people. I won't give them that power."

Kate agreed to a piece of pie after that; It seemed that forcing something past the butterflies in her stomach might get her through the rest of the evening without passing out.

By the time she left Diane's, snow was beginning to stick to the grass and trees, but the sand trucks had been out and the roads were wet and clear.

Gigi's Mustang was in the driveway when Kate pulled in, and Kate found her restless friend pacing through the kitchen in her leather jacket, the pearl handle of her .22 caliber revolver protruding from the waist of her pants.

"I wasn't planning on a shoot out," Kate said.

"Better safe than sorry. We don't know where the hell we're going. Hurry up," she said, "the roads are starting to ice up."

"We should take the Jeep," Kate said.

"Give me the keys. I don't want you driving tonight."

Kate picked up the phone. "Just let me call Diane. I promised to ring once when I got in."

"Oh, geez...Kate. Don't tell me you went there."

"What? I didn't tell her anything. I just got some history on the Hebrons—I'll tell you on the way."

The quarry was located about seven miles outside of town. Gigi took the back roads slowly but, even so, managed to bypass Wolf Road. Snow clouds had blotted out the light of the moon, and the sign itself was obscured by a leaning snag, its woodpeckered trunk and brittle branches hanging over the letters. Gigi backed up to the entrance, then made a sharp turn into the darkness. The Jeep went bouncing over bumps and rocks and ruts filled with icy mud from the morning rain. The road leveled off then, and they drove straight ahead for the better part of a mile; until, that is, a distant booming resonated from the interior of the woods. It sounded almost like thunder, only continuous and strangely rhythmic.

"Shh!" Gigi suddenly stopped the Jeep. "You hear that?" She rolled down the window and cocked her head. "It's music."

Whirling white snowflakes shone in the headlights, making it seem as though they were driving through some fantastical kaleidoscope. "I can't see a damned thing," Gigi growled.

"Turn the headlights off," Kate suggested, and once Gigi did, the snow became invisible. They leaned forward, straining their eyes and moving their heads back and forth, until Kate spotted a flicker of light shining in a rise of woods ahead. "Look," she pointed, "up there."

Gigi took her foot off the brake. "That's it, that's got to be it," she said, putting the lights on again. "Here we go. Hold on." She steered the bouncing Jeep up the gravelly incline, taking it like a cowgirl breaking a bronco. "Shit..." she mumbled to herself.

As they approached the top, a driveway with two entrances came into view. Several imported cars were parked, and beyond them stood a Victorian house. It was painted smoky gray and appeared newly renovated, the ground floor windows seeming to have been purposely obliterated in the process. The booming of the muffled music was louder now, and they listened for a moment to the familiar sounds of club music.

Nerves jangled, all Kate could think to do was tidy her face in the mirror so that Allegra wouldn't see her looking terribly unkempt. Allegra...the thought of seeing her made the hordes of butterflies in her stomach flutter so wildly, that it seemed they might fly right out her mouth any moment. "Let's do it." Gigi gestured with her chin. "We'll sneak around back, check for windows—see who's in there."

Quietly, they pressed the Jeep doors closed, walking softly over the light snow covering, and around the front of the house. But no sooner had they made the turn, than a man's voice spoke from behind. "Good evening, Dr. Gallagher...."

Kate cringed, knowing good and well who it was without even having to look. And when she did look, she wished she hadn't; Dewitt's black suit seemed blacker than ever against the white snow.

"Allegra isn't here," he said, "But I suppose you may as well come in out of the cold." Then he glanced at Kate's bandage, shook his head, and continued shaking it as he led them through the door.

"Wait here," he said, leaving Kate and Gigi standing side by side next to a long coat rack. They looked at each other with uncertainty, then turned their focus to the Victorian's contemporary interior. Silver and black lacquer predominated, and here and there, standing vases of pink and white silk flowers decorated the floor. A circular bar took up most of the space, and around it sat a dozen or so women. A small group of dark-skinned dwarves with riding boots and hair as long as they were tall, sat hugging their drinks and spying Kate and Gigi with curious, black eyes. The other women were of average height. One had auburn hair cut short to show off her pretty face and pointy ears; another was unusually long-necked, or so it seemed, with rosy skin and fine-spun hair like cotton candy. At the side of the bar, a rather tall woman stood looking Gigi up and down. She was attractive, no doubt, except her curly top was snow white, the irises of her eyes just as white and colorless.

"Hey there, sweet cheeks," she said to Gigi, making a kissing sound with her lips. "Can I get you something?"

Gigi's eyes opened in wonder, as the woman winked and flashed a smile to reveal long, sparkling cuspids. Gigi's own lips grew wide as her eyes. She blushed, smiled awkwardly, then looked away, saved from the white-eyed woman by Dewitt's speedy return.

A beautiful woman followed behind him, lean but muscular legs carrying her with the ease and grace of a seasoned huntress. Long golden hair, flowing down to her buttocks, shimmered and swished as she moved. And when she finally came face to face with the two, both Kate and Gigi stared hypnotically into her—what were they? Purple eyes.

"Hello, Dr. Gallagher...." There was a long pause, then, "I'm Allegra's cousin...Keziah." She took Kate's hand with empathy. "How's your head?"

"Not a...not too bad, thank you," she stammered, then pointed to Gigi. "This is, uh...my friend...Gigi—"

"Gabriella Giovanni," Gigi broke in, almost pushing Kate aside in order to offer her own hand.

Keziah nodded, smiled teasingly, appraisingly and, it seemed, held Gigi's hand much longer than she had held Kate's. "That's a pretty pistol you have there, Gabriella, but it makes me awfully nervous," she said, in a voice that didn't sound a bit nervous. "I'd feel much more comfortable if you left it in Dewitt's temporary care...and allowed me to buy you a drink. If any shots are fired here tonight, I trust they will be shots of spirits."

Gigi's eyes twinkled. She broke out in a stupid grin, her tongue slightly protruding from between her teeth, as she willingly pulled the snub-nosed revolver from her waistband and handed it to Dewitt.

Kate's body stiffened. She knew that look; knew when Gigi was under the influence of a woman. If Gigi lost her good sense now, Kate wouldn't know what to do, should things start going badly. She wondered, in fact, if she'd ever see the front door again.

Keziah led them past a spacious black and white tiled area, where a few other mysterious characters danced. From the back, Allegra's cousin seemed equal parts of golden hair and legs.

"What a *long* drink of water that woman is...." Gigi whispered, staring Keziah up and down. "She's gorgeous!"

Kate nudged her sternly. "*Please*, Gigi," she hissed under her breath. "Get a *grip*...! For *my* sake!"

"Yeah, yeah. Don't worry about it," Gigi answered, not paying serious attention to Kate. "Everything's under control. Relax."

They entered another small room, a private dining area where Keziah then offered them seats around a circular table. The purple-eyed woman ordered cappucino, and Kate and Gigi agreed to the same. The waitress—strange in her own right, although Kate couldn't quite put a finger on it—promptly returned with three piping hot cups of the stuff.

"The drinks are on Dewitt," the waitress said, then she looked at Gigi. "He asked if you'd be so kind as to give him the recipe for your..." she squinted at the scribbling on her pad. "...*black ravioli*...?"

"Uh...sure," Gigi said, swelling with pride. "No problem."

Keziah smiled. "He's been raving about the doggy bag you sent him home with on Halloween." She teasingly licked the steamed milk dripping over the edge of her cup, staring at Gigi as she did. "I must compliment you both on your resourcefulness—how ever did you find this place?"

Gigi hesitated. "Mildred Lutz—she didn't mean to, though. She thought you and Allegra had sent us to rough her up, so to speak." Gigi put a cigarette in her mouth, and Keziah quickly reached and lit it for her.

Keziah's movements were so easy, so flowingly smooth, that it seemed to Kate she was born of wind and water.

"Mildred?" Keziah inquired. "What else did she tell you?"

"That you tried to kill her with spiders."

"Is that why you brought the gun, Gabriella? Because you thought we might kill you?" She shook her head and softly chuckled. "There are good and evil in every group, but we are not malevolent people...for the most part." Keziah drank from her cup, then set it down again. "For thousands of years we have been ostracized because of our unique...appearances, if you will. Fortunately, financial wealth has bought and preserved our privacy. And along comes Mrs. Lutz, minding everyone else's business and witnessing...a bit of harmless dwarf magic, you might say."

Kate thoughts immediately shifted to the opal. "Magic?"

Keziah smiled. "Surely you are familiar with Celtic folklore, Dr. Gallagher? Dwarves, if you remember, can disappear at will...they delight in walking around invisible on occasion..." she paused, regarding Gigi playfully. "Just as some people enjoy shedding their clothes and walking around naked in the privacy of their home."

Gigi grinned sideways, her cheeks turning raspberry-red.

Keziah nodded. "One day, during a summer solstice party, Mildred was snooping, I suppose, and caught sight of Arba and Teasel engaging in frolicsome disappearing acts while they danced around an outdoor fire. Mildred accused the Hebrons of being devils— threatened to expose them."

Keziah looked at them. "You are minorities, too, ladies, so I need not explain the pain of oppression, nor the fear of exposure. When someone suddenly threatens to destroy your home, your haven...self-preservation takes over, as it did with me. I followed Mildred and, to my delight, watched her go into a women's bar. I decided I could easily court and seduce her, and win her allegiance just to keep her quiet. But, as you know, its hard to keep Mildred quiet." Keziah rolled her eyes. "I couldn't bear her company, and in the end, couldn't bring myself to sleep with her as planned. My rejection enraged her. She began searching our mountain, spied on Allegra's cottage behind the evergreen stands, then eventually found her way to my house. She paid me a friendly visit—just to let me know about her plans to publicly destroy my people." Keziah's purple eyes shifted from Gigi to Kate. "You know the rest...."

"Man..." Gigi frowned with sympathy. "Under the circumstances, I probably would have done the same thing."

Kate nodded in agreement. She was relieved to discover no one had intentions of killing her, and Keziah's hospitality was certainly comforting, but it was Allegra she had come to see. "Where's Allegra?" she asked. But as soon as she did, she wasn't sure she wanted to know; each answered question only served to deepen her sense of loss, confirm the impossibility of ever having the treasure she had found in Allegra. It almost made Kate wish she had not seen, nor heard from Allegra after Halloween; at least that way she could have lived with the fantasy. Now she had lost that, too. Apparently, no one had even heard Kate's question. Gigi and the purple-eyed woman were entranced, and Kate worried that Gigi, too, was falling under some sort of sexual enchantment. "What about Allegra?" Kate asked again, this time louder. "Do you expect her?"

Keziah tore her eyes away from Gigi. "She hasn't been here much this month." Keziah tilted her head and smiled, then gestured toward the telephone. "We can call her from here, if you like. She'll be pleased to know you cared enough to seek her out...considering what happened this morning."

"I'd appreciate it," Kate said. "I want her to know I have no desire to cause her trouble. I just thought that if...well, you know—the spell."

"Pardon?"

"The dwarf magic you mentioned...if she'd take back whatever sort of spell she put on me..."

Keziah furrowed her brow. "Spell?" she inquired, clearly puzzled.

"Yes," Kate said, suddenly unsure of herself and feeling a bit foolish. "The *love* spell."

Keziah's countenance instantly changed, and she suddenly seemed emotionally distant. "Is that your reason for coming?"

Gigi kicked Kate underneath the table.

Kate looked helplessly at her friend, then turned hesitantly back to Keziah. "Well...yes," she shrugged, "I—"

Disappointment reflected in Keziah's eyes. "Dr. Gallagher," she slowly began, "if anyone is under a spell, I'm afraid it is Allegra who has fallen under yours." She sat back and rested an elbow on her chair. "Oh, we have powers—each of us different ones—that lie in our capacity to understand and harness the earth's magic...God-given magic."

Keziah sighed heavily and bit her knuckle, as if quickly rethinking things. "Perhaps there is little point in telling Allegra you were here at all tonight. Between missing you, and grieving over her grandmother's demise...."

"Grandmother?" Kate was at a complete loss how to respond. "That was her *grandmother's* funeral? Rachel Hebron? I...I'm so sorry...."

"Don't be," Keziah said. "There's no way you could have known. Nonetheless, I think that knowing only the fear of magic brought you here would be a bit too much for her right now." Kate hung her head in shame, thoughtlessly tracing the lines in her palm. "I never would have chased her in the cemetery..."

"Go home and get some rest, Dr. Gallagher. You've been through a lot, too—go home to your life, and rest assured that there is no magic at play."

The warm and friendly atmosphere suddenly dissipated, the general mood at the table becoming depressed. Even Gigi's face appeared a bit droopy to Kate. She pushed back her chair, stood, then solemnly thanked Keziah for her time and courtesy.

"Why don't you wait in the car," Gigi said in a low, expressionless voice. "Let me get my gun and give Dewitt his recipe."

Kate nodded, and with her head still hung, moped out dispiritedly, oblivious to the unique faces watching her go by.

Gigi was silent when she got back in the Jeep, her fingers tensely gripping the steering wheel, as they rolled down the incline and bounced through the tunnel of dark trees. "Dewitt's not such a bad guy," she finally said. "A little shy...but not a bad guy."

Kate did not respond, and after another few minutes had passed, Gigi spoke again. "So what are you going to do now?"

"Nothing. What do you expect me to do?"

Gigi shot her a sour face. "You know, sometimes you can really be insensitive."

Kate grew wide-eyed. "Just what is that supposed to mean?"

"This was love at first sight, right? A woman came along and touched your heart the way no one ever could." Gigi lit a cigarette and forcefully blew out her smoke with a hint of irritation. "And now Allegra's hurting, probably *needs* you, and you can't be there for her."

"This is hard enough for me, Gigi. I'm sick over this. What do you expect me to do—she isn't *normal*."

"Normal? You want *normal*? Tell you what, let's take a ride around the county tomorrow—survey all the freaking nuclear families—and see how many of them consider us normal. You're being a bigot," she grumbled.

"A *bigot*? Because Allegra's *green*, I'm suddenly a bigot?"

"So...? She's a woman of color. So what?"

"This is *hardly* an interracial relationship we're talking about, *Gigi*!" Kate looked out the window, running agitated fingers through her hair. She's *green*, dammit. Green...with magical powers. *Geez*...!" The snow was falling heavily now, and the night now seemed so cold and desolate to Kate.

"That's not the point," Gigi pressed. "You've been with women for—how long—almost twenty years? And never been in love. Then, unexpectedly, you fall hard for someone who's beautiful, wealthy, interesting and *crazy* for you. Someone who loves nature and animals and all the things you love. Then, *bing-bang*, it's over because she's visibly different. I don't get it."

"I don't want to be having this conversation," Kate said, as they approached her house. Merlin and Gandalf were sitting in the dimly lit window, with what looked to Kate to be sour faces, too. It felt as though everyone was ganging up on her, and Kate was beginning to feel sorry for herself.

"Baby, look..." Gigi opened her hands and shrugged. "I want to see you happy, okay? So you do what you need to do—but don't lie to yourself, that's all."

Kate hung her head again. "Do you want to come in for tea, or something?"

"Nah...I'm pretty beat, myself," Gigi said, her eyes a bit shifty.

Kate gave her a sideways look. "I hope you're not planning on going back there, Gigi. Gigi...? Are you...?"

"No! Why would I? Come on, Doc...I'm going home. Really. I need to get some sleep." She still couldn't manage to look Kate in the eye. "I'll call you in the morning. Maybe we can have dinner and talk, if you're up for it."

Low in spirit, Kate nodded and got out, listlessly making her way inside. She managed to shake a box of nibblets into the cat bowl, then staggered upstairs to find the answering machine blinking.

"...Hi, Kaitlyn, it's Mom—guess you're not in. Gigi called...I came across a wonderful article in one of my journals on letting go. I'll drop a copy in the mail on my way home. I'm in session for the next hour. Call me after that if you like..."

Kate fell face down on the bed. "Gee, Mom, thanks. Just what I need," she mumbled into the comforter. "Send me a nice little article, put a neat little Band-aid on the boo-boo—"

Kate would have continued her muffled soliloquy into the feathery comforter, if not for the phone ringing just then.

"Katie, darlin'? Is that you?"

"Hi, Gram..."

"I didn't mean to call this late—you don't sound too good. Is Gigi there with you?" Her voice was high and sweet.

Kate flipped over on her back. "She just left."

"Did you straighten things out with Aleg...the green one? It's just amazing, I tell you. Your grandfather still can't believe it. It's a miracle. We've spent our lives writing about *little people* in the forests—never thought we'd meet one, though. It's a miracle...!"

Kate opened her mouth in a silent groan. "Gram, I don't think you'll be meeting her. I won't be seeing her again. I can't really talk about it right now. It's too much to deal with —I'm...I'm..." Kate's voice began to break. "I'm ready to go over the edge."

"What edge is that?"

"*The* edge." Kate rolled her eyes at the ceiling.

"Well, have you ever been over the edge before? What's waiting over the edge that makes it sound so terrible, darlin'?"

Kate clenched her teeth. "I *don't* know."

"Well, then maybe you should try going over it," she said, her tone easy. "You just might discover that you have wings... might find yourself flying over a lot of beautiful things."

Kate had to smile at the lunacy; it was the only thing left to do, save for going crazy. "Gram...listen, I *really* need to sleep."

"Then sleep. If you need us to come up before Christmas, just call and we'll be on our way."

"I'll keep it in mind...thanks, Gram."

"See you later, Kater-Gator," her grandmother squeaked, and then she blew a kiss into the phone.

Kate had hardly enough energy to hang up the phone. Half asleep from exhaustion, she kicked off her shoes and lay with the receiver resting on her chest.

☾ ☾ ☾

The snow fell all night long, and Kate seemed to have the same dream for hours; a dream in which she was standing in a garden overgrown with lavender. She was barefoot, watering the garden in a T-shirt and rolled up jeans, when suddenly a roaring motorcycle pulled up. The rider wore black leather, her face obscured behind her tinted shield. But Kate knew it was Allegra. In the dream, Kate dropped her watering can, rushed to straddle the bike, and wrapped her arms tightly, affectionately around the rider. The motorcycle took off, slow at first, then moving faster and faster until, suddenly, Kate realized the biker had turned into a witch, the bike into a broom, and all the houses below were growing smaller as they flew higher.

Higher and farther they flew, Kate hugging Allegra tightly, blinking her eyes against the wind and wisps of raven hair blowing back into her face. Then the ground grew near again, and soon they landed in a forest, smack in front of a gingerbread house. Allegra smiled as she placed a gum drop on the tip of Kate's waiting tongue, then led her through a candy door and into a warm, fire-lit bedroom. Teasingly, Allegra pushed her to the bed, then stepped back to slowly disrobe herself. She felt herself aroused, as she lay watching, reaching for Allegra's beautifully green body. Then she woke with a start, her T-shirt wet with perspiration.

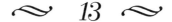

13

*K*ate was still sweating when she got to the office. She tried convincing herself it was a simple matter of physical exertion, of having shoveled snow, but who was she kidding? It was the dream—that forbidden desire which had aroused her all night long, and now left her with the discomfort of having failed to hide from herself in her sleep.

Appointments were scheduled back to back all day, and even during lunch, her desperate need to sort things out, think things through, was interrupted by one emergency after another. By three o'clock, her mind felt like an unravelling ball of yarn; a jumbled mess of guilt and sorrow and, most of all, a haunting and irrepressible urge to be with her green witch again.

Kate drove home lost in thought, finally deciding to leave any further decisions to her subconscious; to that nocturnal entity that had so cunningly invaded her sleep, only to strip her of her emotional guard, then entertain her with such a pleasurably unsettling dream.

Without much thought, Kate fed the cats, changed into a red cotton sweater, pushed her feet into clumsy boots and threw on her coat. Her first winter in the country had arrived unexpectedly, and she hadn't time to search her miscellaneous boxes for a good pair of gloves. She did, however, find one skimpy one in her closet, the mate to which was probably lying on some forgotten highway amidst all those pairless shoes she often saw abandoned by the roadside. She regarded the glove, then tossed it back, thinking that maybe she didn't need gloves, after all.

The phone caught her eye as she left the bedroom, and for a moment Kate was deeply tempted to call Gigi. There were, however, some things a woman just had to do alone—well, maybe not *entirely* alone if there happened to be an amulet staring you in the face. She stared back at the opal, aware of her growing attachment to the colorful stone...to the way it strangely pacified and entertained her these past few restless nights. She plucked it up from the dresser, tossed it in the air a few times, and remembered Arba's words on Halloween; something about faith and getting lost and finding your way. Kate decided she was lost, in an emotional sense, anyway, and so she pocketed the gem just in case.

Next thing she knew, she was traveling up the mountain, the wheels of the Jeep gripping the snow-packed road, Allegra's bat house bouncing along on the passenger seat. Kate hadn't planned on giving it to her today, but was glad she had kept it in the Jeep all month. Maybe it had something to do with not liking to show up empty-handed. And failing wine or pastries or flowers, she decided a bat house would suffice.

Behind the rising peaks of a winter mountain, a blood-red sun had begun to set. She squinted against its painful glare, searching the desolate landscape in hopes of sighting the witch's evergreen stand—the one Keziah had described, the one Mildred had so unwisely invaded. Kate felt light-headed all of a sudden, as if she were still dreaming; as if she were a marionette on a universal stage, her invisible strings being pulled and urged along by some omnipotent puppeteer.

Slowly, steadily, the Jeep climbed and climbed, and Kate was nervously scanning the rolling hills when, just off to the east, she spied a cluster of pines; a thick and darkened patch rising high above the lighter splashes of bare oak and birch and maple trees. Kate studied it, making a mental note of its general location, then continued to the top of the mountain where the trees now leveled off, obscuring her far-sighted view of things.

Veering right, she followed a vegetative maze of nameless, tertiary roads, overgrown and tapering off until they prevented further passage. Kate looked around, estimating the hidden stand of pines to be four, maybe five hundred feet into the wooded interior. She turned off the motor, climbed out with the bat house in her hand—although it now seemed a rather silly gift for her hostess—and approached the tangled darkness.

An arctic presence had turned the late afternoon air bitter. The temperature on the mountain was a good ten degrees lower than it had been in the valley, and steadily dropped with the coming of nightfall. A deep breath seemed instantly to stiffen the hairs in Kate's nose, freeze the moisture on her eyelashes. But at the same time it cleared her lungs, revitalized her mind, and she marched ahead with new-found energy and purpose. Kate hadn't the slightest idea what she would say when she did arrive at Allegra's. She only prayed she'd have her wits about her; that something appropriate would come to mind.

Of course, there was always the possibility of the witch choosing not to let Kate speak her mind at all. Maybe she'd welcome her in with beckoning eyes, commanding eyes, perhaps chant something frighteningly devilish, or—who knew?—even trick Kate into drinking from some bubbly, shape-shifting potion that might change her into a sorry little frog. Maybe that's why Mildred looked as amphibious as she did, Kate surmised. Of course, Mildred's potion had probably passed its expiration date, and so only succeeded in altering her face. Kate knew she wouldn't be so lucky. Her potion would no doubt come from a fresh brew. And then what? Allegra would coo sweet pet names, scoop her up, plop her in a fish bowl. And there, sentenced to live out her natural life in the witch's thrall, Kate would sit back on her slippery feet, just staring at her mistress through never-blinking, golden eyes; ranting and raving and ribbeting incoherently from time to time. It was a horrifying prospect; one Kate instantly argued herself out of, as she shook her head, took another breath of icy air, and warily continued over the smooth blanket of snow.

Prints of rabbits and grouse and fox were all about the forest floor, along with deeper tracks looking as if they were the signature of a stealthy coyote. Kate pressed on, pushing against branches, all the while watching her feet to avoid tripping over scabrous roots. But her feet, she soon realized, were getting awfully cold, and it occurred to her that maybe she had traveled too far. With all her twisting and weaving and turning, it was quite likely she had lost all sense of distance and direction. Kate stopped, feeling a shiver in her bones, her hands beginning to stiffen with cold pain.

Everything looked the same, one tree after the next, with no end in sight. The woods grew darker. Within minutes, it seemed, twilight washed the snow and all the satin-white birches a hazy blue. It was actually beautiful, Kate thought—in a mystical sort of way—but the pain in her feet and hands quickly convinced her this was a scene best viewed from the windows of a fire-lit cabin. If only she could find one. She put the bat house down to briskly rub her hands and, as she did, wondered at the sight of a waning moon through the branches. '...*Follow the moon which will rise in the east...*'

Kate looked about her, relieved, at least, to be able to follow *something* east. But if she *had* been traveling east, then perhaps she would need to backtrack west; and if while moving west, she'd unknowingly walked north...why then, she'd have to walk south before heading east—who could say? Damn the moon! She was more confused than ever.

Lost and freezing, her vision stolen by the night, Kate hopped from foot to foot, trying to keep the blood circulating to her toes. She patted her coat pockets and felt for the lighter she'd foolishly left behind in the Jeep, then wondered what her chances were of possibly *feeling* her way back to safety. Very poor, she decided—what with all that north and south and east and west business.

In the cold shadows of the moon she moved ahead, batting her eyes against the twigs that so rudely sprung and slapped and stung her face. And just as a branch switched her hard across the cheek, another stinging pain grabbed her somewhere in the groin, and she put a hand to herself. But in between her hand and the pain was the bulging impression of her opal—an unusually *hot* opal. Kate flinched and yelped and jerked her hand away, peering down in shocked disbelief at a line of orange light emanating along the slit of her pants pocket. Her eyes popped at the sight of it, and with one cold and stiff and very ambivalent thumb, she pulled the pocket open just wide enough to watch the stone's turbulent light filling her pocket like a pool of fire. *Dwarf magic*...and the magic was in her *pocket*. Kate yelped again, yanked her thumb back, thinking to run wildly through the woods. But her legs wouldn't move, so she stood still instead, the whites of her eyes shifting suspiciously in the dim moonlight, her eyeballs rotating roundabout to catch sight of—what?—a dwarfish prankster hiding in the trees? A sultry witch circling on a broom above? She couldn't be sure.

Kate's body grew colder, her groin hotter until, finally, she cringed, held her breath, and did what she had to do. With fingers so cold they were barely able to cooperate with her brain, Kate struggled to shove her hand in the pocket and, after three misses, withdrew the fiery sphere. Far too stunned to drop it, she watched as the bewitching light seeped through her clutched fingers like a hand held over a flashlight. Almost instantly, its welcomed heat dissipated her fears, rid her mind of any intentions she might have had of flinging the enchanted opal far into the woods. Dwarf magic, she reconsidered, might not be such *bad* magic if only it would ward off frostbite until she found her way somewhere. She wanted to flop down, rip off her boots, let her feet wallow in its magical heat. But she hadn't any time to sit. Not now. Fueled by nervous energy, Kate opened her hand, exposing the orb to the night, and from her palm let its energy radiate and cast a soft light all about the blackened woods. No batteries, no electrical cord; if only Pat the forest ranger could see her now. The thought made Kate want to giggle insanely for a moment.

Kate took tiny, apprehensive steps in the light of her magical stone-lantern, walking this way and that way, with really no idea where to go until, up ahead, she sighted a twinkling of tiny lights, like stars mirrored in the snow. Kate moved toward them, vaguely aware of changes in the earth, of the icy ground crackling and turning hollow beneath her boots. And then a few more feet, and she found both her path and the twinkles blocked by a tall and ominous deadfall. Fallen trees, randomly locked and intertwined, arched themselves nearly four feet high. Kate stretched her head, examining what seemed to be boggy land beyond. And there, reflecting and sparkling the blue light of the moon, were nothing more than frozen raindrops clinging to stalks of reeds and cattails. Kate frowned at the beckoning twinkles, then quit breathing long enough to hear eerie creaks and pops issuing from the freezing marsh. It sounded to Kate as though all those tangled marsh weeds were creeping about—stretching and yawning and crawling into one big icy bed to sleep their way through winter dreams. Kate wished she were in *her* bed, yawning or stretching—it didn't matter which.

Shifting her weight, she passed the glowing opal from side to side, struggling to make out the shapes that lay on the far side of the marsh. But neither the moon, nor even the gem's orange light could penetrate the curtain of shadows along its edge because...the forest was too thick, the branches too densely clustered...because...Kate used her hand to block the glare of the opal...because...they were evergreens. Hemlocks. The *stand*, she was certain. And somewhere, lurking in their shadows, was her witch.

Kate couldn't figure out how to get around the marsh, and in the end decided she had no choice but to journey across it. But that meant crossing the deadfall. And deadfalls, she'd been told, were dangerous; why, one slip, and your leg could be eaten up and snapped in two. Immediately, Kate abandoned Allegra's bat house to free her arms for balance. Cautiously then, and holding tightly to her magical orb, she stepped atop the first log. The log was sheerly coated with ice, though, and she managed only to steady herself for a moment before slipping off. One boot came down hard, sinking into the icy muck and soaking her foot clear up to her ankle. Gasping, she yanked out her boot with such sudden movement that it sent the opal popping right out of her hand, and forced Kate to take a hard-won seat on the ground.

In darkness again, Kate got to her knees, groping for the displaced opal until she spotted its light glowing around the rim of a melted hole in the snow. She crawled to the orb, plucked it from the wet depression, and was just straightening up when she spied, from the corner of her eye, a fleeting shadow pass somewhere through the trees. Kate swiveled, seeing nothing, then swore she saw the same shadow pass swiftly on the other side.

Then, there it came again, racing past her a bit closer this time. And then again it flashed through the woods, even closer now, so that Kate could feel the vibrations of its thunderous sprinting. A bear, she thought; a bear circling in as bears will tend to do—first large circles, then spiraling in to make smaller, tighter ones before closing in on its confused and panicky prey. *Something* was closing in.

Kate's first instinct was to opt for a primal scream, but her bellowing, she speculated, would only send out a message of fear and defeat. Of course, fear and defeat seemed destined tonight, so she shouted anyway. "*Help!*" she yelled to no one in particular. But her shout did nothing to interrupt the shadow's rhythmic movement. It grew bigger now, gaining speed with each successive passing.

Frozen by both the merciless elements and her own fear, Kate waited motionless, hearing the increasing volume of the beast's slobbery panting, the swishing and whooshing of paws raking the snow. Then, without further warning, it rushed at her.

In the space of a second the creature heaved and lunged, its massive body leaving the ground as it leapt from darkness. It growled a raging growl, bared hateful fangs—fangs that shone a sickly yellow in the opal's orange light—before solid paws came crashing against her chest. The impact knocked the wind out of Kate and she fell, blinded by sprays of snow, her back slamming hard against the ground. She fought and kicked and swung aimlessly, and in her mindless frenzy it was a good minute before she realized nothing was fighting back. There was a reprieve, a sudden silence, although the threatening weight still bore heavily upon her. She blinked her snow filled eyes, then blinked and blinked again, finally coming to stare with disbelief at the drooling predator pinning her shoulders from above. Its face was just as shocked as her own.

"...*you*? Ly...Ly..." Kate fell back. "Oh...geez...*Oh God...Lycos!*" Kate moaned.

The black dog whined, a long tongue dangling from the side of her mouth, her goofy head cocked in confused apology, as if to say, *What the hell are you doin' here, Doc? You could get yourself killed sneaking around the woods like that.*

With a grunt and a sigh, Kate tried to roll herself over, then flopped back in the snow and moaned and groaned and rolled some more. "Oh...Lycos. I saved your life and...and...you just took ten years off mine. Get me out of here," she said, pulling herself into a sitting position and brushing snow from her hair. "Lycos? Where's *Arba...Teasel...*? Go get *Arba* before I freeze to death."

The black dog's ears twitched at the mention of the dwarves, but she only sat back and whimpered and pawed Kate's pants.

"Okay, okay...I'm coming," Kate mumbled. "Let's go find Ar..." Kate paused, cocking her head at the panting dog, then silently recited her pen pal's arcane message: *Fear not the fates who weave from above, lest you destroy a tapestry woven with love. Follow the moon which will rise in the east, led by the stone and the wit of the...*

Kate's eyebrows dropped a notch, and she studied Lycos suspiciously. "Are you...could you be the beast? Then her stomach sank and she shut her eyes for a moment. "Lycos...? Where's...*Allegra*? Do you know *Allegra*?"

Lycos tilted her head then, her mouth widening in something of a toothy smile, and she began prancing and spinning and doing a hurry-up-Doc-I-can't-wait-much-longer dance.

"You *do*, don't you?" Kate wanted to laugh and sob and holler—all at the same time. "Let's *find* her, Lycos—Let's go find *Allegra*."

Kate pushed herself up, dusted snow from her pants and jacket, then retrieved her opal and the bat house she had discarded along the deadfall. Walking on the sides of her boots to ease the pain in her toes, Kate followed cautiously behind, relying on the opal for light and warmth, the beast-dog for guidance. And with an intuitive understanding of the doctor's predicament, Lycos safely led her across the icy marsh, giving a concerned, backwards glance to make sure her spiritual doctor-friend was keeping pace. Soon after, they entered a maze of birch and willow and poplar trees, then wove their way through what seemed a never-ending labyrinth of dark and looming hemlocks. The tall evergreens closed in on the travelers, their shadows collecting with threatening aspect; an aspect which, Kate suspected, typically lifted with the light of day.

It was difficult to tell exactly how far they journeyed; Kate seemed to have lost all track of time. But after a long and grueling while, she found herself stepping out of the shadowed stand and into a deep field.

The open air felt heavy; oddly insulated, as though it might snow again. And as she took a breath of arctic air, it in turn, seemed to strangely breathe the breath in her. She looked roundabout, her heart suddenly lunging at the sight of a stone cottage.

A warm and hopeful light shone through frosted windows. Thick smoke wafted from its chimney, drifting dreamily toward the blue moon and lacing the air with a fine and woody aroma. It was safe, Kate thought, to assume the witch was in tonight. With a nervous swallow, she took her first step toward the cottage.

Only a handful of stars flickered overhead, and the field seemed unnaturally quiet, save for the distant creaking of tree boughs, and the sound of snow crunching and squeaking beneath Kate's boots. Lycos took the lead again, as she impatiently rushed between Kate and the cottage, stopping now and again to howl with her lips kissing the blue moon. Then she stopped, looked back with those imposing eyes, and swung her head with a jerking motion to urge Kate along. But soon she gave up on her hobbling doctor, and raced ahead instead to scratch on the front door.

Nothing happened at first, but then the door swung slowly open, and from afar Kate saw Allegra's full-length figure silhouetted in the doorway. The witch stood motionless, perhaps unsure of the stranger approaching in the darkness. Kate wondered if perhaps Allegra might rightly mistake her for an old man, shuffling along on the sides of her soles.

In blue jeans and a white shirt rolled up at the sleeves, Allegra stepped out, blocking the blinding porch light with a hand held to her forehead. Lycos whined at her mistress, then darted back to Kate's side, as though wanting full credit for her doctor's unlikely arrival.

"Kate...?" the witch intoned, her voice an octave higher with disbelief. "Hello...? ...Kate? Is that you...?"

"Hi, honey, I'm home," Kate said, giving an inane wave of her hand. And then her ankle turned in and sent her falling face first into the snow.

With that, Allegra rushed out, bending down beside Kate in the snow. She looked at Lycos, then glanced with puzzlement at the dark line of hemlocks. "How did you—where did you *come* from? ...Are you injured? Kate...? *Kate!*"

Kate was too busy spewing snow from her mouth to answer. "I'm okay," she finally muttered, giving her tongue a final wipe. "I think my foot is frozen dead. I might have frost-bite."

Allegra sighed—a heavy, quivering sigh—then helped Kate up, guiding her to the cottage with a secure arm wrapped gently around her waist. "Your foot...does it still hurt?"

"Badly," Kate confessed.

"Well, that's a good sign. As long as you can still feel the pain, you know it's alive." She regarded Kate with something of a doleful smile.

Kate shook her head in confusion, as she limped up the three stone steps, frowning all the way at both Lycos and the witch. "She's *yours*? Your dog...?"

"Wolf," Allegra admitted guiltily. "Mostly wolf, anyway." And then, as if to ease Kate's dismay, she said, "I never dreamed I'd have the chance to see the two of you together." She released her grip on Kate and gestured with an arm toward the open doorway.

Blazing flames and a Tiffany lamp lit the cottage. It was wonderfully warm—much larger than it appeared from the outside—with high, rustic walls and a stone fireplace reaching clear to the ceiling. And mingling with the sweet smell of burning cherry wood, was the faint and spicy scent of lavender.

Allegra led her straight to the hearth. "Get these clothes off," she said. And then, shifting her eyes with sudden embarrassment, said, "Your coat and boots, I mean."

Kate would have blushed, except that her face was already red from being out in the cold. She nodded nervously and handed the bat house to Allegra. "Just a little something I picked up for you last month."

"A *bat* house? Oh, Kate..." she said approvingly, "I have *one*, but not like *this*. This one's *beautiful*."

Kate gave a nervous smile, the corners of her mouth twitching as she struggled to unfasten her jacket. The zipper got jammed at the bottom, though, and when it looked as if Kate wouldn't be able to finish the job, Allegra pursed her lips with stern affection, came up close, and shook the zipper free. But just as she did, there came a scratching sound at the front door, and they both turned to see Lycos edging her way in, the opal now crimson red between her teeth and setting her whole mouth aglow. She whined, first at her mistress, then at her doctor, possibly undecided as to who the rightful owner might be.

"Lycos, my *opal*..." Allegra called out.

"Huh?" Kate broke in. "It's *mine*. Teasel gave it to me when...when..." She paused and made a face at Allegra. "...when she came to get your *wolf* on Halloween."

"But I don't understand. My grandmother kept it safe for me in her..." The witch's voice trailed off, and she stared abstractedly into space. "The stone was created for me, Kate. It responds to my...proximity," she said weakly, as though afraid any mention of magic might spook Kate into running away all over again. "My godmother...Teasel...must have gotten to it somehow. She's a hopeless matchmaker, but I'm afraid her meddling did more harm than good." She regarded Kate with those forest green eyes, an apologetic smile coming to her beautiful pale green face. "It's good to see you, though," she said, taking Kate's coat. She reached and gently touched the cut above her eye. "I'm so very sorry."

Kate hung her head, not unlike the woeful Barney Banks. "I think I'm the one who needs to apologize, Allegra...I never meant to cause you such grief. I...I had no idea Rachel was your grandmother," she said, raising her eyes to meet the witch's gaze.

Quiet pain flickered in Allegra's eyes, but something else flickered in them, too; something warm and joyful like sunlit leaves after too long a rain. Silently then, she led Kate to the sofa where the black wolf eagerly waited for company. Allegra shook her head. "Lycos, has your etiquette failed you? It's not every day a doctor makes house calls, you know. Move over."

"Leave her," Kate said. But Lycos had already jumped down, settling, instead, for sitting on the floor with her head in her doctor's lap. "I can't believe she's yours...I just can't..." She took the opal from between Lycos's paws and placed it on the table.

Allegra didn't say a word. Instead, she took a deep breath, nodded thoughtfully, and bent down to help Kate pull off her boots. When she stood, she flung back her wavy, raven hair, disappeared into another room, and returned with a fresh pair of dry socks. "I'll get us something hot to drink," she said.

With unsteady hands, Kate peeled off her own wet and nearly frozen socks, then pulled on the dry ones. *Witch socks*, she thought, and began fiddling nervously with Lycos's ears. Her eyes roamed all about the room. She stared at the colors of the stained glass lamp, studied the dome-shaped window and leafy plants; the oaken furniture, the curious art pieces which seemed to come from all over the world. She even studied the floors and ceiling; after all, she had never been inside a *real* witch's house before. The fact of it made her dizzy. But the burning sensation in her feet had a stabilizing effect—defrosting was always such a painful process.

In a few minutes Allegra was back with two hot toddies, orange slices floating decoratively on the surface of each steamy glass. As soon as Kate was offered one, she took a long swallow, forgetting her earlier fears of bubbly potions and slippery frogs; the worst thing about being turned into a frog now, Kate admitted to herself, was that it would render her physically unattractive to Allegra. And really, underneath it all, she didn't want the witch to stop wanting her. Kate choked and coughed a bit, her eyes watering as the hot liquid slid down her throat, coating her gullet with fire.

"Slow down..." the witch said, casting her a sideways glance. "There's whiskey in there—drink that fast, and you might find yourself growing a beard by morning."

Morning.... Kate didn't know where she'd be come morning—either in her bed, on Allegra's sofa, or in a fish bowl, she concluded. She coughed again, gave an embarrassed smile, and set the glass down. Kate's awkwardness, that endearing quality which would have amused Allegra under different circumstances, now seemed cause for deep concern. She gave a bittersweet smile, took a seat diagonally across from Kate in a high-backed oaken chair, then propped her elbows and brought the palms of her hands together. With fingertips raised to her lips, she peered into her estranged lover's face for what seemed to Kate an awfully long time before speaking. "Why did you come?" she flatly asked.

Kate wasn't sure whether it was the question or the witch's sudden formality that set her heart to pounding. She shrugged, regarded the floating orange in her glass, took another swallow—a sip, this time—then countered Allegra's stare. Ruggedly dressed in jeans and brown boots, her white shirt unbuttoned just enough to hint at her cleavage, Allegra looked as though she'd just climbed off a horse; off a horse and onto a throne. In her high-backed chair she was so poised, so regal, so terribly attractive—no matter that she was still green and it wasn't Halloween.

Butterflies stirred in Kate's belly, and she put an inconspicuous arm around herself, deciding there wasn't any more use in pretending she hadn't lost her heart and half her mind to love. It *had* to be love, or something with the potential for love, at least. Why, it wasn't every day that a woman came along and made you feel sick to your stomach. Only a woman who had you falling crazy in love could do such things.

Kate shifted her eyes to the orange in her glass again. With a nervous finger she poked at it, submerged it, watched stupidly as it floated to the surface, then took another swig. And then, thinking she ought to answer Allegra's question, she went ahead and blurted out all that had happened that month: her meeting with Mildred, her visit to Diane's, even her and Gigi's clandestine trip to the Widow's Peak last night. She pulled out the anonymous note kept folded in her wallet and handed it to the witch.

Allegra's brow dropped as she traced thoughtful fingers over the paper, seeming to recognize the stationery. Slowly she unfolded it, read it, and when she had finished, closed her eyes and tightened her lips. "My grandmother..." She began, her voice a hoarse whisper, "...it's her handwriting."

Kate felt herself choke up just a bit. "But why? She didn't even know me. How—"

"She knew about you." Allegra got up, a far away look in her eyes, and walked to the window. A fine snow was just beginning to fall, and here and there, tiny ice crystals stuck to the frosted panes. "She knew how much you meant to me, Kate. I can only imagine that she wanted things to work in our favor, and so solicited Teasel's help." Allegra turned and moved sinuously across the room to the fireplace, the contour of her lithe body catching both the light and shadows of the dancing flames.

"Kate..." she said, taking hold of a poker, "Our meeting on Halloween was not a chance encounter...." She poked the fire, then turned with a sigh and looked directly into Kate's face. "I was waiting there for you."

Kate met the witch's stare and thought to say something, but the lump in her throat made speaking impossible.

"I told you I take long walks in the woods," Allegra continued. "It was one early September morning that I first saw you by the pond...and I watched. I watched you watching birds...picking wild flowers...wondering at the living things about you. I even watched you lose your balance and fall in the water the day you handled that listless snapping turtle." Allegra bit her lip, as if trying not to smile at the sweet memories, but a smile broke softly on her face anyway. "I guess you thought the turtle was dead, until it woke up and snapped at your finger."

Kate forced a half-hearted grin, acknowledging the tiny scar on her pinky. She would have preferred not to be reminded of the shelled beast.

"I watched you loving life, Kate. And *I* fell in love with *you*...though from a distance. So many mornings I came in secrecy—it became something of a ritual. But then it was no longer enough. I wanted to know you, talk with you...be with you. Of course..." Allegra said, looking down at her green hands, "I couldn't very well have let you see me like *this*. You would have shrieked and run, no doubt." She regarded Kate with a slight, sarcastic roll of her eyes that made Kate wince.

Allegra returned to her seat and reached for a lavender cigarette. She offered one to Kate, lit them both, then took her glass and settled regally into her chair again. "When Lycos was shot, there was no time to waste on makeup, so Teasel and Arba rushed her down to you." She looked affectionately down at Lycos, then adoringly into Kate's eyes. "You saved her, gave so much of yourself, that it only endeared you to me more. I don't know what happened after that, Kate—my heart grew selfish, I suppose, and as Halloween approached, I decided that if only for one night, I would risk a romantic interlude with you. It was the only day of the year I could be myself, you see...and I didn't think beyond that one day, didn't think of the consequences to either of us."

The mention of Halloween brought Kate back to that warm and windy and enchanted night, flooding her with intrusive visions of their lovemaking. Kate's eyes shifted from Allegra's bare hands and forearms to the pale green flesh of her partially exposed chest—flesh that had appeared, and now again seemed so sensual. It was the color of life itself; but a color, Kate reminded herself, which hinted at the supernatural; a symptom of some higher and formidable power that eluded mortal comprehension. And as Kate sat there trying to conceive of the inconceivable, she realized she was still fearing Allegra as much as she was loving her. A classical case of approach-avoidance, is what her mother would have called it.

"You're staring," Allegra said, "just as hard as you stared the first time you ever saw me...my color frightens you, doesn't it?"

"I'm staring because you're as beautiful as you were the first time I saw you." Their eyes came to lock in an equally penetrating gaze that made Kate's stomach turn and her mind go suddenly blank. And while she struggled to collect her thoughts, she was glad to let the sounds of the crackling fire fill the conversational silence. "Allegra, it's not the...the...*greenery*," Kate said, not knowing what else to call it, "it's the unknown, the unexpectedness of it all. When I first saw you...in the rain, in the cemetery...I didn't know *what* you were going to do to me."

Allegra arched one eyebrow incredulously, her countenance one of disbelief mingled with insult. "And *what* exactly did you imagine I might do, Kate? Zap you? Turn you into a toad, or something?"

"Um-hmm."

Allegra's other eyebrow went up in surprise. "No...you can't be serious." A *toad*...?"

"A frog."

"A *frog*?" Allegra stood up, opening her arms wide. "Oh, for *heavens sake*, Kate!"

Kate winced. "Sorry," she said, suddenly feeling like some sort of simpleton.

Allegra's arms dropped to her sides, and she slowly shook her head in a way that suggested she just couldn't fathom Kate's imagination. "I know all that I put you through was wrong and very unfair. But how could you...?"

"Allegra..." Kate broke in, thinking she ought to defend her current state of mind. "So maybe I overreacted. Can you blame me, though? I mean, what did you expect? I don't have any frame of reference for all that's gone on since Halloween. I've never had a green lover, never slept with a witch before."

"I'm not a witch," Allegra said, raising her voice a bit, then dropping it to an agreeable whisper. "Well...descriptively, maybe, but not technically."

A categorical mistake, Kate thought. A short time ago she hadn't believed in fairy tale witches. Now there was all this categorical business to straighten out about descriptive witches and technical witches and... "Then why...why are you..."

"Green?" Allegra finished for her. She sighed and gave a conceding nod. "I will tell you, Kate, but *not* as long as you're sitting there fearing my magic." She turned and walked back to the window, stopping beside a tall, dark plant with shiny leaves. "Do you like gardenias?" she casually asked.

Unsure of Allegra's intentions, Kate made an I-suppose-so type of gesture, and watched as Allegra took hold of a branch of the potted shrub. She looked sideways at Kate, then for a brief moment closed her eyes and gently tightened her grip. Kate's eyes, on the contrary, never closed once; they oscillated with anticipation between Allegra and the leafy branch, without an inkling as to what they were watching for. Suddenly though, the shrub gave a shudder and a rustle, as if some incorporeal guest had, just at that very moment, walked past the plant and stubbed his toe on the planter. Allegra appeared to be in a study, her green eyes glowing like emeralds in the firelight. She released her grip, then spread her fingers over a creamy white bud which, Kate was certain, hadn't been there a second ago.

Allegra raised her hand, slowly inclining her fingers like a magician; summoning, drawing forth the new life that her power stirred. Kate felt as though she were traveling back in time, back to her tenth-year birthday party; sitting Indian-style, the mouths of all her guests hanging open in awe as a hired illusionist pulled tricks from his hat. But she was a woman now; the magician was her lover; and the magician's magic was real.

Seemingly in rhythm with the pinging of snowflakes against the outside window, the budding flower began to miraculously bloom. From between Allegra's spread fingers, the leaf cluster quivered. First one, and then another milky petal exposed itself, swelling and unfolding itself like a woman beneath the skilled hands of a lover. Its sweet essence began to spread and permeate the room. But Kate was only vaguely aware of the smell, and more aware of the tic which seemed to have developed just below her eye. She brushed a hand across her cheek to wipe away the fluttering sensation.

The gardenia bloomed luscious and full, Allegra supporting its weight with her fingertips. "Magic...exquisite magic, wouldn't you say?" she asked, as the flower gave all it could give of itself. "It's what you once told me you were missing in your life." She smiled reassuringly, almost teasingly, then gently slid her hand up the stem and pinched off the exquisite flower.

Once again, she sinuously crossed the room, this time taking a seat on the sofa, and presented the gardenia to Kate, "And this magic," she whispered, "is nothing you should fear." She peered into Kate's eyes, her own green eyes and her tone growing quite serious. "Please don't *ever* fear me...."

Kate thought back to their moonlit walk, then grinned—a nervous grin, but a grin nonetheless—and accepted the big, buttery-looking flower in both her hands. The mysterious fragrance, so close and potent now, was a bit overwhelming. It set her mind in a whirl.

Allegra took her glass and shifted her body toward Kate, who waited politely with the gardenia resting in her lap.

"My story is complicated," Allegra began. "I suppose you wouldn't be able to sit here and tell me much about *your* ancestors who lived thousands, even hundreds of years ago."

Kate had never thought beyond her great grandparents, and so she shook her head no.

Allegra nodded. "All I can tell you is what has been handed down to me." She searched Kate's eyes, as if wondering exactly how much Kate was prepared to cope with right now. "Your friend Diane — she wasn't too far off," Allegra said, her countenance turning almost stoical as it had in the cemetery. "Our race...my race is said to have descended from...from angels, Kate—fairy-like guardians, if it's more comfortable for you to think in those terms. They were spiritual guardians sent to walk the Earth on, well...*business*, if you will."

Allegra paused, giving Kate a studied glance, then continued. "But instead, they fell in love with the Earth's physical beauty, with the notion of possessing mortal bodies with which to experience the sensory delights of this world."

"Picture, for a moment, what it would be like to exist only in spiritual form, and then, one day you are granted an incarnation with which to carry out a mission in this physical dimension. Imagine how exhilarating it would be," she said, a flicker of passion filling her eyes, "to run with the speed and grace of a gazelle, to be touched by the wind, by the caressing hands of another human being. Imagine the sensations of breathing in the fragrance of a thousand flowers...of eating, tasting, drinking from a spring; of having, for the first time, eyes with which to see the wonders, ears with which to hear the sweetness of a song...a body with which to dance barefoot on a sun-warmed beach. This world may be tainted, Kate, but it is glorious, you know."

Allegra stopped, waiting perhaps, for a response. But Kate sat poker-faced, listening with silent interest. Surprisingly, she wasn't overly surprised at all; in fact, she seriously wondered if anything would surprise her ever again. Probably not in this lifetime, she told herself.

"And so these angels...fairies...fell from grace and bred with humans. Their progeny—hybrids of the flesh and spirit, you might say—came to be known as the race of giants, though not so much in size, as in psychic strength and superhuman power." Allegra lifted an open hand, then let it drop to her lap. "Something in our DNA went awry, though. It seems we were cursed with genes of the various life forms; of those earthly things that originally seduced us into partaking of this world in the first place; recessive genes which arbitrarily surfaced from generation to generation. *My* skin, Kate, contains a natural pigment similar to that found in plants."

Allegra lowered her head. "My father is like me...but most of us manage to conceal our superhuman legacy. Keziah, for instance, possesses optical powers which enable her to see constellations invisible to the naked eye. And Dewitt...he has extraordinary night vision, more acute than any cat or owl. If you saw him in the day, though, you'd take notice of his vertical pupils. Of course, he must hide from the sunlight...it is blindingly painful for him and, needless to say, restricts his social life to more...nocturnal activities.

"Our curses are our gifts, our gifts our curses, I suppose. It all depends on how we perceive what we have been given." Allegra took a long breath and glanced at the crackling fire, and as she did a burning log just happened to slip and sputter and hiss. Kate regarded it with a quick glance, exchanged her gardenia for her glass on the table, and in one final gulp polished off her hot toddy.

"This *mighty* race—*Nephilim* we are called—were not an evil people," Allegra explained, "but their freakish powers turned the world against them, forced them to spend their lives at war. Naturally, they gained a reputation as being hateful, destructive warriors."

Kate looked down, nonchalantly examining her fingernails. "So you're not...hu...human...?" she stammered.

"Human?" A soft smile broke on Allegra's face. "Mostly. I was born and I will die, Kate. I bleed when I am cut, my heart hurts when it is broken, and...I make an awful lot of mistakes— even *with* the magic. Is that human enough?"

Kate looked down at Allegra's hand, slowly touched it, then took it into her own, as if doing so would help signify the beginning of acceptance. And the warmth of Allegra's hand, a hand she had longed to hold, instantly flooded Kate with memories of how soft and moist and good that skin had felt against her own. With a deep sigh, she squeezed it, then gave a sideways glance. "I suppose..." she said. " And Teasel and Arba? They're relatives?" "Oh, no. The dwarves are not *blood* relatives. They're just regular dwarves. You see, when the giants were eventually conquered in battle and the city of Hebron was taken from them, the few surviving ones were sealed in caverns, sentenced to live in darkness until death. Dwarves, however, if you remember your mythology, are instinctive diggers with a fondness for subterranean life, for creating elaborate underground networks. As the family story goes, it was such a group of dwarves who accidently unearthed the giants—fed them, gave them homes, protection...became their keepers. They grew to love us, even took names associated with the race, and learned the ways of our powers. Nephilum, you see, by way of magic, succeeded in achieving the failed dream of every alchemist—turning lead into gold."

Allegra shrugged quite nonchalantly. "Our relationship with the dwarves is rather symbiotic. We have always lived closely with them. Today they share our wealth and serve as our proxies, enabling us to maintain full, however reclusive lives—here and overseas, where most of my people live."

Kate didn't have much to say at the moment; she was trying to imagine Dewitt with vertical pupils.

Allegra patted Kate's thigh. "You don't have to say anything, Kate. And you don't have to stay. But maybe one day, when you've had a chance to sort through all of this..." Allegra paused, her voice beginning to quiver and betray the would-be stoic. "Maybe one day," she continued, "we could find a way to keep the friendship. It would mean so very much to me."

Kate stared at her green angel-witch, a woman who was probably more woman than Kate could ever hope to handle. And if, indeed, all that had been said in the cemetery about sins and crimes of the hearts held true, then Allegra was, without a doubt, the sweetest sin she would ever taste. "What are you telling me?" Kate asked.

"I'm telling you you're free to go." Allegra held her arms out. "No tricks, no frogs, no magic...no strings attached." Allegra got up and wandered to the window; unable, for the first time to meet Kate's eyes.

"You don't want me here?"

Allegra's voice grew weakly hoarse. "That's hardly it, Kate."

"Then why are you telling me to go?"

"I'm not *telling* you to go...I said you were *free* to go."

Kate felt the devil playfully stirring from within, and she determined to play her cards right this time; no matter that she didn't, and hadn't had a full deck to play with in—what was it?—several weeks now. "Well, good..."

she said innocently, "I thought that maybe you were suggesting I'd over-stayed my welcome...."

Allegra made a face. "Do you *really* think I would tire of you so easily?"

"Oh, *no*..." Kate answered playfully. She softly smacked her lips, feeling suddenly confident and glib and oddly at ease, although for the life of her she couldn't imagine why. "I'd *never* think that of you. In fact...if I remember correctly, it was *I* who tired first on Halloween...."

Allegra did something of a double-take, then lowered her head to hide her sudden embarrassment.

"Allegra..." Kate pushed, her tone turning serious, "We made love...."

"Once."

"Twice..." Kate corrected.

Allegra looked up with those shy and sexy and half-closed eyes. "Twice..." she was forced to agree.

"And I had hoped it wouldn't be the last time."

Allegra looked shocked for a moment, and then a spark of joy broke in her eyes. But she quickly shut them as if to contain an overflow of emotion. "Oh, Kate..." she said, shaking her head hesitantly, "I'm afraid these recent days have left us both emotionally exhausted. I don't think you know what you're saying....

"I would love to be with you, Kate, and I believe I could make you happy. I could give you things, show you things beyond your wildest dreams. But in terms of an ordinary life?" She shook her head. "I have magic, Kate...but not the magic to change who I am, or how I appear. Even magic has its limitations."

Allegra smiled regretfully. "It takes me two, sometimes three hours of preparation before I can pass in public. There aren't many places where I can be myself. A normal life, I'm afraid, is the one thing I could never offer you."

"Gigi taught me an important lesson about *normalcy*," Kate said softly.

Allegra regarded her quizzically.

"In the woods that night..." Kate began, "when you asked if I would run when I found my magic...?" She glanced at Allegra, then shook her head. "I don't want to run from it anymore. It would be a senseless race, you know?" Kate shrugged. "Sort of like..."

"Running from your shadow?"

"Yes..." Kate laughed just a bit. "Something like that."

Allegra came back over to her, trailed her finger underneath her chin, then took Kate's hand in her own.

"Kate looked down at her hand, then up at Allegra again. "You read palms, too?"

Allegra smiled. "I'd much rather read your mind." Then, "Come with me," she said, raising one expectant eyebrow, "there is something I need to show you."

Kate's lips parted and she felt her stomach flip. She looked up at Allegra's body, then toward the bedroom door, then at their hands again and swallowed hard.

Without another word, she led Kate into her softly lit bedroom. The carpet was cream colored plush—sort of like a cloud, Kate thought—and in the middle was a brass bed, crystal lamps adorning each night stand and casting rainbows across the stuccoed ceiling. And on one of the tables sat a vase with a purple rose, the same rose Kate had given her on Halloween. It was still living; perfect, in fact, as if it had just been picked. "Oh God..." Kate mumbled.

"What?"

"Nothing."

Allegra looked over her shoulder, acknowledged the lavender rose with a mischievous glance, then turned back to Kate. "I told you I would keep it always...."

At the foot of the bed Allegra studied Kate, their arms loosely draped around one another's waist. Kate felt the pull between their eyes; an unexplainable force that seemed to reach in and touch the core of her being. It enveloped her, made her gasp slightly, made her want to drown in the magic and tenderness of her lover. And just as it had happened in Kate's erotic dream, Allegra gently pushed her down upon the bed.

"Look at me," she said, her words slow and deliberate as she stood above Kate, nervously unbuttoning her shirt, and drawing in a quick breath. "I want you to take a look at me...and tell me, honestly, if you want this."

In silence, Kate reached up, spreading Allegra's shirt far enough so that her eyes came to rest on her pale green breasts. Kate felt her own body respond to Allegra's nearness, to the feel of her flesh...the scent of lavender mingling with her body heat. Kate smiled softly. "I've been aching for you, Allegra...my *heart* has been aching. Lie with me," she managed to whisper.

Allegra slowly lowered herself over Kate, her lustrous hair falling forward, her forest green eyes so serious in their passion. "Oh, my sweetheart...how I have missed you, too. Every night and every day my soul has longed for you...."

And just then, a single tear surfaced in Allegra's eye and rolled down her cheek. Kate pulled Allegra on top of her, caught the tear with the tip of her tongue—and a funny thing happened; it seemed to turn right around and come back out of Kate's eye.

"Yes, I *want* this," Kate said, sliding her hands inside Allegra's shirt and running them over her bare shoulders. "I want all of it. I could love you, Allegra Hebron...really, *really* love you. Just give me a chance to *try*."

And as their lips came together in a warm, heartfelt kiss, it occurred to Kate that *trying* might not be so hard, after all.

⤳ *Epilogue* ⤳

*E*veryone seemed to be commenting on how vibrant Kate was
looking these past couple of days. She had been seeing patients back to
back—no word from Barney, though—and had neglected to return Gigi's
call. But despite a hectic two days, not to mention two wonderfully sleepless
nights with Allegra, Kate had to admit that she was looking remarkably well.

Dinner at Allegra's was for seven o'clock, but at five, she had called
to apologize for the addition of two unexpected dinner guests. Kate gladly
agreed to pick up an extra bottle of wine, then ran to the pet shop for a bone,
and even managed to slip into the bakery before it closed, for a chocolate
truffle cake.

The cats seemed highly disappointed that Allegra would not be
coming over tonight. Gandalf, especially. It seemed he was prepared to make
a habit of showing off when Allegra was around. and it occurred to Kate that
he might have developed something of a crush on her.

At seven o'clock on the button, Kate was showered and dressed and
up the mountain, parking her Jeep alongside an unfamiliar car on Allegra's
property. And no sooner had Kate closed the car door, than Allegra was
greeting her at the front door with what seemed to Kate, a spark of mischief
in her eyes.

"Hi, love," she whispered, pulling Kate close to place a welcoming
kiss on her lips. "God...I've missed you all day long."

"Likewise," Kate whispered, smiling and kissing her and burying her
face in Allegra's fragrant neck. But then, as she stood hugging her lover, she
opened her eyes to see the beautiful, purple-eyed Keziah sitting in the next
room beside an all too familiar face. "Gigi!" Kate said with a start.

"What—?"

Gigi grinned broadly. "Hey, don't give me any of this *what* stuff. If you'd returned my call, you wouldn't be standing there with your mouth hanging open, Doc."

Kate looked at them both with dumbfounded wonder. "You two?" she gestured with a moving finger between her best friend and Allegra's cousin.

Keziah smiled at Kate, then waited for Gigi to respond.

"So?" Gigi said playfully, "So what about it?" she squeezed Keziah's hand and, placing it in her lap, winked at Kate. "Remember all that stuff I was saying about being normal?" She gestured at Keziah with her head. "Well, this is the first *normal* one I've met in months, probably years."

Kate turned to her lover for some sort of explanation. But Allegra, slipping her arm around Kate's waist, only smiled at her lover and winked.

Kate looked around, then down at the black, grinning wolf; hoping maybe that Lycos might offer some explanation. But just then, a tiny particle of fairy dust must have been floating in the air, because something miniscule whirled and spiraled down, and caught itself right on the tip of the wolf's eyelash. And Lycos winked, too.

The End

ABOUT THE AUTHOR

Karen Williams holds a BA in media studies and philosophy, a master's degree in social work, and--as if there were any connection--lectures and has published numerous articles on pets, nature, and the human-animal bond. She divides her time between the city and the mountains of New York, but prefers the country by far. Despite public warnings, she admits to feeding the wild things that live under her house: a raccoon couple, a well-mannered skunk, (and although she has never seen it, is quite sure) a highly reclusive, female nymph.

In her spare time, Ms. Williams likes to read, walk, grow herbs and hunt for witches. If you have any in your possession—witches, that is—she asks that you please forward them immediately.

If You Liked This Book...

Authors seldom get to hear what readers like about their work. If you enjoyed reading this novel, why not let the author know? Simply write the author:

Author's name
c/o Rising Tide Press
5 Kivy Street
Huntington Station, NY 11746

MORE EXCITING FICTION FROM RISING TIDE PRESS

ROMANCING THE DREAM
Heidi Johanna

This imaginative tale begins when Jacqui St. John leaves northern California looking for a new home, and cruises into the seemingly ordinary town of Kulshan, on the Oregon coast. Seeing the lilac bushes in bloom along the roadside, she suddenly remembers the recurring dream that has been tantalizing her for months—a dream of a house full of women, radiating warmth and welcome, and of one special woman, dressed in silk and leather.... But why has Jacqui, like so many other women, been drawn to this place? The answer is simple but wonderful—the women plan to take over the town and make a lesbian haven. A captivating and erotic love story with an unusual plot. A novel that will charm you with its gentle humor and fine writing.

ISBN 0-9628938-0-3;176 Pages; $8.95

YOU LIGHT THE FIRE
Kristen Garrett

Here's a grown-up *Rubyfruit Jungle*--sexy, spicy, and side-splittingly funny. Garrett, a fresh new voice in lesbian fiction, has created two memorable characters in Mindy Brinson and Cheerio Monroe. Can a gorgeous, sexy, high school math teacher and a raunchy, commitment-shy ex singer, make it last, in mainstream USA? With a little help from their friends, they can. This humorous, erotic and unpredictable love story will keep you laughing, and marveling at the variety of lesbian love.

ISBN 0-9628938-5-4; 176 Pages; $8.95

EDGE OF PASSION
Shelley Smith

The author of **Horizon of the Heart** presents another absorbing and sexy novel! From the moment Angela saw Micki sitting at the end of the smoky bar, she was consumed with desire for this cool and sophisticated woman, and determined to have her...at any cost. Set against the backdrop of colorful Provincetown and Boston, this sizzling novel will draw you into the all-consuming love affair between an older and a younger woman. A gripping love story, which is both fierce and tender. It will keep you breathless until the last page.

ISBN 0-9628938-1-1; 192 Pages; $8.95

CORNERS OF THE HEART
Leslie Grey

This captivating novel of love and suspense introduces two unforgettable characters whose diverse paths have finally led them to each other. It is Spring, season of promise, when beautiful, French-born Chris Benet wanders into Katya Michaels' life. But their budding love is shadowed by a baffling mystery which they must solve. You will read with bated breath as they work together to outwit the menace that threatens Deer Falls; your heart will pound as the story races to its heart-stopping climax. Vivid, sensitive writing and an intriguing plot are the hallmarks of this exciting new writer.

ISBN 0-9628938-3-8; 208 Pages; $9.95

RETURN TO ISIS
Jean Stewart

The year is 2093. In this fantasy zone where sword and superstition meet sci-fi adventure, two women make a daring escape to freedom. Whit, a bold warrior from an Amazon nation, rescues Amelia from a dismal world where females are either breeders or drones. Together, they journey over grueling terrain, to the shining world of Artemis, and in their struggle to survive, find themselves unexpectedly drawn to each other. But it is in the safety of Artemis, Whit's home colony, that danger truly lurks. And it is in the ruins of Isis that the secret of how it was mysteriously destroyed waits to be uncovered. Here's adventure, mystery and romance all rolled into one.

ISBN 0-9628938-6-2; 192 Pages; $8.95

FACES OF LOVE
Sharon Gilligan

A wise and sensitive novel which takes us into the lives of Maggie, Karen, Cory, and their community of friends. Maggie Halloran, a prominent women's rights advocate, and Karen Weston, a brilliant attorney, have been together for 10 years in a relationship which is full of love, but is also often stormy. When Maggie's heart is captured by the young and beautiful Cory, she must take stock of her life and make some decisions.

Set against the backdrop of Madison, Wisconsin, and its dynamic women's community, the characters in this engaging novel are bright, involved, '90s women dealing with universal issues of love, commitment and friendship. A wonderful read!

ISBN 0-9628938-4-6 ; 192 Pages; $8.95

DANGER IN HIGH PLACES:
An Alix Nicholson Mystery
Sharon Gilligan

Free-lance photographer Alix Nicholson was expecting some great photos of the AIDS Quilt— what she got was a corpse with a story to tell! Set against the backdrop of Washington, DC, the bestselling author of **Faces of Love** delivers a riveting mystery. When Alix accidentally stumbles on a deadly scheme surrounding AIDS funding, she is catapulted into the seamy underbelly of Washington politics. With the help of Mac, lesbian congressional aide, Alix gradually untangles the plot, has a romantic interlude, and learns of the dangers in high places.

ISBN 0-9628938-7-0; 192 Pages; $9.95

ISIS RISING
Jean Stewart

The eagerly awaited sequel to the immensely popular **Return to Isis** is here at last! In this stirring romantic fantasy, Jean Stewart continues the adventures of Whit (every woman's heart-throb), her beloved Kali, and a cast of colorful characters, as they rebuild Isis from the ashes. But all does not go smoothly in this brave new world, and Whit, with the help of her friends, must battle the forces that threaten. A rousing futuristic adventure and an endearing love story all rolled into one. Destined to capture your heart.

ISBN 0-9628938-8-9;192 Pages; $9.95.

SHADOWS AFTER DARK
Ouida Crozier

Wings of death are spreading over the world of Körnagy and Kyril's mission on Earth is to find the cure. Here, she meets the beautiful but lonely Kathryn, who has been yearning for a deep and enduring love with just such a woman as Kyril. But to her horror, Kathryn learns that her darkly exotic new lover has been sent to Earth with a purpose—to save her own dying vampire world. A tender and richly poetic novel. *ISBN 1-883061-50-4; 224 Pages; $9.95*

How To Order:

Rising Tide Press books are available from you local women's bookstore or directly from Rising Tide Press. Send check, money order, or Visa/MC account number, with expiration date and signature to: Rising Tide Press, 5 Kivy St., Huntington Sta., New York 11746. **Credit card** orders must be **over $25. Remember** to include shipping and handling charges: $4.95 for the first book plus $1.00 for each additional book. ***Credit Card Orders** Call our Toll Free # **1-800-648-5333**.* For UPS delivery, provide street address.

Our Publishing Philosophy

Rising Tide Press is a lesbian-owned and operated publishing company committed to publishing books by, for, and about lesbians and their lives. We are not only committed to readers, but also to lesbian writers who need nurturing and support, whether or not their manuscripts are accepted for publication. Through quality writing, the press aims to entertain, educate, and empower readers, whether they are women-loving-women or heterosexual. It is our intention to promote lesbian culture, community, and civil rights, nationwide, through the printed word.

In addition, RTP will seek to provide readers with images of lesbians aspiring to be more than their prescribed roles dictate. The novels selected for publication will aim to portray women from all walks of life, (regardless of class, ethnicity, religion or race), women who are strong, not just victims, women who can and do aspire to be more, and not just settle, women who will fight injustice with courage. Hopefully, our novels will provide new ideas for creating change in a heterosexist and homophobic society. Finally, we hope our books will encourage lesbians to respect and love themselves more, and at the same time, convey this love and respect of self to the society at large. It is our belief that this philosophy can best be actualized through fine writing that entertains, as well as educates the reader. Books, even lesbian books, can be fun, as well as liberating.

WRITERS WANTED!!!

*Rising Tide Press, Publisher of
Lesbian Novels,
is Soliciting Quality Fiction Manuscripts*

Rising Tide Press is interested in publishing quality Lesbian fiction: romance, mystery, and science-fiction/fantasy. Non-fiction is also welcome, but please, no poetry or short stories.

Please send us the following:

- One page synopsis of plot
- The manuscript
- A brief autobiographical sketch
- Large manila envelope with sufficient return postage

RISING TIDE PRESS

5 KIVY ST.
HUNTINGTON STATION,
N.Y. 11746